Dedicated to my daughter, Rahma

ERA

OF

NITOCRIS

By

Mervat Mohsen

Era of Nitocris

Copyrights @UKinkers 2024

The following is a work of fiction. Any names, characters, places and incidents are the product of the author's imagination. Any resemblance to persons, living or dead, is entirely coincidental.

Book editing & formatting: JV Author Services

www.ukinkers.com

Acknowledgements

Many thanks to my daughter, Rahma, Sherif El Hotabiy, Pico and Nada, John and Vicky Regan from JV Author Services.

Contents

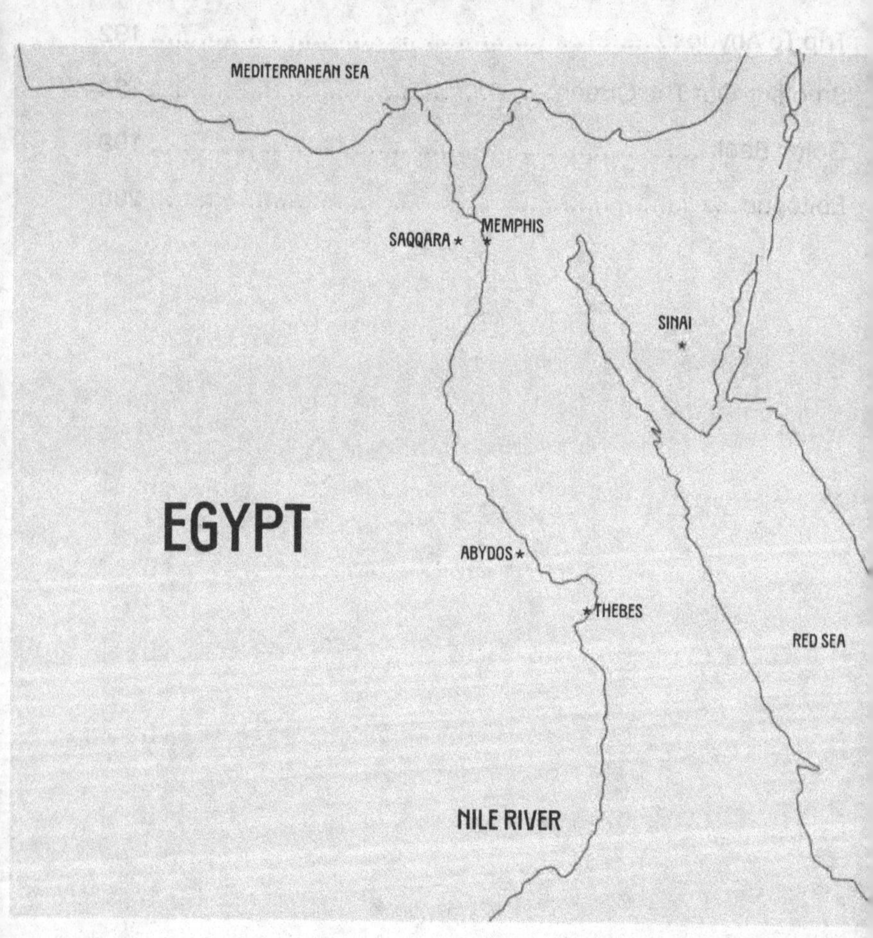

MEDITERRANEAN SEA
SAQQARA
MEMPHIS
SINAI
EGYPT
ABYDOS
THEBES
RED SEA
NILE RIVER

Prologue

King Pepi II lay on the floor covered in blood at the foot of his throne. Nitocris, dishevelled in a bloody diaphanous robe, bent over the King with a dagger in her hand. A few feet away lay her brother, Merenre, curled in agony, fighting for breath as hot fumes emanated from his lips and pores across his shrivelling skin.

"Why?" he asked as the poison continued to consume the crown prince, draining his vital bodily fluids.

Nitocris held the dagger to his throat and sneered. "You won't live long enough in this life to find out." With a flash of the blade, she slit her brother's throat. She watched on as the viscous red fluid pumped from the severed artery before she turned and swiftly fled towards the exit she had forged a long time ago.

She remembered the warning that a member of the elite guard, who was loyal to her, had given during the last full moon regarding the King's suspicions about his daughter. "Mistress," he said, "I have heard sentinels in drunken stupor discussing the King's orders for vigilance when you visit the royal quarters. They are under strict command to interrupt your audience with the King within the first shadow on the timepiece."

Nitocris smiled to herself. Their vigilance had proved useless.

Hurriedly, Nitocris removed a stone brick with a plaster duck face scribed on its surface from the floor behind the throne. She pulled another brick with a painted lotus flower marked with a sceptre and prepared for her escape. The palace, built above the cascading waters of the Nile, did not stop the fearless assassin from jumping – missing the rocks by a hair – abandoning herself to the force of the water and cleansing the diaphanous robe from the killings.

Riva

Twenty-year-old Riva took the road to the left instead of crossing over to the opposite side of the street and made a right to pick up regular home supplies around the corner from her house. In her absent-mindedness, the aspiring actress kept on walking through a narrow, empty street as the sun set. The young girl, with rounded eyes, thick eyebrows and curly hair, recalled an earlier conversation she had had with a beautician.

"Your eye makeup needs toning above the eye," Sarah said. The beautician had made the comments at the auditioning of a number of girls, including Riva, for a tourism documentary. "Marine is not your colour,' she continued. "Perhaps baby blue will show your complexion to better advantage if you insist on using those tones." Riva had waited her turn among the applicants while trying to assess her chances among the slender, tall and stunningly attractive group. She looked different from the others – curvier and fuller-figured. Did they like what they saw? Would they like her rounded cheeks, circular lips and eyes?

Lost in thought, while remembering the beautician's comments, Riva failed to notice the gun-toting man across the street. It was only when he fired, and his suited-up victim hit the pavement, quite dead, that Riva gasped. She gazed at the killer, unable to move. The short, lithe assailant, tattooed, with black hair and glassy eyes, picked up the corpse like a potato sack and thumped it inside the boot of the waiting vehicle.

"Hurry up,' he said to the driver. "Get us out of here." Riva's eyes lowered to a tattoo on the gunman's hand – a sceptre etched at his thumb – that still held the fatal instrument. The killer stood under the streetlight and stopped in his tracks when he saw Riva standing just a few feet from him, but before she could scream, he struck and bundled her into the car before it sped away.

Riva woke up on a sofa in an office with a glass partition overlooking the bar and dance floor of a high-end club below. Trendsetting fashionistas swayed on the other side of the wall from where she sat as loud music filtered through, jewellery flashed, and people gyrated to the throb of a familiar tune.

"You brought her here!" A man shouted through the speaker on her assailant's mobile.

The tattooed man's face went pale as he tried to placate whoever was on the other end. Riva put a hand to her head and gently touched the bump where he had struck her. She unsteadily sat up.

The tattooed man reached behind his back and pulled his gun from his belt. 'Do you want me to get rid of her?'

"Have you completely lost it?" the voice on the phone screamed. "You want to kill a witness at my respectable club? Any of the scumbags in the club would make a better manager than you."

"But Boss—"

He growled down the phone. "I told you not to be seen, you idiot." He swore. Riva turned her head as she heard screaming, then silence. "Drop her where you found her," he ordered. "The man's dead and can't be traced back to us. Just don't mess up again."

The phone clicked into silence, and the killer turned and saw the now-seated Riva, but before she could do anything, he dropped his gun and phone onto the table and grabbed her. Riva struggled to break free from his grip as a piece of cloth was pushed over her mouth, muffling her screams. She kicked out and, wrestling with her assailant, the pair fell to the floor. Her head swam as she fought to remain conscious, but slowly, her resistance lessened as her limp body fell away from him, and Riva's world went black.

Riva opened her eyes and stared up at a young girl looking down at her.

"Are you OK?" she said. Riva nodded and struggled to her feet. She wanted to scream murder, but what had happened seemed so absurd. Had she imagined it? If it was real, she could have been murdered. It was only the intervention of the guy on the telephone that saved her, and if she went to the police, what would she say? She thanked the woman and headed off. The poor dead guy, though, she thought. Who was he? It was like a movie, and what had happened would make a great one.

A full moon shone down as Riva headed home. She heard a sound behind her and spun around but could do nothing as a greyish, egg-shaped object rolled down the pavement and knocked her off her feet. Riva watched as it continued on, hit a wall, and slowly came to rest nearby. She picked it up, and her entire body shivered. In that fraction of a second, a life flashed before her eyes. Chariots pulled by running horses went into battle, and an image of a crocodile head on a human form looked on from the bank of a river as farmers tilled the fields. Women in long black braids wearing pristine linen garments played music on harps with such dedication that Riva could almost hear the tune as other tall, elegant women played various instruments. A crowd of regally-dressed men and women nodded enthusiastically as the music continued. Black smoke moved among the oblivious crowd, but as Riva concentrated on the amorphous form, the image in her mind faded and then disappeared. The egg-shaped stone fell from her hand and rolled along the pavement again. Shaken from the reverie, Riva hurried after the now-coloured stone until she finally caught it.

The Power of the Stones

Stellar star Riva headed to the pyramids with director Steven, producer Moses, John Abel – the screenwriter, and a team of makeup artists, designers and technicians to inspect the setting for a new sequel to a feature film on ancient Egypt. The actress had come a long way since she stumbled upon the stone.

Several years had passed since the chance encounter with the enchanted gem. Riva's acting skills had improved dramatically, and she had become an overnight sensation. The night she returned home with the unusual object, she tossed her clothes in the washing machine and took a hot shower. Later, she slumped on a couch with a bag of chips, hot coffee, and a tuna sandwich and settled in front of the television.

Believing she had done terribly at the audition and, still somewhat shaken from the ordeal of being kidnapped, she consoled herself with the fact she was still alive. While still considering whether to involve the police, she was startled by her mobile ringing and almost dropped her coffee.

"Is this Riva?" the familiar voice of the director from the audition asked.

Riva gulped as her heart raced. "Y-e-s."

"Can you come again tomorrow?" he said.

"Of course."

"Please read the script carefully," he said mechanically, "and watch out for the nuances."

The next day, Riva's presence on set appeared to surprise the crew as she sheepishly made her way around the set. Steven, the director, had apparently cast her as a reporter in the documentary. As she became accustomed to her role, the crew and cast appeared to warm to her, and as she played more roles, her name soon spread through the acting community, and her reputation as an up-and-coming talent with genuine prospects grew. Although other filmmakers soon sought Riva to play parts in feature films rather than documentaries, her big breaks came from working with

Steven. Together, they worked on increasingly bigger and bigger productions, moving beyond documentaries and onto blockbusters.

Steven had left Britain after college and marriage to Jane, found work at an advertising agency in the capital, Cairo, fell in love with the city, and never left. His wife and son visited a few times but never stayed. This put a strain on their marriage, and eventually, it broke down when his wife met someone else.

Relieved, rather than disappointed, Steven managed to establish himself by making tourism documentaries exploring the tombs and sights around the city. On occasion, he worked on shady occult films, which had to be funded by private parties in advance. His efforts to forge relationships with natives or ex-pats failed, and Steven decided to remain focused on the tombs and friends.

Tall and muscular, he towered over most. His shoulder-length brown hair, handsome features, well-spoken voice, and politeness made him stand out amongst people.

Steven met Riva at an audition for a documentary on Karnak Temple, which revolved around the adventures of a television journalist who uncovers fertility rites among the stronger and weaker pharaohs. The director rejected Riva at first, then changed his mind, but he never knew why.

The performance of the aspiring actress improved dramatically the second time he employed her, which caught the attention of others within the studio. Steven and Riva soon formed a formidable partnership, mesmerising audiences with gripping performances and fabulous direction. Steven became attracted to Riva, but the feelings were never reciprocated. Riva found him a bore except when they worked on a project together.

The crew set up camp at dawn by the sphinx to avoid the warm September sun. John Abel, the screenwriter, worked on the storyline while on location, discussing the plot with the lead actress, which helped to visualise how the screenplay would work.

As for Steven, he readily deviated from the storyline, eliminating or adding scenes when Riva would have sudden bursts of inspiration, convincing department heads from the studio, cast and the screenwriter to move to bigger and better locations, much to the annoyance of some.

One day, a row erupted between John Abel and Steven over changes made by Riva on location. While filming a scene, Riva walked as if in a trance to a slab of marble in the Karnak Temple and pointed at a painted scene on the granite slab.

"This is how the King's virility has been tested by using the leaves of acacia," she said, as if in a stupor.

Furious, John Abel stormed out of the temple, pushing through the crowd of tourists that had assembled to watch the filming.

Steven had hurried after the irate scriptwriter and attempted to mollify him. "Giving into the whims of an actor who turns dust to gold is not a bad idea, don't you agree?" Steven said. "It is still your script, and your name is on it."

Abel and Steven had worked together for some time after a chance meeting at a hangout, popular among ex-pats, in an affluent neighbourhood in Cairo. Abel liked to write his scripts on his laptop while sitting at a table and was furious with anybody who dared speak to him when he was working. Stout and potbellied, Abel usually resembled an unmade bed with creased clothing, unruly, curly black hair atop a heavy face, thick lips and a small nose that appeared out of place within his features.

He came up to Steven one day and handed him a script. "I think that will catapult you, us, to fame," he said, beaming. "Read it."

The story revolved around a power struggle in a tumultuous period in ancient Egyptian history. Steven, enthralled and excited by the gripping narrative, spent all night reading the story. As early as he dared, he telephoned Moses, the producer and entrepreneur. "Moses, listen," he said with barely concealed excitement. "This is a game-changer."

Moses, a shrewd and wily businessman who financed anything that would make money –from meat packing to weekly journals to movies – readily agreed, such was Steven's enthusiasm.

Steven cast Riva in Abel's first sequel, which was about a rocky period in the era of the pharaohs. The movie created quite a stir, and soon, the clique of four, Steven, Riva, Abel and Moses, grew closer as they continued to make franchises. The mysteriousness of their leading actress intrigued and worried the three men, so they tried to keep her under wraps from the increasingly curious press.

"Riva!" Steven shouted at Riva, who was shivering uncontrollably despite the warm night, as they filmed in the temple during the first sequel. Riva then stopped her trembling and walked to a spot near a temple outside Cairo. "This is where murder takes place," she said.

John Abel frowned. "How could you possibly know? The story about a queen who kills her father has never been confirmed."

Riva placed a hand on one of the columns. "I feel it."

The men exchanged glances with each other but said nothing. Having agreed, wisely, that it was best to ignore Riva's strange episodes, especially when the sudden seizures proved constructive to the plot. In time, Riva's idiosyncrasies became a regular habit, and the films rapidly transformed the cast and crew into a formidable filmmaking enterprise.

"Fire, move," Riva said as she turned wide-eyed to face the cast and crew. She turned away from them as she looked across at the pyramids. "Can't you see the curves?" she shrieked.

Abel listened intently. He had grown accustomed to Riva's disclosures and welcomed them, incorporating them into the lines he wrote.

Riva continued to stare as a flame erupted in front of her. Hundreds of burning shapes emerged from the fire and ran past the oblivious crew. Then, the blaze transformed into a shimmering retinue of bare-chested warriors wearing polished armour and elaborate headdresses. The shape of a woman wearing a long, golden dress, which flowed majestically down to her ankles, came into view. Riva stared into a pair of young, powerful eyes which appeared to burrow into her core. The two girls stood, studying each other while the sun cast a coruscating beam across the pair.

"Who are you?" Riva asked.

"I belong to an ancient court," she said. "I am the daughter of a mighty king," she continued before disappearing.

"Wake up, Riva. Wake up." John Abel gently shook the confused actress. Steven stood a few steps behind, biting his lip. Riva sat up as everyone looked on.

"I am all right," she said as John Abel helped her to her feet. "I think I have been given an audience with a princess." Riva glanced between the writer and director. "She has a name. Nebet. Her name is Princess Nebet. She needs our help, and we need a good story." She glanced again at their worried faces. "Have I been out longer than the last time?" The two men nodded.

Riva turned and moved across to the spot where the Princess had appeared, worried that she would forget what she had told her. Riva pirouetted with her arms out wide. "The story begins here. This is the angle we should film from. I don't know why yet."

Riva looked at the scenic view of the three pyramids at a distance from the sphinx. Different from generic postcard photos.

Steven joined her. "The opening shot will be fantastic," he said, "but we will have to find several locations."

"Look at the smaller construct over there," Riva said, pointing to a smaller pyramid. "Can you see it? It is close to the great pyramids, at the base of the largest."

John Abel busily wrote down a storyline depicting a runaway Princess reuniting with a long-lost love under the rising sun. "I must be telepathic," Abel said, beaming.

"You want me to follow?" Riva said to some unseen entity. She ran into the desert in the direction of the structure as Steven and the rest of the crew followed.

The apparition reappeared, floating ahead of Riva as she tried to keep pace with the spectre. Steven matched her stride, but the panting producer could not keep up the pace. Then, tiring, the actress slowed as the ancient being quickened, making it impossible to follow on foot.

"We'll take the cars," Riva said. "We must not lose her."

The convoy reached the smallest of the three pyramids and stopped. Riva jumped from the vehicle and gazed at the Princess, who was pointing at the sandy earth. Driven by the spirit, the actress dropped to her knees and began to dig. Steven and Abel hurried across to her and watched as she clawed at the sand.

"What is it?" Steven said, dropping down next to her. Riva ignored him as she continued her frantic digging. Abel and some of the others did likewise as a flurry of hands pulled back the sand until something appeared, glimmering at the bottom of the excavated hole. A colourful stone, the size of an eyeball with a carved ruby on top, rose above the surface, and Riva grasped the gem before the sand slipped back into the hole.

"The stone is almost alive," Riva said. "Can't you see?" A ray of light burst from the stone. Her colleagues ignored the comments. They had heard Riva's pronouncements previously. For them, it simply heralded another box office hit.

The sun came up, which meant that filming could progress once more.

Riva gazed down at the twinkling stone as she remembered the gem she had found previously. "It is time to start writing, please, John." Riva took a deep breath and, repeating what Princess Nebet was saying, she began. "In ancient times, I led a privileged royal life. I studied the fine arts and danced with such grace that I put other dancers to shame," Riva continued as the scriptwriter scribbled away. "I adored my family." The Princess smiled at Riva. "I studied fighting techniques and became an excellent combatant, mastering grappling, jousting and javelin throwing. My ability with a bow was unrivalled. One day, the goddess Hathor fired the arrow of love deep into my heart during a game attended by my father, the King. My newfound love, a brave fighter, was expeditiously promoted into the clique of strong-bodied guards around the King. He had joined as a volunteer soldier from a southern Nome. My father wouldn't consent to the marriage. The love of my life had no lineage of any kind, noble or other."

Riva paused briefly and continued with the Princess's words. "When my father discovered my love for the fighter, he threw him out and ordered his exile. I forbid you to see him, he said. He is a stray, and because of you, I will throw him to the dogs despite the fact that he is my best fighter. He has given the love of my life to the palace sorcerer to make sure I never find him. But he did not count on me being as strong-headed and stubborn as himself. I have vowed to find my warrior no matter where and how long it takes." Riva watched as the Princess lowered her eyes. "I will help immortalise your name in my realm if you help me return home," the Princess said to Riva. "In my search, I have lost my way back. Nor can I find the love of my life." She started to sob.

Riva had no idea how to help and wisely remained silent as the Princess continued with her story. Riva, in turn, translated the events to John Abel.

"I am stuck in the present. My home is the red stone you are holding in your hand. It carries a fine ruby that sheds a red light on the stone, given to me by my mentor, the hour priest Wenefer. The gem shelters me during my travels in space and time, but it will soon lose its life, and I shall not be sheltered anymore." The Princess continued the narrative as Riva recounted it. Abel excitedly scribbled it down as endless possibilities for the new script flooded his mind.

"Wenefer," explained the Princess, "had enchanted the stone with a potent potion using the strongest herbs and magical powers. Such magic is perfected only by high priests, and Wenefer, a senior priest, knew how to wield a potion. Father trusts him and has asked him to come to serve in the palace."

Wenefer explained to the Princess that once beyond the palace gates, the stone would provide shelter outside the court, and she would forfeit the right of his magical protection. She was weakened once she was away from the energy of the palace, and only the red stone kept her alive.

He informed the Princess that the gem would only be a safe home for a short time, and then she had to find her way back. The stone contained a map that responded to the beating of the Princess's heart and would show her the way back to the palace.

Priest Wenefer's skills were impressive, and he was able to predict when the floods took place. He foresaw the demise of kings, the fertility of harems and was highly sought after to identify potential love interests and arrange marriages. He dedicated some of his skills to cast protective spells on mummies and alleviate the pain of man and woman on their way to the heavens or the underworld. Although he was a master of incantations and sorcery and a trusted confidante among the residents of the palace, he had limitations.

"He gave me warnings, too," the Princess said. "The stone draws maps to show you the way home, but I cannot foresee life beyond the times I know. Upon your return, if you return, when you find what you are looking for, I suggest you ready yourself to face the consequences. Your father will be furious." Agonised, the Princess also recalled the warnings of the priest not to be tricked into turning to the dark forces for assistance.

Wenefer had attached the ruby in the invincible stone, both of which were forged from alien magic and the sun thousands of years ago. The priest discovered the stone by chance, near the temple he served at before joining the palace. One night, he witnessed an object as it fell, burning to earth from the sky. He stood mesmerised and later wrote down the litany he chanted at the time, which may have contributed to the birth of the red stone.

Wenefer bent and picked up the still-hot stone, which had the ruby loosely mounted into it. Using his garment to gather the object, he hurried back to where he lived. Then, using all his experience, expertise and supernatural qualities, he trained the stone to serve him before carving a place in the stone for the ruby to keep both inseparable, like mother and child.

In truth, child, Wenefer had told her, I do not believe I shall see you or the stones again. Perhaps it is meant to be. Wenefer then shook his head and walked away, leaving the Princess to her fate.

The kind priest, Wenefer, found peace in the desert, praying under star-studded skies and the priesthood at Karnak Temple in Thebes and Memphis in Upper Egypt. He focused on the study of the Ka, the life force and the qualities of stars, much to the dismay of his disciples. They understood, however, that he followed a much-needed path to find cures and good magic.

Normally, generations of priests kept descendants informed about the universe. They left behind secret documents for those disciples to stay vigilant about sorcery. Older priests discussed the stars and the types of magic that lived before their times. They made sure they passed on their finds in case such discoveries came in useful. When the King summoned Wenefer to teach the Princess some of his secrets, he promised that he would allow the reluctant priest to go to the silence of the nights once he had completed the Princess's teachings. Wenefer schooled the Princess in religion, medicine, and the history of their land and also trained her to speak to the stone through the beating of the heart so the stone could respond. Which it did.

"The gem uncovered the routes I had to take," the Princess said. "It drew maps of kingdoms and people living across different time zones. Now, the stone has pointed a road to the south, which means I have to travel towards the Cataracts to find my lost lover."

Riva listened to all those tales as John Abel continued to write his storyline, which told the story of the love-struck Princess. The events took place in the Middle Kingdom thousands of years ago. A story about love and passion at the foot of the Pyramid. Princess Nebet appeared to trust Riva implicitly.

Riva had kept the first stone that she had found when still a struggling actress safe in her bedroom. She had an affinity with the gem that she couldn't put into words. It was as if the stone had chosen her under the full moon on that fateful night and had proven to be a lucky charm for her. Since that day, stories and images had arrived unbidden and flowed through her mind. These images and stories were refined into scripts by John Abel.

Riva

Riva looked into the mirror as visions of the Princess and events from the past stared back. The face of a woman with thick black eyebrows and dark-painted eyes briefly appeared before being replaced with a view of a battlefield with Egyptian soldiers in mortal combat with foreign legions. The noise was deafening as blades swished while swords and daggers crashed against one another. There was a whoosh as arrows were liberated from their bows while the fighting continued all around. The scenes arrived unbidden – a tumult of images cascaded over her as helplessly she looked on.

The phantom princess of the desert had also changed. Riva could sense her liking for the world she now inhabited. "If I stay," she confided in Riva, "I will have to find another home and relinquish the red stone, for it is about to die. As Wenefer told me, like people, the stone has a set lifespan."

Riva bore witness to the Princess's conversation as she continued to gaze into the mirror.

"Eventually," Wenefer said as he looked affectionately at his protégé. "You will have to send word to your father to help bring you back." The Princess froze at these ominous words. She was aware that Royals, lost or in need of help in foreign realms, were forced to summon the dark realm of the demons, who acted most dishonourably. The Princess would have to cut a part of her soul with a blade sealed with the majestic insignia hidden deep in the ring around her finger and hand it over to the force operating the gate to get her messages through to the other world. The action meant the Princess agreed to relinquish part of her beauty and cut many seasons from her life. When she died, she would be forced to spend time in the nether world before gaining admittance into eternal bliss. Wenefer would also face death by torture for breaking the trust of the King and abetting the royal in crime.

In the meantime, the ethereal Princess implored Riva to watch out for her home, the red stone. "I have to spend part of the night within the walls of the red gem," she told Riva. "I must remain from midnight till dawn or lose my royal aura. Please keep my home safe."

Unknown to Riva at the time, when she had found the stone in the desert, she unwittingly opened a minuscule gate, becoming, in a sense, a guardian to the Princess and holder of secrets.

"You are putting a lot of trust in me," Riva told the Princess. "I am merely an actress who wants to play roles." Riva was both humbled and frightened in taking charge of the stone and all the sorcery contained within it. The Princess omitted to tell the mortal girl that as long as Riva held the stone, the Princess was able to rest in her human body. The Princess, unbeknown to Riva, had paused in her quest to find her lover by stealthily moving inside Riva in order to rest her tired soul.

The filming crew travelled to Luxor in the south to shoot a promising sequel to the film, standing excitedly in line among endless tourists and locals. Riva discussed her plan with Steven and John Abel.

After listening intently to the actress, Steven clasped his hands together. "We shall head to the Temple of Karnak and take the scene from the sacred lake," he explained to the team. The crew and cast chatted enthusiastically as Riva became lightheaded and staggered before collapsing to the floor.

The Princess fled Riva's body, realising that the mortal proved too weak to hold her energy for more than a few minutes. For now, the Princess would give Riva time to film her sequel. Riva opened her eyes as if nothing had happened and proceeded to the gate – with the nonplussed director and entourage looking on.

The team arrived in ancient Thebes, the city of Luxor, which clung to the Nile bank, coiling and snaking around the land for centuries as if they were lovers, locked in an embrace.

The crew moved, almost unfettered, back and forth along the Nile banks, making the movie. Their power and influence increased as the movie franchise revenues skyrocketed at the box office.

"We shall take a break after the shoot," John Abel snapped. "I need to visit an archaeologist friend of mine to go over some of the facts before we fly to Memphis and back to Thebes for a sequel. I cannot depend on these visions alone for my facts."

Riva sensed his rising annoyance. Although his writing output had increased like never before, she suspected his reliance on her visions was beginning to rile the writer. He was clearly jealous, but she could only hope that this would change as they progressed.

In Luxor, the script once again delivered itself as John Abel wrote down the words dictated to Riva by the Princess. This time, the actress searched for a lost parchment that led to a power of sorts in the Temple of Karnak. Riva, carrying the stone which harboured the Princess, led the crew into the temple to an alabaster slab with hieroglyphics etched into the ancient stone. As Riva stood above it, the slab revealed a three-dimensional parchment preserved inside an alabaster jar. A painting on the jar showed a king drinking from a cup beside the deity Osiris.

"The potion in the cup gives pharaohs extended lives," the Princess whispered to Riva. "It is gifted with physical and mental powers. Inside the jar is a parchment with writings and symbols which need to be deciphered."

Steven gazed at the beautiful jar. "If such attention to detail is on display on the outside," he said, "then the contents, by reason, should be even more precious." As Steven spoke, the red stone held by Riva glowed, illuminating the contents preserved within.

"A cautious priest saved the document in unguent and ancient oils in an alabaster jar," Riva said as she retold the story that the Princess recounted. This ritual had become essential with each sequel. "Priests of my world go to many lengths to protect their information," she continued. "If one of them is caught by the wrong followers, especially Seth, they will be tortured and burnt until the smoke from their skin uncovers the secrets of the parchments."

The Princess commanded Riva to break the slab and fetch the contents.

John Abel turned white. "We cannot break the law for a ghost," he said to Riva. "We have to call in the antiquities department and forget about your muse. I can write a script without her."

Riva and the others protested, and after some discussion, John Abel left. He did not want anything more to do with the phantom.

Riva and Steven now had to consider how far they were prepared to go.

"We will return with tools at midnight," Steven said solemnly, knowing that the parchment could put their following picture on a totally higher level of success. "Frankly, I find the prospects irresistible," he said.

At the hotel by the Nile, they helped themselves to a light meal of unsalted white cheese immersed in olive oil, lemon, and spiced with thyme and black pepper. They washed this down with copious amounts of mint tea to help them stay awake and refreshed.

By nightfall, the soft breeze encouraged tourists and natives to stroll along the Nile bank. Riva and Steven took a walk into the market downtown, which, in Luxor, remained in a constant state of flux, especially at night when the weather cooled. To avoid suspicious eyes, Riva and Steven first browsed stores bursting with replicas of the busts of kings, queens and cats. They bought silver-crafted jewellery and semi-precious gems, mainly agate, rumoured to bestow its owner with self-confidence. Later, they collected a cordless drill and spare batteries, secreted inside Riva's tote bag, and headed for the temple.

Allowing the Princess's stone to guide them and assisted by a full moon, they made their way undetected to an entrance below what resembled a clerestory. Quickly finding their way to the alabaster stone and using the drill at low speed, they began their work. To their surprise, the slab cracked from the small hole they had drilled, almost as if they had unknowingly pushed a button. A piece of glass was revealed, and Riva carefully placed her hands between the alabaster pieces and picked it up. As she held it in her hands, it metamorphosed into a jar with a piece of paper visible inside. Riva and Steven put the two pieces of alabaster together and hurried back to the hotel the same way they had arrived.

As they reached the hotel, Riva remembered something that had happened to her years before. When she was about ten, during a trip to London, she met Peter, an English man whom Riva's mother had trained to be a journalist with. Peter had met and finally married a beautiful woman who had divorced her husband, a baron, to be with him. Peter appeared to be an average British member of the press, except for one thing. He claimed to have befriended a ghost. One day, he made a strange comment to her. "You must decipher the parchment," he said. "Save your roots." Riva did not understand what he had said and made light of the entire episode, thinking Peter was joking, but for some reason, she had been reminded of the incident now. It appeared connected in some way.

In the morning, Riva planned to show the jar to a revered Egyptologist and assess the significance of the find. Steven worried about the time wasted on this and also involving someone else. He had to finish the film, and due to pressure from the production company, he had to begin another with little time for rest. "This is not part of my job description, way above my pay grade," he had said to Riva. "We are colluding with a phantom to rob a temple in the middle of the night," he had continued.

But in truth, he knew their adventures had changed their lives, bringing about box office hits. He decided to relax, and the next day, Steven took a horse carriage, a favourite pastime in Luxor, leaving ahead of Riva. Once there, he met with Dr Imran, an expert on ancient Egypt, and waited for Riva and John Abel.

Riva and John Abel had agreed to join later. Riva collected John Abel from his hotel and showed him what she and Steven had found, assuring him that there were no hard feelings on her part for his previous day's behaviour. In truth, he did not need much cajoling, realising, after a night's sleep, that the scripts written with Riva's help were the best he had ever done. Her visions had opened up the golden gates to success. Since working with the young actress, producers were falling over themselves to get him to write screenplays for them. A far cry from his humble beginnings when he would wait all night outside the door of directors and beg them to read his scripts.

Riva and John Abel arrived at the historian's residence with the jar. She was desperately hoping for both an explanation and an opportunity to enrich the script. Perhaps even helping the Princess to find her lover and return home. Then, thought Riva, she could put the entire matter behind her.

The professor worked near the Temple of Karnak. On the pair's arrival, they found the door to his office slightly open. Dr Imran was slumped on his desk. His skin was shrivelled, and next to him, on the floor, lay a sceptre. Papers and books were scattered everywhere around the body, and Steven, appearing to be in a trance, stood close by – his eyes fixed in a stare. John Abel gently shook him.

"What is happening?" Steven said. "Why are you pushing me? Keep that dagger away." John Abel and Riva glanced at each other as the scriptwriter led Steven to a chair. They listened as he recounted what had happened. But he was unable to tell them much. Unable to remember if the doctor was dead on his arrival or if anyone else was there.

Before calling the police, Riva convinced Steven to say they had all arrived together and stumbled upon the crime scene. "The police may suspect you," she said, "if they know you were alone with the doctor."

Dr Imran studied Egyptology for most of his adult life. He received numerous accolades for archaeological finds based on his breakthrough essays about the ancient world. In short, no one understood ancient Egyptian life and the magic therein better. Over decades, he thoroughly investigated the relationship between the history of the pharaohs and their architecture. He even dabbled in conjuration to trace the evolution of the ancient's magic. When he taught students at universities around the world, he would occasionally amuse them, demonstrating how the pharaohs used their magic to divine which women could bear them children, who proved to be a fitting match, and what potions prolonged their lives. Now he lay dead.

The police arrived at the scene shortly after Riva's call.

"What are the three of you doing in the archaeologist's office?" asked the detective in charge.

"We meet with Dr Imran before any filming," John Abel said. "We discuss historical credibility, and then we fictionalise the data."

"I consult with the doctor on the adequacy of the settings to the times," Steven said solemnly. He glanced at Riva, who held the urn with the secret parchment immersed in a potion.

Riva tried to remain calm, recalling the unauthorised excavation and the relic she carried and did not report. She steadied herself, trying to push away the thought that they had stumbled onto a crime scene. She slumped onto a nearby chair. "I'm sorry," she said. "This is such a shock. Dr Imran was a dear friend. He was a lovely man, and his knowledge of ancient Egypt was unrivalled. His work will never be forgotten, and he will be greatly missed." Riva answered the other questions posed by the police as calmly as she could. But her mind remained on their find and the possible breakthrough in magic spells carried out in ancient rituals.

The detective eyed Riva and the item she held suspiciously, then glanced between the three of them, deep in thought. It could prove awkward if the famous actress and her colleagues went missing. Her presence amused the natives, who followed her every move. Also, a film shoot in Luxor attracted businesses and entertained Thebans and tourists. "I expect you at the police station tomorrow for a statement," he snapped. "You can come alone."

Riva had to decipher the parchment, the writings on the urn and the strange liquid inside. Sometimes, the contents looked like floating gas, doodling incomprehensible sketches inside the alabaster cage. The unusual urn made of pieces of glass threaded together by a silver thread stood straight, inspiring the possibility of a new script, setting the scene for a crime genre – a joyride for the director.

Once back in her hotel room, she almost dropped the jar at the sight of the Princess. The apparition never failed to surprise her, appearing out of nowhere. But this time, something was different. The Princess was so terrified when she saw the moving objects inside the jar that Riva stepped back, tripped and fell, smashing the jar to smithereens. Fumes from the vessel filled the room before escaping through the open door. The smoke spread fast, forcing frightened residents from their beds. Some crowded in the lobby – others fled outside. Firefighters quickly arrived, but as soon as they did, the odourless fumes dispersed, leaving the confused manager to calm the residents. He took a microphone from the reception area and attempted to appease the excited patrons. "This is a false alarm," he said. "The hotel has hired a new magician, and he is trying out a new trick for the show tonight. Please return to your rooms."

In the mayhem, no one had paid attention to Riva – who inhaled a great deal of smoke – and as she looked on, a parchment unfolded before her eyes, spawning images and scribbling words with an invisible hand before setting free an insect, and then, as quickly as it arrived, it vanished.

"What a beautiful scarab," she said to herself. "Or is that a falcon on top of Osiris?"

The insect reminded her of the mosquito bite that caused the death of Lord Carnarvon – The Earl financed excavation work in Luxor, which led to the breakthrough discovery of the Tomb of King Tutankhamun. Carnarvon died horrifically, and his family returned the relics he had taken, wanting nothing to do with them after he died. Fearing that they were cursed. Riva thought of the Osirians who, led by Osiris, worked hard, cultivated the land, tended cattle, and taught farming to their children. Osiris taught love and fertility and, most importantly, encouraged good magic.

"Osirian magic," she whispered. "Incredible. But who is the beautiful woman in the background carrying a sceptre?" Riva saw a luminous female wearing a bloodied white robe threatening Osiris with a staff and pushing away the falcon.

The images that washed over Riva from the broken jar, proved too much, and she fainted.

She had become accustomed to the sight of John Abel looking down worryingly at her when she was roused from her unconsciousness, with an equally concerned Steven dutifully waiting for her to explain the visions.

"The dreams narrated lifetimes," she said. "Did you see the flying mosquito?"

Other concerned colleagues joined the director and writer. Riva looked down at the smashed jar, but she still had the parchment, which had landed in her lap. Maybe some residue from the vaporised potion had clung to the papyrus roll, protecting it somehow, she concluded.

Riva moved a hand to her elbow. The venomous insect had wounded her deeply, leaving a vicious, snarling hole.

The next day, Riva, pleased to be alive despite losing a piece of evidence, headed to the police station to give a second statement. The detective, as well as asking about the discovery of the body, had enquired if she knew anything about the fumes that had started in her room. Riva had told him she didn't. Telling the detective nothing of her visions or attack by the insect.

She joined the crew later in Karnak to start the filming. Mechanically, she led her team to the exact location where she had retrieved the canopic jar. Shooting took place, and the Princess assisted Riva with playing the demonic Queen to perfection. When Riva checked her makeup, she perfectly resembled the Queen from the jar. How many ghosts did she embrace?

The crew wrapped the scene before dawn and headed exhausted back to their hotel on the Nile.

Steven looked out of the window before he fell asleep. Rubbing his eyes in disbelief, he could have sworn he saw shadows vaporising out of the Nile. He shook his head, putting it down to his tiredness and fell into a deep slumber.

So soundly did he sleep that he did not wake when a group of armed assailants stormed into Riva's room. Their bodies transformed into beasts with claws. An old man wreathed in wrinkles strolled under the window and alerted by the shadows in the room – the silhouettes of the dark beings exposed – he sighed. His eyes shone with an alien brightness as he walked on. It began.

"Wake up!" The Princess had roused the sleeping Riva minutes before the attack, giving her enough time to pull on her pyjamas and escape through the window to the lower floor with the sound of furniture breaking echoing above her.

The police came within minutes, and the inspector, who had taken Riva's statement, was calm on his arrival. The actress created too much noise for her own good and also for the guests at the esteemed hotel. Fortunately, the tourists seemed amused by what had happened. Had it not been for the publicity the film generated for the city, he would have booked her on the first plane out of Luxor, along with her crew, for good. His suspicion surrounding the mysterious actress had increased, prompting him to have her followed around the clock since she had landed. He was well aware of her nighttime venture into the Karnak Temple.

He had previously met with his informant. "Both the actress and her companion inspected locations for the shoot," the informant said.

But the detective remained unconvinced – born into an old family that handled tomb raiders and smugglers of ancient artefacts.

"Have you seen them stop somewhere in the temple?" he asked his spy.

"Oh yes. They have but…" The young boy furrowed his brow, unable to continue. He did not remember. His memory was there one minute and gone the next. "I can't remember," he said to the detective.

The boy must have been hypnotised somehow during the discovery, mused the detective. More seasoned sources had informed him that the celebrity guests seemingly had their hands on a wealth of information – a historical trajectory no one had ever explored before. The chances of solving the mystery in Riva's room seemed unlikely, as did finding the vaporised killer of the Egyptologist Dr Imran.

Detective Abanoub examined Riva's room for clues, picking up a piece of broken glass. He grimaced as he felt the residual power of the glass and wondered how many old-school police officers still lived like him – with one foot in the spirit world. He closed his eyes, and a vision of a soulless queen appeared but quickly vanished. Abanoub froze for a moment, for this demon differed from the ones he had previously encountered. With a heavy heart, he prepared for one last battle, one last journey into the surreal. The room had all the clues he needed, but ignoring them, he decided to leave. He eyed Riva, pushed his notebook into his pocket, handed her a card with his details on it, and advised her to call him if she needed help. Riva smiled, and the pair parted.

Abanoub – The Detective

Abanoub deduced that the murder and the attack on Riva had roots way back in time, and he had witnessed only the tip of an iceberg. His job as a detective provided an appropriate cover for the actual work he undertook as guardian of the gate to the ancients. He hoped that one of his sons would carry the workload after him and follow in his stead. In fact, he wished to retire.

"I want to stay home, watch over the land and plant trees," he said.

His wife gave him a smile – the same tender smile she had given him over the past forty years whenever he expressed the desire to leave the force.

If he had read the clues correctly, and he believed that he had, they acted as a summons to ward off another bout of sorcery which plagued the city for many years. He had lived through incredible events, ironing out wrinkles in time, and had gained an impressive reputation as an expert interpreter of ancient crimes. His knack for wrapping up age-old cold cases without alerting the media and his services were viewed as indispensable by his superiors on both sides of time.

Abanoub was a quiet man pushing sixty-five. The detective's family went back thousands of years, all the way to the Intermediate Period when havoc and darkness clouded the country. This forced the whole Abanoubian tribe to migrate from the ancient capital, Memphis, to the Delta when it had become too difficult to stay down south. Those days were dark for many families when weaker pharaohs ruled. Power had been handed to even weaker nomarchs, and sorcery threatened to destabilise the kingdom and upset the Nile. The river became so sad that its waters coiled upon itself, writhing like an angry python and retreated. Predators, crocodiles, and snakes walked out of dried-up shores and were mercilessly hunted by priests from the dark side. The animals became fodder for magic that crippled, maimed and set people against each other. Those priests who opted for blackness and dark magic excavated headquarters underground to recruit tainted hearts and expanded their forces exponentially. They allied themselves with the deity Seth, who lived with the sole purpose of bringing down everything fruitful his brother Osiris worked for all his life.

Abanoub had many tales to tell, which would delight a gullible actress such as Riva, who clearly hungered after fame. His family had vowed since time immemorial to fend off the evil forces with as little magic as possible. At least they used green magic – potions made from herbs, tree leaves, and grass, exhumed from corals bought from sailors and blessed by priests to heal tortured souls. Some people who came into contact with peaceful magic converted from wickedness into indolence. Friends and foes alike, once subjected to such a potent potion, threw down their javelins rather than fight and inflict harm on each other. Abanoub's people became renowned centurions until the coming of age of the New Kingdom, which gave them respite from the dark magic.

Abanoub concluded that the murder and the trashing of the Egyptologist's home bore the marks of the deity Seth all over again, ever determined to seize the throne he thought his by right. Seth, the cunning force, had used civilians and lost souls eager for petty riches to change the course of history. Abanoub, a close friend of Imran, had formed a clique of devoted veterans who combated alien deconstructionists of history. Someone or something killed him for the information he possessed. "I bet it is the woman I saw in the shard," he said to himself.

Abanoub ran over the events in his mind, attempting to establish if there were similarities between the mayhem in Riva's room and another case he had worked on. He had helped two ancient lovers who had been brought forth by mistake during a séance orchestrated by a former convict and dabbler in raw magic. While trying to send them back to where they came from, the sorcerer ushered in a Nubian warrior who sought the girl, Carmen, for himself and intended to kill the lover. Seventeen-year-old Carmen had visited Abanoub in his dream, imploring him for help. Abanoub, sorry for the spirit wandering alone in a strange realm, approached the convict, turned sorcerer, and ordered him to reverse the spell.

Abanoub gave the dabbler a piece of ancient timber, inherited from a great-grandmother when he was a child, but kept a small amount for himself. He ordered the man to burn it during the conjuring.

The convict stared at the detective in disbelief. "Are we going to work together?" he asked.

"Now," Abanoub bellowed as he stared at the stunned man who did exactly as he was told.

The old detective watched on, directing the convict on how to turn back the clock and isolate the warrior before he murdered the girl's lover. The magic session ended well. The lovers were reunited and returned to their ancient time zone in Memphis while the warrior remained banished, roaming the realms for eternity. The convict, awed by Abanoub's magical prowess, devoted himself to the detective. He employed the man's son, Obeid, as an errand boy in the precinct. Abanoub, however, no longer found solace in saving helpless souls. He felt sorry for all the beings who roamed along the abyss of realms, lost in time and space without closure, disturbing some of the living who unknowingly crossed their paths. He could not help them all.

Disturbances during mystical gatherings became frequent in Luxor, and the natives became accustomed to mishaps which sometimes unleashed disturbing spirits. Abanoub and the magician became close and pulled in mutual favours from acquaintances. The detective removed the final piece of magical timber from his pocket and gave it to the convict to assist the helpless spirits. The wood, immersed in sorcery, had been gifted by a high priest to his mother's side and ended up in the ex-convict's hands. But Abanoub knew that the less the souls rattled, the less the earth shook, and demons were rendered powerless.

In all honesty, Abanoub felt sorry for his friend having to endure the daily torment inflicted by the Nubian warrior. The trapped warrior harassed the convict constantly and made his life a living hell. The exiled ghost hurled furniture and made noises, beseeching the convict to help him get back home. The convict, unable to sleep, went mad with rage. Things came to a head after his landlord complained to the police many times, and the convict was at the end of his tether.

"This is your ultimatum," the landlord warned. "Either you stop the noise, or I'll throw you out."

The Nubian warrior, anguished over his plight, screamed constantly, pleading with the sorcerer to send him back with vows never to come near the girl. The timber eased the pain of the banished Nubian, but because of his poisoned spirit, the goodness of the timber helped his transition to the underworld, but he lived no more.

The mess in Riva's room portended a far worse scenario, not a simple case he could resolve with inherited timber and the convict's help.

Riva

Riva sat in a corner in her pyjamas, scared but determined. She must be close to discovering if criminals openly attacked a famed hub for high-end tourists.

In the morning, the crew assembled at the same spot in Karnak Temple where Riva seized the jar.

Abanoub sent his errand boy, the magician's son, Obeid, to keep an eye on Riva while he went to alert another member of the clique of vigilantes, Rahim. His old friend must have seen the signs of devils rattling doors to bring Nitocris, the witch, to the throne, he thought.

Riva waited impatiently for daybreak, hoping the Princess could help, but a dark presence gnawed at her brain, attempting to gain access to her psyche. Riva stared into the mirror and watched on as her eyes turned as black as the dead of night as if the sinister entity was trying to gain control of her. She fought to stop it and watched as her eyes returned to their usual hue.

The Princess guided Riva to a spice store metres away from Karnak, hidden behind the giant temple.

A middle-aged man appeared and looked at Riva suspiciously before smiling. "My herbs are as old as the pyramids," he said, pointing to the shelves. "How can I help you? I have potions to make men stronger and women more fertile. What is it you require." The shopkeeper had owned the shop for many years. A vast selection of arcane spices littered the humble shelves. The herbal shop was kept alive with the constant footfall of desperate natives, eager for inexpensive remedies for protection against the other side.

"There is a princess who has contacted me," Riva blurted out. "Princess Nebet lives in a stone, and she wants to return home." She lowered her eyes. "I just want my life back, but in order to get it back, I have to free the Princess from the dying stone and help her find her lover."

The shopkeeper sat Riva down on a stool carved in hieroglyphics and handed her a red coral. He frowned. "Corals exude strength," he said, "but this stone has more power."

Riva examined the coral as it vibrated gently in her hands. "Where did you obtain such a beautiful thing,' she said.

"From a sailor who had travelled to the farthest eastern shores. He often brought back exotic stones with no clear idea about their true power and value. The sailor told me that the coral spoke to him at night in a language he did not recognise." The storekeeper chuckled. "One of his fellow sailors had warned him that the captain would not tolerate such foolish talk, so I was able to obtain the coral for a reasonable price. I did not want the sailor to realise its true worth." The storekeeper took back the coral and held it against the Princess's red stone.

The Princess appeared in full regalia and pointed at Karnak Temple. Riva and the shopkeeper followed as she fled the shop, quickly catching up with her. She paused as if she did not know what direction to take, and the shopkeeper tossed a handful of truth seeds in front of the trio to cajole temple spirits into helping the Princess find her way. They moved off again and reached the pylons, but as they did, a man with a scarf around his face appeared from nowhere. He grabbed Riva by the throat and began strangling her. The storekeeper barrelled into the man, and the pair of them crashed to the ground. The two men fought, and the storekeeper reached into his pocket for the coral and hit his assailant in the face with it. The man screamed, bringing his hands to where the coral had struck him. Mortally wounded, he staggered away from the shopkeeper and burst into flames. Within seconds, he was reduced to a pile of ashes.

"Who was he?" Riva said.

The storekeeper clambered to his feet. "A fellow salesman," he said. "For years, he has pestered me, asking for free herbs. He was a nuisance but harmless. He was a silver craftsman …" The storekeeper looked down at the pile of ashes. "His handiwork is unrivalled."

The shopkeeper understood the ominous signs of supernatural forces at play – the silversmith, an unnecessary casualty, one of many who would die in the ensuing battle. The storekeeper belonged to a fine class of ageing gatekeepers, too old now to battle against the metaphysical. Together with Abanoub, the dead historian Dr Imran, and a few others, they had formed a tiny cult of their own to do what they could. Their families had descended from a long line of Thebans and Memphites. Somewhere along the way, they had connected with other migrants from the south and east to fight the malignant forces that had evolved over time into unforgiving and brutal enemies. Remedies had to be mastered, and poisons more potent. The cult had been forced to employ dangerous tactics, using venom from the fangs of the deadliest snakes that lived in the marshes below the cataracts, for green magic no longer worked. Many young men and women sent by the shopkeeper to fetch the venom had met a tragic end. Others had been corrupted and turned to the darker side when touched by the poison they travelled to find.

As the shopkeeper, Riva and the Princess waited, images of Dr Imran appeared before them. As they watched, the murder scene unfolded, showing how the acclaimed historian had died the day before. Riva gasped as she realised that the person who had killed him was the director. Steven, holding a sceptre, his eyes unblinking, breathed a cloud of smoke into the professor's room. The Doctor put a hand to his throat as the billowing clouds surrounded him. His breathing laboured as he fought for breath before finally closing his eyes and slumping onto the desk. Steven placed the sceptre onto the floor, straightened himself and stood motionless.

The Princess brought a hand up to her mouth as she stared at Steven. "This is the Libyan prince who wanted my hand in marriage. I refused." She lowered her head. "I have left my family in the throes of a killer. I must go back. The demons are multiplying in number and power."

The Princess continued speaking. Recounting more tales as the truth seeds loosened her tongue. "My father is in great danger," she said. "The Libyan prince wants to forge, by marrying me, a political alliance which would stabilise Egypt's western border. This will not only bolster his tribal ties but safeguard trade routes of herbs and cattle through the realm." She turned to Riva and the shopkeeper. "But he will gain a foothold for his demons in my kingdom." Her eyes widened. "He is seeking revenge for being scorned."

"What can you do?" Riva said.

The Princess smiled. "If I return to my realm with this information, my father will forgive me. He may even allow me to marry my beloved bodyguard. He will be greatly angered by the actions of the Libyan prince."

The Dead Professor – Dr Imran

Egyptologist Dr Imran probably died the way he lived, immersed in magic, after a life devoted to finding a formula that would kill all the demons on earth. The shopkeeper thought back to the last time he had visited his friend, Dr Imran.

"Actually, it is a simple task, really," he had told Aminee, the shopkeeper and best friend. "Find the hideouts and smoke them out with my potion." Imran held up his blue fingers and pointed to a purple ointment in a jar. "I can use my invention as ink, too. That could prove useful."

"Well, my friend," Aminee said more to himself than Riva, who had accompanied him to where Dr Imram had been murdered. "You let your guard down. Despite your impeccable knowledge of dark sorcery, you allowed yourself to be killed."

The shopkeeper, respected and admired by the entire police precinct for his healing abilities, had called in some favours and stood at the crime scene with the actress. He needed to check some of the books the professor was working on at the time of his death. The police officer guarding Imran's flat had looked the other way when he arrived. Clearly, the officer had been told to allow the shopkeeper unfettered access. He threw a few truth seeds across the floor, and waving the coral stone in front of himself, he swiftly located the last book the Egyptologist was reading before his demise.

The shopkeeper approached the case of the murdered man differently from the authorities. The truth, he knew, was more twisted than they believed. He had met with his friend on many occasions, usually in the dead of night, and would study ancient books until daybreak. The books, sealed with intricate spells that could only be broken by seasoned sorcerers, needed to be carefully treated, or the consequences could be dire.

"I think it is this crimson volume." The shopkeeper held aloft a book with old, yellowed paper written in Hieroglyphics that described the history of a wandering princess. "I believe the Princess communicated with Dr Imran," he said, "but an entity may have scared her from the office." He leafed through the pages and stopped at a page containing dried petals mixed with fine gem shards. "Look at the page," he said to Riva. "My friend has left me breadcrumbs. Imran stumbled on new evidence."

Within the pages, the shopkeeper discovered a charm made from blue stones and wrapped in the skin of a long-dead leopard that lived beyond the Cataracts. He stared down at the ancient, crimson page within the aged volume with words transcribed on the sheet. From this page, he pulled a papyrus roll which contained memoirs from the court jotted down by various scribes who worked for senior priests. The intimate lives of those who lived inside the palaces and humble dwellings were only to be accessed by a handful of sorcerers. The encrypted records, in direct contrast to publicly registered feats of pharaohs on walls, educated the clergy secretly on how to either help their kings or overpower them.

"These rare books," he said to Riva, tapping the mighty volume, "are sprinkled with holy tomb ash from senior icons to ensure they are not read by the wrong eyes." As the shopkeeper passed the coral across the pages, more disturbing truths were revealed. His friend had left a clue for him. Etched on the front, with shaky hands, was a sceptre which signalled imminent danger.

"Can you see the face sketched over Steven's?" he said to Riva. She nodded, and he continued. "It is not the face of the Libyan suitor. Someone else murdered the doctor and used magic to mask his face. The perpetrator must have left in a hurry, thinking Imran was already dead. Your footsteps may have scared him off, giving my poor friend time to scribble a few notes."

"Do you know who it is?" Riva said.

The shopkeeper rubbed his chin. "No, but the Princess may be able to identify the true perpetrator."

"Shall I summon the Princess?" Riva said. The shopkeeper nodded, and Riva took hold of the stone and gently shook it.

The Princess had not left yet and was still considering how to track and find her lover to bring him back to her realm to assist her in fighting the prince.

On hearing the calling of the stone, she appeared at the crime scene, frowned at Riva and the shopkeeper, and looked down at the book. "This is the face of the lover I am searching for. What does this mean?" she said through tear-laden eyes.

The shopkeeper explained that the warrior she had been following had turned rogue. The King had sent the Libyan prince to save the Princess. "As a foreigner on Egyptian soil," the shopkeeper said, "the prince might have mistaken the Egyptologist for a scribe because of the books littering his office. I have relived the night the doctor died, and the presence of the book confirms that my visions are true." The shopkeeper scattered a powder in front of the three of them, and the events of the night unfolded. "As you see, Steven, the director, is dressed as the prince and is in a peaceful conversation with Dr Imran."

"But how did he know to come here?" the Princess said.

"Serendipity may have played a big role," he said. "The Libyan spirit travelled here in search of you at around the same time Steven visited to discuss the movie. Conveniently, the prince must have possessed Steven long enough to discuss where you were. As we can see from the visions, Dr Imran does not appear threatened and is communicating amicably with the prince." The shopkeeper smiled. "My friend is enjoying talking with an ancient royal from the West." The shopkeeper leant closer. "I can, I think, decipher some of the words he is saying to the warrior. You will find her here, in the city of Thebes, roaming the Temple of Karnak. It would help if you took this amulet, woven in copper threads. It will open the Princess's eyes to the dark spell she is under, which distorts your true nature and return her to her father."

As they continued to watch the vision, the prince vaporised, leaving Dr Imran bemused.

The shopkeeper opened the scroll on the desk. "The rogue warrior has joined with much darker forces. Their followers have a sceptre on their thumb." The shopkeeper turned to the princess. "The warrior was furious that your father had broken up your relationship and that Dr Imran had discovered the truth. It was almost certainly this that got him killed."

The Princess gasped. "I did not know."

"The bodyguard you fell for," the shopkeeper said, "is somewhere close to his own home. He intends to brew a spell which will prevent you from returning home. If he is successful, he will blackmail your father and order him to make him chief minister and architect." The shopkeeper shook his head.

"What is it?" Riva said.

"Dr Imran has, in good faith, conjured the spirit of the warrior to reprimand him and, foolishly, believed he could steer him away from black magic. He may well have succeeded, but the arrival of Steven sadly interrupted his spell. The warrior seized his opportunity by possessing Steven. This has given him cover, and he will attempt to poison the Princess." He smiled. "You may have a new story for the movie, Riva."

The shopkeeper narrowed his eyes, lowered his head and inspected something on the desk. "It is the residue of a type of venom. A rare venom indeed," he said. "Expertly brewed from the secretion of a pregnant hippo and a cobra from the Far East. Poor Dr Imram did well in scribbling a message before being overcome. It is indeed a potent poison. The warrior placed a small sceptre by the dead man in rude defiance to, in his eyes, the legitimate authority. Revealing where his loyalty truly lies." He thumped the desk. "The dark forces are flexing their muscles. We must be vigilant."

"This is heartbreaking," the Princess said and stood upright, not shedding a tear. "I am still a princess of Egypt. I have to find my Libyan suitor. Can you help?"

Riva studied the Princess, who appeared to have matured beyond her days with her revelations of betrayal and bravery. Her posture and bearing stiffened, and she seemed more majestic. She had also appeared to have demanded their help rather than ask for it.

"I will return to my father, apologise and beg his forgiveness," the Princess said. "I will marry the Libyan prince as he wishes. But first, I must fight the dark forces which have been unleashed as atonement for my behaviour." She looked at the others. "Order has to prevail."

The shopkeeper plucked a book from his friend's library and turned the pages to a spell he had performed with his friend on many occasions. With help from Riva, he lit a small fire on a plate and threw some seeds into the flames. Then, picking up a bag with symbols adorning it, he blended some seeds with ground ibis's eyes to assist the Princess in finding the whereabouts of her future partner and offer some protection. "Come near to the flames, my lady," he said. "You must care enough to find him before he is captured by the demons."

Once the fire had died out, he collected the ashes into a small cotton purse and placed them on the desk. "You must inhale the ashes," he said. The Princess collected the purse and left to find the Libyan prince, while Riva bid goodbye to the shopkeeper and returned to the hotel.

Abanoub was waiting for her with Obeid. His errand boy had briefed him on the bizarre happenings at the temple, but he had been unable to see all that occurred.

"It is as if they have had a conversation with the air," Obeid said. "I saw nothing but the old man and the actress. It was all very strange." Abanoub smiled. He was able to fill in the gaps.

Riva finally reached the hotel and pushed her way through the paparazzi that had assembled in the lobby, much to the amusement of the tourists and the annoyance of the detective, Abanoub. He had been ordered by his superiors to hold press conferences and issue a statement denying or confirming some of the reports.

"Is it true, Riva?" one of the reporters shouted as she entered, "that you're getting married in a pharaonic swimsuit within the sacred lake using ibises as bridesmaids?" Riva ignored the comment and joined the detective.

"There are rumours of murderous rogues running around the city in ancient garbs," another said. "What is the truth, detective?"

Abanoub held up his hands. "At this moment, I am not able to verify what happened. Our investigation is ongoing, and you will have to be patient. Riva is assisting us." He nodded to two plain-clothes officers who steered the actress away from the press and into a side room.

Abanoub followed his juniors inside and closed the door.

"I am meeting Steven, my director, and writer John Abel in the adjacent room," she said. "We have to set a schedule for the next shoot."

Abanoub smiled at her. "Don't mind me. I'll tag along If that is all right."

Riva forced a smile of her own. "If you must." Riva headed through a second door and into a room where Steven and John Abel were waiting.

"Ah, good," Steven said, eyeing the detective.

"Don't worry about me," Abanoub said. "I'm just carrying out an investigation as to what happened to Dr Imran and also the events in Riva's room. I won't interrupt." He moved over to a corner and sat.

Steven turned to Riva and ran through the itinerary for the next day's shoot. John Abel and Riva set about discussing how the story would develop while the detective watched on.

After half an hour, Steven was wrapping up the meeting when he stopped talking.

"Are you OK?" Riva said as she looked at the director, who appeared in a trance.

John Abel moved across to him. "Steven?" he said. "What's wrong?"

Steven ignored him. He groaned, and the others watched on in silence as blood seeped from his forehead. A blue light emanated from him, and gradually, the amorphous shape of the Libyan prince stepped free of his body, faded and disappeared. Slowly, the director roused from his stupor, frowned and then fell to the floor.

Riva put a hand to her forehead as a lightning bolt of pain shot across her temple. She eased herself into a chair. These incidents with the metaphysical had increased almost daily, and Riva was struggling to cope with them. She watched the two men help Steven to his feet and sat him next to her.

"What happened?" John Abel asked Steven.

"I'm not sure," he said.

"Are you both all right?" the detective said to Steven and Riva, who both nodded.

Abanoub's mobile sounded, and he took the call. A brief conversation took place with the caller before he turned to the other three. "I will allow you to recover," he said. "I have another meeting. I will interview you when you're feeling better." With that, he promptly left as the other three watched on, speechless.

Abanoub travelled to the coroner's office and collected the result of Dr Imram's post-mortem. He briefly studied the documents that concluded that the doctor had died of heart failure. He considered this. Clearly, neither the director nor the actress had anything to do with his death.

Time moved on, and the movie was completed, which proved to be another great success, increasing Riva's fame further. But despite her burgeoning popularity, she could not shake the feeling that someone or something was watching her. She would catch a glimpse, occasionally, when she passed a mirror, but when she looked, there was nothing there. With her nerves on edge, Riva carried on with her role as an actress.

On premiere night, Riva was visited by the Princess. She thanked Riva for her help and handed her a small bottle containing a powder that the Princess claimed would slow down ageing. After thanking the Princess, the two of them parted, and Riva made her way to the premiere.

Not Over Yet

An acclaimed critic remarked as he shook hands with the director. "Hosting the opening night here, where it all begins, is a smart move, Steven," he said.

Steven smiled. "There is another showing later in the month at the foot of the Giza pyramids. You must come," he said as he moved busily among the crowd, pausing occasionally to listen to some of the comments and talk with guests. He joined Riva and the other cast members as photographers snapped away.

"Everything all right?" he said to Riva.

"I'm a little tired,' she said. "I'll give it another half hour, and then I'm turning in."

"Riva," someone from the paparazzi shouted, and she dutifully turned to face them with a smile on her face.

She finally reached the hotel and collected her key. Within minutes, she was sound asleep in her bed, still wearing the evening gown from the premiere.

Riva was awoken as she tumbled to the floor and sleepily surveyed the room in an effort to discover what had pushed her from her bed. A hippopotamus stood at the far end of the room, trying desperately to evade the fisherman's net. She gasped as she looked around at the carnage that the animal had caused. The phone beside her bed rang, and someone hammered at the door as the fisherman, oblivious to his surroundings, continued his hunt.

She picked up the phone and ignored the door. "Miss Riva," a voice said, "the guests are complaining. Is everything all right? Shall I send security? Your party is too loud. I will have to notify the police if it continues." Riva slammed the phone down without answering and rubbed the sleepiness from her eyes. The fisherman was still trying to capture the elusive animal. She had read somewhere that hippos were considered evil in ancient Egypt and driven away from the rivers. The animal's mouth gaped open in a show of strength, bearing his age-old foot-long tusks. She picked up a pillow and stuffed it inside the beast's open mouth. The muscled fisherman bowed, thanked Riva for her help, tossed something towards her, smiled and vaporised along with the hippo. Riva picked up a red talisman shaped like a wallet, and the room regained its former tidiness.

The banging on her door continued. She made her way over to it and pulled it open. Two security guards stood there.

Riva collected her wits and smiled innocently at her two visitors. "Yes?" she said.

The two men looked beyond her and into the empty room. "I'm sorry to bother you, one of them said, "but we've complaints about noise coming from your room."

Riva moved aside, allowing them to enter. "Noise?"

The two guards exchanged glances with each other. 'Yes," they said in unison.

"Maybe the commotion is in the room upstairs," she said. "I believe there is a guitarist from a rock group staying above, and he plays music in the middle of the night. Perhaps it is him that is causing the commotion. I have only just returned from the movie's first performance. Everyone is talking about it."

The men glanced at each other again, apologised and left as Riva slammed the door behind them. She allowed herself a smile, removed her dress and slid back into bed, still holding on tightly to the talisman.

She glanced at the bedside drawer where the stone that had kept the Princess safe lay. The Princess had refused to take it with her, and Riva suspected that she had no plans to leave yet. "I'll need a bigger bag with all these things," she muttered to herself before falling into a deep sleep.

Riva's sleep, although fitful, was full of dreams. She was running through the Temple of Abydos in Upper Egypt, a funerary ground of the kings of ancient Egypt. She reached a chapel, sat down, and, in her dream, opened a parchment revealing a bright red map. Inking its way from Abydos, it passed through Luxor and finally reached Sakkara – the other favoured cemetery marked by kings south of the capital, Cairo. A little dot flashed on the map, and Riva pressed the spot with her finger, uncovering a three-dimensional pyramid. Many pyramids dotted the ancient kingdom, but which one did the map intend? Riva touched the Pyramid again to reveal an image of a king she did not recognise. It might have been Senefru, father of King Cheops and builder of the largest pyramid, but she had to be sure. She touched the image again, and the map transformed into a pharaoh who ushered her into a chamber – the same chamber inside the Pyramid of Cheops, which had been filmed by a robot for a television network in the nineties. Nothing had been found beyond the walls, with rumours circulating at the time that a cache of treasures as large and valuable as those of King Tut lay behind the partition. The map folded itself up and slid into the red wallet given to Riva by the fisherman.

Riva woke, determined to take a look at the closed chamber in the pyramids. She hurried downstairs and found Steven and John Abel enjoying breakfast. She explained her dream to them, and as usual, Steven took little persuasion. "What have we got to lose?" he said. "We may have a new storyline for another movie."

"I shall wait here at the hotel for your safe return," John Abel said. "I will trust the narrative you come back with, but please, leave the writing to me."

"If you're sure?" Riva said.

John Abel nodded. In truth, he was worried about venturing inside the pyramids or other places he did not know well, especially after the death of the archaeologist. However, creative writing posed no danger. How could he refuse all fame and fortune?

The crew booked flights to Cairo, leaving behind a happy hotel manager, pleased with the revenue the film crew brought to his hotel but tired of the chaos that accompanied them. Bookings had been made well in advance by the production company, and he was grateful for the respite, not to mention the effect the crew being at his establishment had on his mental health. The manager, from Cairo, raised by a hard-working family of scientists who lived in the United States for some time, had migrated to Luxor to become a hotelier. Little did he realise how demanding his profession would be. Magic did not constitute a part of his makeup.

On the way to the airport, Riva recounted her dream to Steven and the others. On arrival, they took a car to a nearby hotel, had coffee and a light meal of cheese, dessert and yoghurt – a far cry from the rich, heavenly breakfast in Luxor – and placed the luggage into their accommodation. Within half an hour, Riva and Steven were heading towards the pyramids. To help her revisit her dream, Riva and Steven booked a guide to take them on a tour inside the walls of the largest pyramid.

Nothing prepared the guide for what he saw, nor did Riva expect the narrative that unfolded once inside. They headed to one of the three chambers, which lay at the lowest point of the Pyramid on solid rock, and quickly surveyed its interior. The other two rooms belonged to the King and Queen. Planned by the King's Vizier, Hemiunu, the architect of the Great Pyramid, Riva and Steven gasped as they entered. In any case, Riva put her hand on the Queen's empty sarcophagus and a sharp pain shot through her head, and then a vision of a life-sized person appeared within a stream of light. At first, Riva thought she was looking at a reflection of herself in an ancient garb, but as the figure became more solid, she stared into the face of a stern-looking, disciplined and regal man.

"Have you received the talisman?" Hemiunu, the King's chief Vizier said. His voice deep and sonorous.

"Yes," she said. "What am I to make of it?"

He stepped closer and briefly appraised the young actress. "Travel to Luxor," he said. "Go to the Temple of Karnak and stand by the holy lake. Wait for my command. My Queen is threatened. Her tomb has been defiled. She must recapture her amulet, the scarab, or she will perish."

Riva's eyes widened. "You mean King Cheop's wife? But her sarcophagus is empty. How am I to save a queen I cannot find? I am only an actress."

"Watch out for the words and the signs. You can help later from Thebes. The good is all there. From Thebes, evil perishes. You must restore our kingdom."

The Vizier disappeared, and Riva turned to face Steven and the terrified guide. Steven smiled and put a hand on Riva's shoulder. "Are you OK?" he said. She nodded. She understood his apprehension each time she went into one of her trances. Despite their frequency, no one seemed to get used to them. Steven assisted

Riva as they walked unsteadily from the pyramid tomb and outside. The guide gratefully accepted his payment and hurried away, muttering as he went.

"Perhaps a drink?" Steven said to Riva. "Strong tea with lots of sugar before we continue?"

"I'm tired, and I'm going to my room for a lie down if that's all right?"

"Of course," Steven said.

Once back at the hotel, sleep had come easy for Riva. Within her slumber, the Vizier had visited her with warnings. Riva sat up in bed and rubbed her eyes as the images from her dreams began to fade. She remembered that she had travelled a millennium perhaps and passed through gates to the ancient world. She looked at the table near her bed. It was clear to her now. The leather wallet and amulet had to be buried with Queen Henutsen, mother of King Khafra and builder of the middle Pyramid. She began piecing together the warnings from the Vizier. If she did not save the fourth dynasty and Queen Mother, Henutsen, a crack would form in the ancient world, weakening the beginning of time and unleashing a cycle of violence and poverty.

Riva jumped from her bed, quickly dressed and made her way to Steven's room. She banged on the door and pushed past the startled director. "Everything connects," she said. "I must travel to Luxor and save the charmed scarab, the protector of the Queen, which lies at the bottom of the sacred lake. Unless the wife to the King, mother to another, unites with the scarab, the pyramids' cemetery is doomed, and so are all of you in the present."

"What?" Steven said as he looked at Riva.

"The Vizier warned me before he faded into the walls."

Steven slumped onto his bed. "What else did he say?"

"According to Hemiunu," Riva began, "someone is sending ripples from the past which will shape the landscape of the future. Help me bury the wallet," she said. "The Queen can be aided by one protective talisman until I can bring back the scarab. I need to improvise."

The pair made their way back to the Pyramid. Steven pretended to read inscriptions at the foot of the Pyramid while Riva dug a small hole with her foot. She looked around, and happy that no one was watching them, she dropped the talisman inside the hole and quickly covered it up.

Steven and Riva booked a flight to Luxor, leaving John Abel behind to carry out additional research.

There is a monster in the lake

The producer, Moses, travelled along with Riva and Steven to the temple at Karnak. He had insisted on being there as he was the one footing the bills for the additional travel.

"We are here for the fame, fortune and franchises," Moses said to them. "But I hope that these additional costs will prove worthwhile." He had heard the stories about Riva and had even witnessed some of the unusual events himself, but his pockets were not bottomless. Yet, Steven had managed to persuade him that his outlay would be worth the extra cost.

From Luxor Airport, Riva and the others headed directly to the Temple of Karnak. Riva paused as a vision appeared of the King, within a boat, rowing himself in celebration of the new year, resplendent in a beautiful golden robe inlaid with the eye of Horus. She studied the King with his muscular physique clearly visible beneath the garb. She slowly stepped into the water, closely followed by Steven, who had no intention of allowing her to enter alone. Moses watched on from the bank as they neared the centre.

Cheop's Vizier appeared in front of them, holding a glowing orb. "Dive into the lake," he commanded. "The Queen's jewels lay deep in the waters. The scarab is all she needs. The rest of the treasure is strongly shielded."

Riva was puzzled. Did he think that she intended to steal the other jewels? Surely, if he did, he would not have told her about the scarab. For some reason, she did not trust the Vizier. Undeterred, she plunged beneath the water, and someone or something took hold of her hand and pulled her gently to the riverbed. Riva could not believe her eyes. Scattered across the floor of the lake were jewels of every kind and shape, glimmering brilliantly – hidden for thousands of years.

The hand guided Riva to an area of the floor where a silver and gold scarab, about five centimetres long and attached to a beaded necklace, lay encrusted with sapphires, lapis lazuli, rubies and corals. Riva snatched up the scarab, but as she turned to swim back to the surface, she caught sight of a creature. It was huge. The lake barely able to accommodate the behemoth. Perhaps it was a merman or a mermaid, she mused as she looked at the creature. Its seemingly endless body, covered in scales, glided freely through the lake. Riva felt her head begin to swim as the lack of air began to sap her consciousness. Finally, she recognised what it was as the enormous jaws of a chimaera, the most feared monster among Egyptians, turned to face her. The head was that of a crocodile, the forelimbs of a lion and the hind part of a hippopotamus. She froze, closed her eyes and slumped to the bottom. Hands reached for her, and Steven pulled her from the water. She gasped for breath but was safe. However, Riva had dropped the scarab.

"What happened?" Steven asked.

"Didn't you see the creature?" Riva said, through panting breaths. Steven shook his head. Riva looked across the clear water of the lake, calm with only a few ripples remaining. "I must go back," she said. 'I must get the scarab."

Steven took hold of her as she attempted to climb to her feet. "Don't be stupid," he said. "You almost drowned."

Security guards from the temple surrounded the pair as Moses looked on.

"What kind of a freak cult are you?" one of the guards shouted at them. The guards were used to seeing visitors do ridiculous things on temple grounds, jeopardising their safety and damaging monuments. However, someone jumping in the lake was a new one for them. "Jumping in like that is the stupidest move I have ever seen," one of the guards said. "Look at you."

"Was that some sort of weird ritual?" another asked. "You can easily drown in there, you know." Then he addressed Steven while Moses stepped away from the guards and feigned looking into a notebook. "Talk some sense into your friend," he said, pointing at Riva. Then, the guards shook their heads and ushered the small group out of the temple grounds.

"What are we going to do now," Steven said to Riva as they got outside.

Riva looked back at the temple. "We'll have to return tonight when there are fewer guards about."

Steven took hold of her arm. "Are you mad? We'll end up

getting arrested."

Riva stared at him. "We must. It is vitally important. Perhaps the Vizier might appear and assist us."

Steven threw up his hands and headed to the waiting car. Riva followed, but something caught her eye. As she turned to look, two men disappeared behind a column.

As the car moved off, the two men stepped back from their hiding place. "We must keep our eyes on her. We may hit the jackpot."

News of Riva's exploits had not gone unnoticed among the relic traffickers. She appeared to have an uncanny knack for finding artefacts. The curious foreign actress who would hand over any finds to authorities or return them to their rightful place among the sleeping ancients. And there were others. Spirits from ancient worlds with a darker agenda, namely power, who coveted these items for their own nefarious deeds.

On the way back to the hotel in Luxor, Riva concocted an unusual method of capturing the scarab. The ancients used the lake to keep sacred geese. If only she could persuade Hemiunu or the princess to reclaim those geese from the past, then the birds could claim the scarab. It was a metaphysical plan, but it might just work.

They reached the hotel, and Riva and Steven met with Moses to partake of food and rest before the dangerous night ahead. They would need calmness and composure for her plan to work.

Karnak Temple closed at six o'clock in the afternoon. Riva, Steven and Moses had decided on one of two courses of action to get them inside and to the lake. Either return to the temple at five pm before closing time, keeping well away from the guards who had ejected them, hide until nightfall and then emerge. Or, Moses suggested, call on an old friend of his who knew of secret tunnels which would gain them entry under cover of darkness. The latter would not come cheap, but Moses agreed to pay what was needed if they decided on that course. After discussing their options for some time, they decided to use the hidden tunnels.

Traffickers had dug the tunnels in older times from the outside, below the long-gone souvenir shops and all the way to the sanctuary at the back of the temple. In a security sweep some years earlier, the entire area around the temple had been opened into a wide path, showing the temple from afar in all its splendour. Years ago, the area had housed a foreign mission, which had been removed, and extensive exploratory work had been done near this sight. Yet, some of the passages had remained suspiciously under the radar.

Aly, the driver, picked up Riva and Steven at midnight. Moses, although he had paid for their endeavour, decided not to go. "I am getting too long in the tooth for all this skulduggery. I have seen enough peculiarities, and I am sure I shall be seeing more, so I am not missing much. Just make sure that you come back safe and sound."

Riva and Steven slipped out of the back of the hotel unnoticed and into Aly's milk and fruit transport truck. Despite all their precautions, Riva sensed that all was not right. She put this down to nerves and tried to ignore her disquieting feeling. The vehicle carried fresh produce from local farms, especially cow and goat milk, which had to be delivered at dawn, so it did not look out of place parked outside the kitchen door.

Aly smiled at his passengers and gratefully accepted the money Moses had given to Steven. "Few people know about the tunnel or where it leads," Aly said. "It is dug below a statue of Queen Isis, mother of King Thutmos III, now in Cairo Museum. The passage serves as a hideout for peaceful spirits. I know how to get you there unnoticed."

Aly's calming assurances did not assuage Riva's fears. However, his knowledge of the spiritual world appeared to impress Steven.

"The spirits here live around Queen Isis, called Iset sometimes," Aly continued. "They are blessed with healing powers." Riva and Steven listened intently as Aly continued his history lesson. Listening to Aly and asking occasional questions helped to calm her nervousness on the way to the temple.

"The Queen loved her son, who loved her back," Aly said, "and when he grew into an adult, he erected a statue in her honour. He also promoted her status from concubine to first wife to his father.

Iset remained on the side of good and practised magic, healing, death, and resurrection."

They finally reached the temple and waited.

They had hidden for what seemed like an eternity before daring to move from their place of safety. They made their way inside through the secret tunnel and to the far end of the temple, to the lake. Riva had brought goggles and a waterproof torchlight – purchased from a shop near the hotel – to help her search the lakebed for the scarab. She had put on a bathing suit beneath her clothes and quickly undressed, leaving her dry clothes with Steven. Knowing her time beneath the water would be limited and would probably require several dives, Riva took a deep breath and dived in. She instantly spotted the gems on the bottom of the lake as the light from the torch coruscated off them. After rising for air several times, she spotted the scarab, swam quickly to the bottom and snatched up the jewel. She turned and kicked for the surface as a hand – she assumed it was Steven's – took hold of her. But instead of pulling her free of the water, the hand pulled her back under. She struggled as her lungs, desperately in need of air, ached. Her heart hammered in her chest as she fought to free herself from what held her. Her head swam, and as her consciousness faded, she dropped the scarab again. Darkness clouded her sight as she felt more hands take hold of her, but this time, they were Steven's. Grasping tightly hold of her bathing suit, he hauled her from the water and onto dry land.

"I thought—" Riva said but turned sharply as arrows shot past them, landing in the soil close by. More arrows arrived from inside the temple, and Steven grabbed hold of Riva and dragged her back to their hiding place. Steven looked at where the arrows had landed, but they were gone. The surreal arrow attack from the temple continued until three in the morning, two hours away from sunrise, and then suddenly stopped. She had one final opportunity to retrieve the scarab, or all would be lost.

"I have to get the scarab," Riva said. "It is now or never."

"But what if the arrows start again?" he said.

"We must take that risk," she said and jumped into the water with the torch.

The scarab shone back at her, and swiftly retrieving it, she pushed it inside her costume and turned for the surface. Someone followed her, but using her last reserves of energy, she kicked harder and, almost choking, managed to maintain the gap between herself and the pursuer. As she reached the surface, she allowed herself a glance backwards. The grotesque eyes of a long-dead man stared back. But something was strange. Instead of legs, he had a crocodile's tail. It made a grab for her leg, but, assisted by Steven, she evaded the creature and crawled free of the water. The hideous beast snarled before slipping back beneath the surface.

"Have you got the scarab?" Steven said.

Riva smiled and patted the small bulge on the side of her swimsuit. She gathered up her clothes, and Steven, wearing only his underwear, snatched up his.

"Good," Steven said as he took her hand and pulled her back to the entrance of the tunnel. Once outside, the pair paused for breath as the sun rose. They dashed for the waiting car, climbed into the back and watched the receding temple fade into the distance as they sped away.

Aly dropped them off at their hotel and hurried away as Riva and Steven crept inside and up to their rooms. Once in her room, Riva examined the scarab. Thoughts came thick and fast. Hemiunu told her that the scarab, the killer of demons, could delay the end of the world for the earlier dynasty. She remembered the words that the Queen had uttered in the Pyramid. "Monarchs must have their charms beside them to rest in peace. Bring the scarab to the Queen, and she will be able to delay the world's end among the ancestors and live to fight Nitocris."

Riva felt too exhausted to think of a safe place to hide the scarab. She shuddered as she remembered the dead man with a crocodile's tail and the swishing arrows of unknown assailants. Riva changed into pyjamas, pushed the gem inside the pocket – until she could find a safer spot – closed her eyes and was quickly asleep. In her dream, she shouted, but no sound came. She pointed to the sanctuary at the back of Karnak Temple, but visions of cobras and a slaughtered falcon remained in her mind.

The Vision

Riva woke up in her bed with a feeling of unease, lifted her hands to rub her eyes and gasped. Her hands were not her own – darker skinned with longer fingers. Putting a hand to her head, she felt the longer hair she now had. She jumped from her bed – the scarab still secreted in her pocket fell to the floor – and hurried across to the mirror. She stared at the image before her. It still looked a lot like her, but there were marked differences. Her long, lustrous hair was black and expertly braided to perfectly sculpt her heart-shaped face. She also felt physically stronger. Riva studied the face for some time, making a mental note of the differences between her reflection and how she usually looked. She picked up a glass of water nearby and greedily drank it before returning to view herself in the mirror. She had on linen trousers and a matching long-sleeved beige shirt. Beneath these, she wore leather shoes which fitted perfectly. On the front of these was a primitive drawing of a lamb.

Riva glided towards the door – her body more agile than she was used to. She became aware of a quiver, full of arrows on her back and around her waist, a belt with a gilded knife tucked securely inside. It came to Riva in a flash. She was a warrior princess or perhaps a huntress – stronger, faster and quicker than previously. Another thought came to her. She had to return to the lake at the Temple of Karnak to receive more instructions and answers, but the moment she stepped outside of her room, she was back in her pyjamas with the scarab inside her pocket. Her hair and features were back to normal. Embarrassed, Riva scurried inside her room and closed the door.

Riva and the crew headed to Karnak Temple and walked through the crowd of tourists to the lake.

"Most of the shots are over there," Steven said to the crew, who were already setting up the equipment. He decided on his angles and settings, then joined Riva in a shaded spot beside the lake. The two of them stared at the lake, home to priests and holy geese in a different life, as the crew got ready for shooting to commence.

"Why does a high-ranking Vizier choose me?" Riva said, speaking to herself rather than to Steven.

"Perhaps he sees you as a messenger," Steven said, "and trusts you. You should enjoy these moments of peace. I think we are in for a showdown, but we shall have a script to die for." Steven chuckled.

As Steven watched the crew complete their tasks, Riva continued to stare across the lake. A vision appeared before her against the backdrop of pylons and statues, and she watched on in silence as the reservoir metamorphosed into a marsh. Papyrus reeds rose majestically from the water, their stalks twelve feet or more. In between the stalks, farmers laboured, cutting down the tallest and bundling them into tightly bound piles on dry land. Riva felt herself being transported to the Delta, north of Luxor, among papyrus leaves – the insignia of Lower Egypt.

In the distance, a large alabaster bowl stood half a metre high with a little hole at the bottom to let the water trickle out, diminishing throughout the day, biding time, measuring the days and the seasons. A man and his wife sat on stools playing a game with little stones as Riva strolled, inspecting the land along the curving banks of the Nile. The mighty river, forever arching through lanes and paths, unravelling stories, and, more importantly, feeding the people with fish from its waters. To better understand the reason for the clandestine visits by the Vizier, Riva reasoned that she needed to observe the old ways, in the fields, the plantations, watching births, the love and the murder…did she say murder?

Everywhere, farmers continued their harvesting of papyrus, bundling and ultimately delivering them to builders who made boats from the stalks. Another group, close by, made ropes from the fibres, while more still collected the edible roots. Her visions continued unabated, taking her to a solitary batch of skiff builders. She was so close to them that she could see the colour of their eyes. One man stood out among the seafarers, looking over his shoulder, hurrying with some of the freshly gathered papyrus stalks. Sheltering in the shade behind trees, a man wearing only a linen loincloth placed the stalks on a flat surface in neatly arranged rows. He squeezed them to expel a substance which sealed the pieces together. Riva stood, mesmerised by his work, as he rubbed and polished the sheet with stone until it resembled paper. When he had completed his work, he gathered up the scrolls of parchment and carried them across to a modest house. The neighbourhood appeared poor to Riva and differed significantly from the houses she knew now.

In her visions, she followed a man who entered a home in a humble village – the stalks held tightly between his hands. He placed them down in front of an older man dressed in faded leopard skin, stooping over a stone desk. She eyed the freshly made marks from a whip at the top of his back, oozing blood onto his garment. He was obviously a member of the clergy since he could write. Plus, he wore the emblematic wild animal coat that had vanished from Egypt in later kingdoms.

What are you escaping from? Riva thought. Judging from the man's garb, he lived in the Old or Middle Kingdom when such hides could still be procured. The runaway priest, unclean, with only a vestige of his once respectable life, had no markings of sophistication. He had probably made a miraculous escape from his former life, she reasoned. Perhaps assisted by his loyal assistant, they were now hiding among the boaters.

"Lay down the stalks and craft a fresh scroll," the old man said to his helper. "The message must be preserved, clean and readable." His assistant did as instructed, laying the stalks in neat rows and then squeezing to seal them as before – the paper quickly dried in the heat. The older man picked up a reed pen with a split nib from the leather pouch he crossed over his shoulder. On his shabby desk, he dipped the end into an ink flask. Riva felt sorry for him. One would have expected a man of his stature to be seated at an impressive desk dotted with colourful ink containers made of numerous ground minerals. Yet, he had ended up in this forsaken place, holding onto his precious flask of ink and documenting a secret piece of information.

Riva watched as the priest went into a trance, conjuring spirits to assist him with his writing. Clearly, he was now too old and fragile to write much himself. The spirits arrived and guided his pen. They did his bidding for as long as he was able to maintain the spell. The older man shook his head and looked skyward as if desperately trying to prolong his writing, but his limited resources rendered him impotent to do more.

His assistant placed a hand on the exhausted man's shoulder. "I have a good memory, my lord," he said, "I shall send a message to our loyal retainers."

The assistant took the pen from his master, and as the hold on the spirits began to dwindle, he quickly wrote down what the dying priest wanted to say.

Riva tried desperately to catch the words the priest whispered to the helper, who repeated the words out loud. King, murder, his son, and scarab, he uttered while continuing his writing. Riva heard times and places, star positions, and spells that showed how a usurper came back from the dead and how to arraign her. She might have heard the name of the Pharaoh Ramsis II, but she wasn't sure. This made no sense to her since the Vizier Hemiunu lived in the earlier days of Cheop's.

Her visions floated through untravelled paths, learning of a grand conspiracy planned by ghostly figures, strolling through time as if on a modern walkway. In her vision, she tried to read the scroll herself, thinking that perhaps the Princess, residing within her brain, would understand. Successfully, the Princess translated words about murder, palace upheaval, and, most importantly, King Ramsis II.

Riva woke from the trance and considered how her visions could be weaved into the movie and at what cost. The trance had lasted longer than usual, a good three minutes, but appeared to cover aeons of time. As she considered this, she spotted a flock of Ibises by the side of the lake inside the temple. Her gaze followed the tallest and strongest looking of them as it disappeared through a crevice behind the lake while the others waited.

"Riva," Steven said, rousing her from her reverie. "The dance scene will be choreographed at night. Your character will be interrupted by her lover."

Her mind wandered again, hardly registering what Steven was

saying. "I have to follow the birds," she said, ignoring his comments. She headed towards where the Ibis had gone, with Steven following in her wake. Only on reaching the crevice did she realise that the gap was small and tight for her to get through. She peered inside at the large bird.

"What did you see?' he asked as he caught her up.

"It cannot be a coincidence that the Ibises appeared after I had seen a dying priest," she said. "He was struggling to write a letter asking for help."

"What priest?' Steven said. "What Ibis?'

"The birds are loyal to Thoth," she said. "He observes the universe for anomalies." She frowned. "How do I know that?"

"The Princess is with you every step of the way," Steven said. "For some reason, she is waiting in this world to help destroy the demons."

Riva looked at him and smiled. "Yes."

Steven glanced back at the crew. "Can you manage to get it by yourself?" He followed Riva's gaze as she peered inside the crevice again. The bird began to peck a hole from which it drew a papyrus scroll.

The Message

Riva saw the message within her mind. A storm of dissent brewed in the ancient world, and the vision detailed the extent of the conspiracy. The narrow fissure in the rock behind the sacred lake, originally built by King Thutmos III, allowed smaller people to pass through, and behind this lay an enormous enclave where dark rituals took place in past millennia.

She could see a skull from a small animal, and her desire to flee was overwhelming. She realised that dark rituals must have taken place in the past and that in every era, a few clergies must have switched allegiances to the dark side. They mastered spells in the underworld to subjugate kings and their subjects, allowing them to steal their treasures. Riva moved through rocks – a track she knew from another life, someone else's life. Steven waited as she made her way along the narrow path.

Spirits of older women shouted between each other as she squeezed her way along the path. These women, she knew, had used the lake in the distant past for treatments. Images of younger infertile women appeared in the lake, seeking that the waters would cure them. These ghosts danced joyously at the gift of procreation, relishing the healing powers of the waters that made them whole again. Arcane magic, which spread across the centuries, helped to free them from their curse.

Riva trod carefully, not wishing to interrupt the women in their ministrations, aware that her presence here could awaken the nemesis of those kind-hearted women trapped between the sacred lake and the dark world. Every step around the lake held a risk of waking up long-dead pharaohs or disturbing evil forces that would delay her finding what she needed to. It appeared that only she could see the Ibis, still holding the parchment in its beak, as the unaware sightseers swarmed the temple. She hoped, at worst, that they would consider her just an eccentric tourist. She could not catch the bird and retrieve the parchment as the tunnel narrowed further. Then she remembered that she had some biscuits inside her bag and pulled one free, hoping to entice the Ibis to bring it to her.

It worked. The regal Ibis came forward, allowing Riva to snatch the parchment from its beak. She dropped a few remaining biscuits at the bird's feet, and it happily ate up the pieces.

Riva edged her way back along the passage with the scroll held tightly. Once free, she undid the leather string holding the parchment and unrolled it. Steven joined her, and the pair gazed at the paper while keeping the document away from prying eyes. Riva couldn't understand the unusual script, so she rolled it back up and retied the string. "We must visit Dr Rahim," she said. "He may be able to decipher the contents."

Rahim – The Happy Doctor

Dr Rahim beamed at Riva. "I am always happy to see you," he said. "Since you have become a huge star, I don't get to see you as often as before."

As an expert on all things pharaonic, directors and writers flocked to see the doctor for directives on set and the casting of their characters. He had first met Riva in the aftermath of her kidnapping and the encounter with the stone. She auditioned for the role of a wily innkeeper in ancient times, and the doctor who'd been at the audition recognised something within her. She was clearly possessed by someone, but he did not know who. He had kept this to himself, though, and maintained a watching brief as her fame and popularity grew. She was destined for greatness. He could feel it.

Using his influence over the director, the doctor had persuaded him to offer her the part. "You must give the role of the innkeeper to the new face over there," he said. "She has promise and will not fail you." Steven, still an assistant at the time, overheard his words of advice and made a mental note. He had already cast Riva in a more minor role and promised himself that he would cast her in the leading role should he get a chance to direct. Steven smiled as he remembered the conversation with the reluctant director and Dr Rahim.

"Rahim, you are losing your mind," the director said. "How many years have we been together? You want me to give the leading role in a big-budget historical film to an unknown?" The director smiled at Rahim. "Perhaps I will take your advice."

Riva shot to fame following that first movie, and she never forgot what Rahim had done for her. Rahim, in fact, had recognised Riva's unique talent for the occult. From that first significant role, Dr Rahim became Riva's confidante, and she confided in him when the spirits spoke to her.

Bygone pharaohs often visited Dr Rahim, and little seemed to surprise him anymore. He lived in a modest flat overlooking the Nile close to Karnak Temple, dedicating his life to the study of the magic of ancient Egypt. When he turned nine, he visited the Temple of Karnak with his mother and slipped past the guards to the ancient lake. He discovered precious stones, and his mother allowed him to keep a small number, shrewdly noting that her son had a good eye for stones and their whereabouts. The rest, she insisted, he put back where he had found them. He selected the lapis lazuli, cherished by sun deity Ra, and a few emeralds that had healing powers. He grew very fond of his mother, who was actually a foster parent. Unable to have children of her own, she came across Rahim on a night when a full moon shone in all its glory on the Nile in the city of Luxor. While out walking with her husband, and having recently married, they decided to take in the breeze along the Nile strip. Both of them were avid readers of ancient Egyptian history and wandered down unfamiliar alleyways while engrossed in conversation.

As they continued on, lulled by the pleasant breeze, they heard a muffled cry and stopped to listen. Then, following the sound along a narrow path, they discovered a chubby baby wrapped in blankets with a shiny scarab brooch holding the linen cloth wrapped around him. In his hands, he held a bottle of milk. The couple looked down at the crying baby, who, to their surprise, stopped crying, smiled, and then chuckled, winning the hearts of the childless couple. The couple desperately wanted to adopt the baby, and Rahim's father, calling in favours from friends he had in the ministry, was able to quickly achieve this. He adored his wife, and knowing how much she wanted a child, they were overjoyed at their good fortune. Rahim's father had known for some time that his wife could not conceive – he possessed a psychic knowledge he did not fully understand – but was so much in love with her that he proposed. His wife, Pearl, came from a broken home. Bright and curious as a child, she found solace in her love of Egyptology. Over time, her knowledge of the ancient world became so extensive that experts from around the globe sought her out.

Pearl met Rahim's father at college. The pair instantly fell in love and became inseparable, researching magic and writing books about their finds.

Rahim, who inherited his parents' interest in magic spells and

Egyptian arcana, walked into their laboratory one day to try out one of his own magic spells based on a formula he managed to decipher. He had corals and lapis lazuli and added a black liquid that his father treasured most. He squatted on a cushion on the floor and read an ancient incantation over the stones before slowly pouring the black liquid on top of it. To his surprise, smoke erupted and enveloped him. Once cleared, a small woman, about thirty centimetres high, stood before him. The conjured woman was dressed as a pharaoh and glanced around the room and at Rahim in shock. She reached out to touch Rahim, who recoiled in horror, spilling the remainder of the black liquid across his face. He screamed in agony as the liquid began to burn his flesh. On seeing this, the woman placed a hand on his face, which stopped the liquid from causing further damage. Despite her help, a scar appeared on Rahim's face, stretching from just under his eye to his chin. From that day on, he became friends with the small pharaonic girl who taught him many ancient spells over many years.

His parents, horrified by what had happened to their son, decided to teach him the correct way to perform magic rather than injure himself again. The ancients grew to accept Rahim, and he continued to learn their magic.

Riva handed the parchment to Rahim. "I thought it better that you keep this," she said. "It will be safer here."

Rahim smiled. "Let me see what Hemiunu wants us to know. Come with me."

Riva and Steven followed the doctor through to the lab that his parents had bequeathed him. While he was still young, his parents had allowed him to use it, but wisely, they had removed the more powerful and dangerous potions to a small room annexed to their bedroom, thinking that he would not dare enter there.

In time, Rahim got into his parents' secret room, unbeknown to them. As the days went by, they grew older, and Rahim bought the next-door apartment and arranged to have them cared for under his supervision. Rahim, a student to remarkable parents, became an expert master of magic in his own right, giving sound counsel to others who dabbled in mysticism.

Rahim beckoned Riva and Steven towards him, placed the scroll on his desk, moved a small lamp next to it, and took out a magnifying glass. He peered through the lens at the ancient parchment's seal and beckoned to Riva to look at it. Little minute scarabs, maybe thousands, could be seen under the lens with a strange red gas emanating from them. Rahim picked up a jar with trapped flies inside and carefully picked one up with a pair of tweezers. He placed the fly near the scarabs. The scarabs instantly swept across the fly, and the insect burst into flames, producing a blue cloud of smoke that mixed with the red. A seal appeared on the parchment.

"The seal can be deadly if not handled properly," he said, "but now it is safe."

Rahim unrolled the parchment and spread it across his desk, exposing incomprehensible writings, some more faded than others. "This parchment has been handed down through generations," he said, scrutinising the scroll. "The hand strokes are different, and some of the letters are more faded than others. "See these words in this corner," he said, tapping the parchment, "they have been scribbled in a hurry. The writer was probably in great peril."

Riva watched, and Rahim continued his work. He cleared his desk and held the edges of the parchment with paperweights of Osiris and Anubis. A part of the writing stood out with ominous red and black hieroglyphic symbols.

Rahim thought back to the time when he had intervened in a fight between the two deities. "I will freeze you with my spells," Osiris warned Anubis, who had recruited a vast number of followers, threatening the might of Osiris.

The discussion took place in Rahim's office when Anubis approached the scientist for support in protecting his dominion. Osiris, learning from travelling spirits that Anubis was trying to spread his dominion across time zones, arrived in modern Luxor to confront the doctor and kill Anubis. Rahim was a much-liked figure among the pharaohs, especially after he struck up a friendship with the tiny female who took to him.

"Kindly, sire, spare Anubis, for he means no harm," Rahim said to Osiris. "Lord Anubis is an expert recruiter and has made friends among the villagers with favours he generously bestows. If you spare him today, he can help find some of your treasures stolen by greedy tomb raiders and bring in news from beyond the realm."

Osiris looked long and hard at the mortal. "You are shrewd," he said. "I will allow Anubis this indiscretion if he promises no more."

Anubis agreed, and the pair put aside their differences. "The world is different here," Osiris said. "We will work together instead of apart. I task you, Anubis, with overseeing the dead." Osiris left in a flood of light as quickly as he had arrived.

Anubis, in gratitude for Rahim's intervention, gifted him a replica of himself and Osiris, which Rahim dutifully accepted. He could not give them to the authorities nor admit that Anubis visited and gifted him with the relics – he would be locked up as a madman or a trafficker. When visitors admired the statues, he would say that they were only replicas and recommend a few gift shops nearby that made such copies.

Riva placed a hand on Rahim's arm. "Is everything all right?" she said.

Rahim turned to face her. "Yes. I was thinking back to an earlier time." He studied the manuscript again. "How did you come by this?" he said.

"It was a present from the Vizier Hemiunu."

Rahim nodded knowingly. "I vow to unite people in love, to balance your world and mine, and keep the Nile happy and bountiful," he remembered saying. With those sincere words he had uttered to the Vizier, Rahim had enjoyed years of respite from strife until today when Riva had arrived with this parchment. Riva and Steven watched on as the doctor closed his eyes, deep in thought. "I will tell you what happened some time ago," he said to them as he finally roused himself from his reverie.

"Rahim, my friend," Hemiunu said to me. "We have a problem that the sorcerers and priests cannot solve. King Cheops is extremely angry that a growing number of maidens are escaping the kingdom. With a heavy heart, I shall tell you what has happened."

Cheops summoned Hemiunu to his majestic throne room and glared at the Vizier.

"Since the days of my father, the King," Cheops told Hemiunu, "maidens have escaped, and no one is concerned. But this mystery baffles me. It must not continue. I trust you will give it your full attention." The King stood and marched off, leaving Hemiunu to his thoughts.

"The Vizier trusted one of the younger priests, Anhurmose," Rahim said. "He had travelled to the land of Assyria to the east and become accustomed to the foreign ways."

"Allow me to suggest a travel through time," Anhurmose said as Hemiunu listened, his heart pounding. Yet the Vizier feigned surprise and acted as if the priest had lost his senses. The young priest told Hemiunu that on his travels to a land with many rivers, he had met a woman named Pearl. She was much revered for her deep knowledge of magic and had a son called Rahim."

"You?" Riva said.

Rahim smiled. "Yes. The priest asked Hemiunu for permission to visit me. Hemiunu agreed."

"Did he visit?" Steven said.

"He did," Rahim said. "I listened to what the Priest Anhurmose had to say. He told me that a time portal had accidently been left open, allowing the maidens to escape the ancient kingdoms. I spoke to my mother – she had experience with escapees – to assist us. Young maidens had sought out my mother when they became disillusioned with the modern world. Most just wanted to return home but feared reprisals on their return. I suggested that a guard was allowing the girls to escape, possibly accepting bribes, and must be caught. We applied a spell to the portal so that only priests could open it, thereby thwarting the maidens' escape attempts and making it difficult for them to cross over, which was causing a temporal imbalance. He was delighted with this. However, there was a second problem. The Vizier found out that Pharaoh Djedefre had fathered one of the girls, Neferhetepes, a priestess of Hathor, the deity of love and fertility. Beautiful and rebellious, she fell in love with a builder and forgot all her teachings and obligations. She refused to marry a Nubian prince who had promised her the world if she accepted his hand. Neferhetepes stubbornly refused, stating that she wanted to marry for love." Rahim paused and took a sip of water.

"What happened to her?" Riva said.

"She tried to convince her father that her sister would be a better match for the prince, but her father, just as obstinate as his daughter, would have none of it. He flew into a rage, telling his headstrong daughter that the prince came from a rich and powerful kingdom. This kingdom, he went on, was important to them because of the goods they supplied. Neferhetepes ran away, escaped through the portal and ended up at the sacred lake in Karnak Temple.

The Princess tried potions and spells to summon her lover to join her, but nothing worked. She blended with the natives to learn the way of their world outside her sheltered life in the palace. The pharaoh, her father, was furious and had the guard who allowed her to escape executed.

Anhurmose recounted the story to me. The Nubian Prince, he continued, had not taken the great insult of being rebuffed well. The King tried everything to assuage his anger, but all failed. The rejected suitor cursed the princess and left with his entourage, taking back all the gifts he had bestowed on the king." Rahim paused again before resuming. "A powerful ally in the south has been lost Anhurmose lamented. The Prince threatened to wage war unless the Princess returned of her own free will. Anhurmose had tried many potions to get the Princess to fall in love with her Nubian suitor, but none of these worked.

The priest recounted to me how he added honey from the King's hives, mixed castor and pomegranates, used highly-toxic minerals, salt, ground horns, and pieces of albino pigs' livers and crushed them with cinnamon. He even mixed molten copper into the potion along with wax, a touch of venom from a foreign serpent and secret herbs. Nothing worked on Neferhetepes. Her magic was too powerful for him. In despair, the priest came to me and told me everything. Perhaps, I told him, what you need lives beyond your own realm."

Rahim looked at Steven and Riva. "I had succeeded once with a powerful potion," Rahim said. "It was able to unite a girl from my village with a suitor she did not care for. Her father persuaded me that it would be desirable for both families." Rahim lowered his head. "I do not like to meddle in the affairs of the heart, but I owed many favours to the girl's mother. She is a nurse and tended to my mother."

"What did you do?" Riva said.

"I gave her a potion for her daughter. She promised not to divulge what she had seen me do when I was preparing the potion, but unbeknown to her, I slipped another potion into her drink. This ensured that she would remember nothing of what I did. I explained to the priest what he had to do and prepared the potion for him, adding a small amount of viper's poison to seal the potion. He had to administer this to the Prince. The spell to get the Princess to fall in love with him was very complicated and took many hours to prepare. Anhurmose was impressed with my work and left extremely happy. He later returned to inform me that he had been successful and a marriage between the couple had been organised by the Princess's elated father. The Nubian Prince returned the original gifts he bestowed on his future father-in-law and added many more. The Princess forgot about her original love, and as far as I know, they lived a long and happy life together."

"What happened to the portal," Riva said.

Rahim smiled. "The King ordered the priest to seal the portal, and assisted by a handful of loyal priests, he did this. These were sworn to secrecy, and the balance returned to the kingdom. To thank me, the priest gifted me this desk made of temple stones." Rahim patted the desk. "It is inscribed with hieroglyphic charms and decorated in gold and silver across its edges. Look."

Riva and Steven moved closer and examined the desk. "It is indeed beautiful," Steven said.

Rahim chuckled. "The temple clergy would have sent a much bigger one, but I explained that it would not fit in my tiny office. I don't live in a temple, I told him. However, I had to come up with a plausible story to explain how I came by it." Rahim waved a hand. "That is for another day. We have this to worry about." He tapped the parchment and began to scrutinise it. "It appears to be a map of Egypt, but some of the names of the cities are misspelt. And these …" He pointed to the different colours on the map. "These could be warning signs. And this zone, marked in red and black, is

Abydos." He scratched his balding head and gave Riva and Steven a long look as he pondered. "The world knows of two wooden tablets housed in the Egyptian Antiquities Museum, the content of which is a record of ordinary life in the ancient world. However, I have possessed a third tablet. It is small, no bigger than the palm of my hand and unknown to the world. It documents the lawful list of kings and is sealed by a secret stamp confirming the right of a king or queen to rule. It also contains significant formulae about the pharaohs' lethal weapons, which changes our perception of what we know about the old world."

"How have you lost it?" Riva said.

Rahim sighed. "The slab is elusive, with a mind of its own. It has changed hands many times over thousands of years. It has protective layers of spells from those who seek to destroy it. This parchment may lead the way to the tablet of Horus."

The Tablet Back Then

For years, Amunet's raw beauty had entranced the villagers where she lived. The girl with plaited hair flowing majestically behind her walked down the same path daily from her humble dwellings on the Theban bank. Oozing charm and flawless beauty, she quickly caught the attention of all farmhands who watched the slender figure stroll along the path. Wearing her simple beige dress, which clung tightly to her body, and with a small amount of her favourite scent, she would go about her work while longing eyes studied her. The poor girl combined her perfume with various herbs, honey from a nearby beehive and saffron obtained from a hopelessly devoted young man who stole the herb from a master, risking a thrashing. Even in her simple clothing, Amunet carried herself with such grace that she put the pharaoh's concubines to shame.

"That girl is the siren that changes men into mindless fools," the mothers would tell their besotted sons. "Find a sensible girl who will bear you children."

Amunet's day arrived as usual. Her walk to her workplace, past the staring men, was like any other. Her scent, which would have been considered cheap on any other woman, filled the air with a captivating fragrance. The sun above, an exquisite gold, shimmered overhead and hung in the cloudless sky, casting silhouettes of her figure as she sauntered across the field.

On this fateful day, Amunet eventually arrived at her place of work and began her task of tilling the soil and removing weeds, thereby allowing her to plant seeds. She was moving about her small patch of land when a heavily pregnant girl, Nieth, who occupied the position next to her own, went into labour. The girl dropped to the ground in agony, and Amunet and others ran to her aid. But as Amunet neared the stricken Nieth, she stepped on a small mound of soil that gave way under her feet. She stumbled and fell, clutching her ankle, which stung as if being attacked by a dozen wasps. As the others tended to the pregnant girl and Amunet sat there rubbing her angry, red foot, she spotted something within the hole she had stood in. She shivered uncontrollably, but after a few seconds, this passed, and the pain in her foot eased. She clambered to her feet, composed herself, and headed across to assist the others, dismissing the strange feeling that was there and then just as quickly gone. Nieth lay on the ground, clearly in labour, as the men were ushered away and more women from the village were summoned. Hot water and cloths were brought forth as the women made the young girl comfortable. A fire was lit nearby, and a large pot hung above it to boil more water.

Amunet held Nieth's hand, and after a brief labour, she delivered a beautiful baby boy whom she named little Apep. The girl, carrying her son, made her way back to the village with Amunet still holding her free hand as the people clapped and cheered. Little Apep, held tightly by his mother, reached out his hand and took hold of Amunet's hair. Amunet smiled and looked deeply into the boy's eyes, but as she did so, a vision appeared. She listened as the baby spoke. "You, Amunet," he said, "have been chosen. Expose the tablet where your foot hit the ground." Amunet's eyes widened, and she looked around at the others, but to her surprise, no one else appeared to have heard it.

She eased herself away from the mother and baby and looked down at her soil-covered foot.

"Move," the overseer shouted to the group of people surrounding the mother and child. "Take Nieth and her baby home. We still have work to do."

The overseer's face darkened, as he studied Amunet. "Resume the work," he shouted at the dispersing crowd.

The overseer, Djau, just as smitten with Amunet as any other man from the village ushered the workers back to their tasks. He had learnt as a child that keeping his thoughts to himself would help him get promoted, and he used his farming knowledge to protect and serve a particular clique of temple priests in Thebes, the mighty capital of the ancient world.

Djau

Djau belonged to a particular group, a cult that prepared for generations to take over the world. Coached by rogue priests, he learnt to use his senses and master a unique set of spells to track down the powerful tablet that had been missing for centuries. His clan lay to the northwest on the Libyan border. Their agents lived along the route to Siwa, an oasis filled with magical tropes, lying to the north and east, many days from Thebes. Djau did not grow up, like his father, on the side of good, choosing instead to commit himself to the darker forces.

"Those hungry, low lives will get me to the palace," he told his mentor before killing him. Unbeknownst to Amunet, she had given him his first clue to the object that could elevate his position in this realm. He despised his father and swore that he would not be meek like him. He would carve out his own destiny in this world.

"I will become great," he told himself over and over.

After Nieth returned home and the work for the day was completed, Djau made his way over to where he had spotted Amunet and began digging a hole. He had witnessed her episode, which gave a clue to the tablet's location. He had watched the girl grow into a young woman, knowing how important she was – the signs were everywhere. But he had to be shrewd. Even his grandma Akila, the great sorceress, had been unable to discover where it lay. He patiently waited until darkness fell, and after midnight, when he was confident the villagers were asleep, he took out his potion and sprinkled it on the ground. He waited for a sign, an indication of where it lay.

Djau put a cloth over his mouth as a vapour escaped from the ground where he had poured the liquid. The vapour made his head spin, but stepping further away from it, he allowed his senses to return to normal and the vapour to disperse before he moved closer. He could see something semi-submerged in a small hole. Excited, Djau dropped to his knees and raked more of the soil from the hole, revealing a rectangular slab partially covered by linen. Djau removed the linen wrap and pulled the slab free. He stood and smiled. "It is clear," he said to himself. "Our time has come," Djau uttered a sacred oath to his occult, gave the village one last look and melted into the night.

Silence reigned across the village, and in one of the houses lay the body. Djau had slipped poison into the older man's drink and arranged the body as if it had died naturally.

The Young Djau

The chief of the village addressed his guards. "Search everything," he ordered. The guards obeyed his orders, frantically going from house to house. No stone was left unturned as they inspected each property meticulously, eventually arriving at the home of Djau's father, User. The terrible murder committed on sacred ground did not make any sense to the authorities.

"My poor mother," the young Djau said to himself. "How will I tell her about my father's death?" Unbeknownst to anyone, he had been at the temple when the body had been discovered. He had broken into the temple and hidden out of sight in one of the Priest's rooms until he could make good his escape. If he was caught with the bloody parchment, he would be blamed.

He slipped out of the temple unseen and hurried home, leaving the guards, who were continuing their search far behind. He arrived back home breathless and made his way into one of the bedrooms. He moved his bed and hid the rolled-up parchment underneath. The scroll contained only a few words when he had hastily read it at the temple. There had been something about a tablet and sceptre, the words he remembered his grandma saying to his father over and over when she was alive. Djau slipped into the room that had belonged to his Grandma, Akila, and selected a potion. 'for protection,' she used to say. Djau made his way back to the room where he had hidden the scroll and sprinkled the powder over the scroll. He carefully covered it with linen and put it inside the hiding place before sliding the bed back.

Djau, worried about his dishevelled and bloody clothing, dashed to the river, cleaned himself up, and then went to bed before the news about his father spread throughout the village.

Ten-year-old Djau instinctively understood that his mother would be safe if she knew nothing about what he had seen at the temple, especially the part about him stealing the document he had fortuitously found at the chaotic murder scene.

I will speak with Apep, the magician, Djau thought. Evil as Apep was, he was the best at putting elements together to create a spell. Some stars, or someone, guided the magician. Djau remembered Akila describing the solitary Apep enviously as a man who knew his magic but could not be trusted. Djau yawned and closed his eyes. Within minutes, he was in a deep sleep.

"The wife and son live here alone," the Magistrate said to the guards. "You have already searched the murdered man's place. Leave the family to mourn. Grandma Akila has been a good friend to all of us."

The murder in the temple had cast a cloud on both the sacred ground and the palace. If the murderer or murderers were not apprehended soon, the people's faith could be tested. For a moment, by the door to User's home, the magistrate affectionately recalled Akila, who had treated himself and his family many times. He remembered how she had given him a potion to help his wife conceive, and she had given birth to seven sons and two daughters. He was shaken from his reverie by one of the guards nearby. He must speak with the priests, he mused and hurried to the temple.

Meanwhile, the villagers prepared User's body for burial and set about organising his funeral. He was eventually laid to rest on the West Bank, in a tomb adorned with simple drawings, and supplied with food and drink to help him through the transition to the next life. The people finally left, leaving the widow to grieve for her husband as her son considered his next move.

"Bring your son to do his father's job," the Priest had said to the widow. "User will be remembered for the great work he has done. In the next life, he will be rewarded." The words were a great comfort to User's wife.

Djau raced home from the funeral, hurried to his bedroom, and pulled the bed away. The parchment had vanished.

Ten years had passed since the scroll had disappeared from under Djau's bed. He had trained hard from that day, becoming well-versed in the way of the priests. He carried out his daily duties diligently, cleaning, cooking, and writing, but all the while, he watched the others. Surreptitiously listening to them as they talked amongst themselves. He would wait until they were drunk on wine and listened as slowly he learnt their secrets. Djau resented them but fulfilled their whims and commands until he was confident he knew enough to practise his own self-made doctrine.

Ten years ago, on the night his father died, Djau remembered how the parchment had glowed in the sanctuary room with a life of its own. Its arcane meanings of which only an exceptional sorcerer might unravel.

Djau prepared himself to trade part of his soul to become a proficient magician, greater even than his grandma Akila. He collected some meagre scraps of food and left for the West Bank, arriving by boat at the cemetery where his dead father had been interred. His intention was to visit a magician Akila had warned him against many times. But undeterred, Djau sealed his fate with the West Bank Wizard and returned to the temple in the East Bank. He needed to keep both sides of the bank satisfied until the papyrus scroll resurfaced.

For thousands of years, labourers and their higher supervisors protected tombs in the Theban West Bank with magic, hoping to keep their belongings intact for the afterlife. The lower echelons of society turned to affordable magicians for protection. In the days of Djau, Apep emerged, versed in wickedness, offering a comfortable transition to the afterlife for a smaller pay.

"Let them have their will with the low-life sorcerers," the priests would say as they grew fatter and more prosperous than the people. Silencing dissenters with threats of reprisals from deities if they overstepped the mark.

Apep, named, like the baby boy born to Nieth, lived alone close to the cemetery, procuring helpful information from the palace and temple about brewing dissent or infiltrating spies from the west. Apep also kept records of time travellers who used the portal without permission and kept himself informed about modern charms, for he excelled in mixing the elements to read the future.

Apep, gifted in the dark side, healed labourers with herbal concoctions, and in return, he expected favours.

"Bring me a fresh liver, or I will take it from your newborn," Apep hissed at the horrified builder. The poor man was forced into stealing a child for Apep. The worker had lost the use of his hand when a large slab fell on it, and he had asked the magician for help, never expecting that he would have to commit such a heinous crime.

Cursed as an infant, Apep limped severely as he walked. Once fully grown, the magician would follow his mother around like a toddler to the extent that it became impossible for her to tend to the house, her husband and the other three siblings.

"I curse you from my heart," his mother had said one day when he angered her. She did not mean to cast the spell, but in her exhausted, dishevelled state and no longer the pretty maiden who played the harp with grace before the marriage, she did not notice a full moon. The next day and for the next forty years, Apep dragged one of his legs as he walked. His mother, seeing the impact of her curse, never again uttered one word of discontent against anyone, even when her husband gave her a sound beating.

Apep, unable to play games with the other children, preferred to read. He garnered sympathy from the priests, and he was given a pen-pushing job. He excelled in his role of bookkeeping historical records and looking after the coffers of the temple. His reading and quest for knowledge knew no bounds, and he quickly learned the names of kings in each dynasty, extolling the virtues of monarchs and queens to anyone who would listen. Sometimes, he entertained the clergy with stories about the concubines of lesser officials whispered to him by spirits he had managed to enslave.

"Do you know the chief consort of the son of the normach in Thebes is having a baby?" he said to the clergy. "But do you know who the father is, the real one?" They laughed at this over beer and asked Apep to tell them more.

Apep was clever, though. He would ply the priests with his homemade wine to loosen their tongues, making a mental note of what they told him. Information, Apep knew, was invaluable.

"That is nothing compared to a bastard who has had herself written on the tablet of kings with no right to you know what," the priest let slip before realising what he had said. The priest, fearful that Apep would tell the others about his indiscretion, allowed him to wander the buildings freely, hoping that, in time, he would forget what he had told him.

Apep's demeanour fooled many priests into thinking him benign. So he grew up quietly in their halls, looking to hear the information which would enable him to perfect his own spell, which he eventually did.

"Magic is changing," one of the Priests said. "The charms are not working as before. We shall need the help of the scumbags. Move on to animal sacrifices." The Priest paused as he heard the telltale sound of the limping Apep close by. "We will pick up on the other subject *later,*" he said, not realising just how good Apep's hearing was.

The wizard's mathematical acuity and orderly registers got him promoted to a cherished, though unofficial, member among the clergy, and he continued to gain knowledge from the priests who foolishly left behind their papers. Apep preferred living in the West Bank, much to the surprise of the priests.

"Don't you wish to stay in clean rooms close to the temple instead of limping back to a filthy hovel all the way to the other side?" the priests never tired of asking.

"I like to stay close to my family," Apep said.

Once back at his cave, Apep would take out the formulae he had stolen from the temple, along with the words he had written down and perfected his own spells with astonishing results. He created beauty oils and a medication for sore throats. He was able to cure common ailments and injuries, and the people would seek him out, little knowing the favours they would have to do.

Apep wrote poetry for the young men to impress and win the hearts of the village girls. He sold smuggled incense from the Land of Punt and further south beyond the second cataract to burn for wooing, weddings, funerals and prayers. Apep had a cure for almost everything.

"I worry my daughters may be lured by Seth," a poor villager said. "If he takes them, they will not marry and die without a promise of the afterlife."

The same complaint recurred among the villagers. Girls had to be protected from the deity Seth, a mischievous creature who spread disorder within the girls. Other potions subverted evil spirits that forced girls to hate matrimony, making them too plain for potential suitors who came to see them. There were, of course, the most popular lotions of all that kept the girls fertile and desirable in the eyes of husbands. In some cases, the potions were designed to keep them strong to till the fields when families were too sick or too poor to provide for the girls. Apep dealt with all complaints but at a price.

"The noise is back," a villager said to her husband. "The wizard is killing girls, I tell you." She prodded him. "Make sure our girls are safe." The simple farmer walked to the cot in the extended mud brick home, and to his relief, the girls slept soundly.

Shrieks often came from Apep's rooms at night, but neighbours never interfered, fearing that their children would be harmed if they spoke out.

One night, the noises were louder than usual. The next day, one of the maidens had gone missing. She had been seen entering Apep's home but had not returned.

"What have you done with Anat?" her mother screamed at him.

Apep smiled. "How could I do anything to a healthy girl like Anat. I am frail. She would be much too strong for me," he said, pointing at his leg. "It requires all of my strength to move."

Anat's friends had seen her enter Apep's den on a full moon, but they never saw her step out. The next day, Apep distributed his best cosmetics amongst the maidens to keep them quiet. When the authorities were summoned, Anat's friends said nothing. They, however, agreed that they would not see Apep on their own.

Soon enough, Apep thought, I will have to sacrifice another of those souls if they want more of my potion to help them stay young and desirable. He chuckled to himself. They did not have to know what the potions contained.

Djau knew of Apep, recalling his parents' blood-curdling stories. The mere mention of his name would enrage them.

As Apep got older, his ability to conjure spirits became increasingly better. He had them travel great distances, stirring up anarchy or robbing people of their cherished possessions. Apep kept these spirits tethered on a mental leash so that they were unable to free themselves from the magician's grasp. He hoped one day to fly one of these demonic souls as far as the Temple of Philae, where festivities took place and people spoke their minds. If he could achieve this and get the spirits as far as the Temple of Abydos, he would be overjoyed. This was the site of the new world order and the burial place of the original rulers of Egypt – the first two dynasties. Imagine the secrets within there.

He grinned. Abydos will provide the healing spell for my leg, he thought. I shall become a high-ranking priest at the temple, telling kings what to do instead of wasting my valuable talent on the lowly.

The ten years that had passed since the death of his father had unleashed the great potential Djau knew he had always possessed. He now had two jobs and was the head of the sorcery department. One day, he would profit from learning about the secrets of life in the present and the eternal one in the hereafter.

Djau, who lived in Thebes, remembered the time he travelled away from the riverbank, reached the eastern bank, and sailed a small boat to the other side of the Nile. He took along Akila's potions to bribe his way into Apep's home. Once at Apep's door, Djau theatrically threw himself onto the floor to impress the magician further. It worked. At first, stunned by the visitor's actions, he soon warmed to him.

"I seek you, my master," Djau pleaded, "to teach me what you know. I shall be your slave and do your bidding."

Apep, amused by the young lad, listened carefully to Djau's rehearsed sentences, nodding slowly as Djau flattered the sorcerer.

"Are you hungry?" he asked Djau while studying him. A fit young man to do his bidding would be welcome, he mused.

Apep prepared a light meal for his guest, and unbeknownst to Djau, he hid some truth seeds in the food. Unable to control his tongue, once the seeds had begun their work, Djau was helpless to stop himself. Apep smiled as the young man told him everything about the massacre he had witnessed at the temple, which left the king, a priest, and his father dead.

"There was a scroll with pictures on it," Djau said. "Someone must have taken it from under my bed."

"What did the pictures look like?"

"I can draw what I remember," Djau said as Apep nodded.

"Tell me more,' he demanded.

"The priests respected my father," Djau continued. "I will start work in the Theban temple soon to repay my father for his work, but I can help you."

Apep's eyes widened at the boy's words. He stroked his chin as he considered what he had been told. This was the dark world answering his prayers, he thought. If Djau had found and lost the parchment close to his home, then maybe he could also find the tablet, the key to conquering the whole of Egypt. "What can you give me, boy, if I teach you all I know?'

Djau shrugged. "I have these potions."

Apep waved them away. "I have no need of those. Have you heard of the king's tablet?"

Over the years, Djau eagerly embraced the teachings of Apep. Together, they worked on rebuilding a replica of the scroll, the contents of which still remained a mystery. Apep lost many of the spirits he entrapped while trying to find the lost parchment. "Someone must have seen or heard something," Apep would often say. Eventually, the two men managed to replicate some of the charms that were contained within the lost scroll – working daily to decipher the hidden text after each of them tended to the villagers, the other to the temple. Every so often, Djau remembered a little more of what he had seen on the original scroll, and Apep aptly completed the rest.

"Boy," Apep said to Djau, "you are growing faster and stronger. I want to try out a new potion I have made. It may help us to further decipher the parchment."

"I trust you, master," Djau said. "How can I assist?"

Apep explained that the new potion contained spirits who might be able to get inside the parchment, but only if Djau concentrated enough on the night of blood and death years ago. The apprentice knew that Apep was wily, only telling him enough so that he would keep returning for more. But Djau, like his master, was cunning and understood the virtue of silence. He looked and learned, allowing his knowledge to grow, secretly reading his master's notes and stealing concoctions when he could. Djau gathered every scrap of information he could. Only with patience would he become the great sorcerer he had always envisioned, and he waited for the opportunity when Apep would drop his guard.

"Prepare my flask," Apep said to Djau one day.

Djau had been given the task of preparing his master's sleeping potion. Despite the older man's wickedness and black heart, he would occasionally suffer from nightmares, which could only be eased with the potion, allowing him to rest.

In time, as Apep aged, he would send Djau to run errands in the temple on the other side of the Nile. Apep grew lazy, older and fatter, becoming more and more addicted to the sleeping potion Djau perfected. But the elderly sorcerer never drank the full amount of potion to ease his pain, preferring to suffer a little at night to allow him to stay alert for anything out of the ordinary. He feared reprisals from the souls of victims he had tortured and also his ever-bolder apprentice. Always suspicious of the younger man, Apep would monitor his preparation of the potion.

But over time, Apep became increasingly dependent on the drug, and his hold on Djau began to weaken. Unable to curb his ambitious apprentice, Djau was free to experiment with Apep's potions.

One day, Djau prepared a potion while Apep slept and threw it over one of the mirrors – something he had secretly seen Apep do. Messages appeared on the mirror, but unbeknown to Djau, these messages could be easily misinterpreted or translated to give the exact opposite meaning. These types of messages, which came from mysterious realms ruled by shapeless alien demons, demanded an expert decipherer. These texts contained unusual hieroglyphics, which, if misconstrued, risked a crippling demise. This, Apep had decided, was beyond Djau's expertise.

One day, the weary warlock beckoned Djau to his side. "Listen, Djau, I want to show you something." Apep, assisted by Djau, eased into the seat behind his desk. He lifted up the lens. The small, rounded piece of polished quartz had been gifted to him by an Assyrian who travelled from the land between two rivers in the east for a cure to a skin disease which was eating him alive.

Apep pointed at the corner of the ceiling. "Look, Djau," he said. Djau looked at the spirits that he had often seen Apep talking with. "The ephemerals you see," Apep said, "are disobeying me because they know I am too weak to make them search for the missing tablet. We need spices. Come with me. I can teach you a thing or two."

Djau assisted as they left the house and walked into the desert beyond the cemetery. Eventually, they stopped, and Apep pointed to a small opening near some rocks. Djau searched and returned with a stone tablet.

"The tablet is made from rays of the sun," Apep said. "I will show you what to do."

Apep tutored Djau on how to prepare green charms – a special kind of spell – which would unlock the tablet and uncover the knowledge within. It took years of practice until Djau got the potion right. By now, Apep was growing weaker, but in his final days, he managed to teach Djau how to find the tablet without the scroll leading to it. The tablet, in the hands of Nitocris, would open the gates to the dark side, blanketing their kingdom.

Gradually, Djau increased the sleeping doses he administered to Apep using his own additives as the older man outgrew his usefulness. Apep increasingly feared sleep, for he feared damnation. The apprentice continued to increase the drug daily, and Apep slept longer and deeper every day. When Apep slept, Djau took the opportunity to use Apep's study across the room from where the sorcerer slept. Acquainting himself with books and Apep's words, Djau learned more about the power of the tablet. Soon, he would not need his master. One night, he increased the dose until Apep closed his eyes for the final time.

The villagers did not miss their creepy sorcerer, assuming he died in his sleep and Djau, the loyal servant, buried him quietly with his own funerary rituals from the dark side. Djau continued to live among the villagers for a few more months after the death of his master and carried out favours for the villagers while wrapping up his studies on the dark world and the elusive queen.

Meanwhile, the poor girls in the neighbourhood who lived close to the cemetery continued to receive their beauty potions from Djau while the rising magician nourished them with the powers of seduction. Their husbands remained tied to their brides, and any incoming suitors couldn't fail to be seduced by the enchanted females.

Older men in the village were supplied with cures for their rheumatic aches, and mothers received gentle potions to quiet their children. All of this ensured that the villagers relied on Djau. Djau also endeared himself to the people on both sides of the Nile banks – a foreman, supervising builders in Thebes, a part-time scribe at the Temple of Luxor and a magician in the West Bank.

One day, Djau felt powerful and confident enough to attempt to locate the tablet. His hard work on the spell book specially prepared indicated that Osiris himself had delivered the tablet from his kingdom. The deity, as strong as ever, prepared for the oncoming battle between good and evil and vowed to put an end to the coming era of Nitocris.

Apep's book told how Osiris needed mortals to expose the fake queen and remove the spell that infamously forged her name into the King's list. For the battle to take place, Nitocris had to be smoked out of her dark temple below Abydos, fought and defeated.

When the battle commenced, the good people of the world would have to stand up for good to help defeat the wicked queen. Thereby eliminating her name from the tablet of kings and making sure it was never written down again. Only then could evil be stopped for good. He collected some of the charmed stones and gems from Apep's wooden shelf and, along with some other potions, set out in search of the slab. According to Apep's calculations, it should be near.

User

Djau's father, User, joined the temple at the age of seven, performing services with great devotion to Priest Kaaper at the Temple of Luxor. He quickly rose to the rank of guardian to the sacred sanctuary and keeper of secrets to hidden rituals performed in the holiest chambers. His mother, Akila, came to Priest Kaaper one day, holding the child's hand. Both versed in the art of sorcery, Priest Kaaper looked at the boy and bent on one knee facing him. "Do you want to work for me, User?" he asked.

"I shall do exactly as my mother tells me to," the boy said.

The child loved Akila deeply, growing up knowing that a solid understanding of right and wrong existed. The opposite sides had no grey areas, no nuances. User had little imagination beyond a simple understanding of human nature. He obeyed rules laid down by an authority chosen by Akila, making him a good person who kept out of trouble. User learnt to disengage from others who refrained from obeying set rules, but he blindly obeyed Kaaper, who, in turn, served in the order of the magic cult of the priesthood.

Kaaper addressed the King and taught the natives only what the people of Egypt should know. User devoted himself to the priest, the tenet and the preservation of secrets. The boy, soon to become a man, understood obedience and the importance of holding his tongue. The concept of a tenet remained an abstract world that made little sense to him. Suffice it to say that the confidential, mysterious rituals and documents that priests, occasionally Kings, had access to existed at the back of the temple behind the shrine and were kept out of sight. One of the two rooms stored the King's ship, while the other served as the offering room, which the King visited on occasion.

"Listen, my boy," Kaaper warned, "you are never to enter the two rooms unless I give you specific instructions to clean up after a ritual." User nodded his understanding.

User, the dedicated servant, collected and chronicled gifts received from subjects and emissaries. He catalogued endowments on papyrus rolls and was proud to have learnt to write at the hands of Kaaper. On very rare occasions, the priest allowed his subject to tend to visiting dignitaries in the chapel where *confidential favours* took place, including help with the King's waning virility, palace agents or deadly potions. User would be quiet, offering drinks to the dignitaries but not really understanding the conversations which took place.

User watched on as a Libyan guest arrived one day. "You want to be positioned in the palace?" Kaaper said, raising his eyebrows.

The western border caused many headaches to successive kings. Regular travellers from the west visited priests to facilitate a Libyan presence within palace walls as concubines or guards and the clergy.

"Your presence in court may not be welcomed," Kaaper said.

"Of course, I mean no offence," the Libyan said. "How about allowing some of my men and women to work with a normach in Thebes? This is what I have in mind. In return, I will show my devotion to the temple. I shall donate one thousand pieces of gold."

The back and forth between Kaaper and the Libyan emissary became the rule in Theban temples. User, however, found the conversation meaningless and cared little about them. Happily, he awaited a gift from the priest – a payment for his work – which he gratefully accepted and delivered to Akila.

When guests from the southern or western borders came to the priest to facilitate trade between the kingdoms, Kaaper would flatter them to enable trade to continue and the coffers to fill. Even the naïve User knew that battles and strife impoverished the temple and put a strain on security. Trade, however, enriched it.

Over many years, User dutifully carried out the assigned duties with diligence. "User," Kaaper said to him one day, "I want you to repeat after me. You are never to enter the King's offering room unless given specific orders by me." User nodded that he understood, but this rule was repeated often to him. Therefore, User kept well clear.

On the eve of one of many celebrations marking the Nile floods, the people of Thebes enjoyed generous donations of food outside the temple walls. Revellers boisterously threw grain and fruits into the Nile to thank the gods for the steady flow of water, which put an end to the drought season. The King threw a banquet for his guests at his palace, and the priests, in turn, enjoyed bountiful offerings from the King.

That night, User waited outside, across from the King's offering room, expecting the priest to tell him to clean up ahead of a royal visit by the monarch himself. Traditionally, the royal, in full regalia, gave thanks for the bountiful waters that replenished the parched ground and heralded a good year. As User waited, he idly watched the clear skies, listening to merry crowds outside the temple walls singing along with professional troupes when something caught his attention. He turned his head towards the symbolic pharaoh's solar boat room and listened. He thought he had heard a muffled scream from within the forbidden area and then another, followed by a loud thud and silence. He waited for the noise to return. Even with his simple mind, he knew enough to realise that the noise sounded like a struggle between at least two people. User waited, unsure how to proceed.

Over the previous thirty years, from little boy to man, he had become accustomed to obeying instructions. He had never had to make a decision himself. User pulled himself back to the present and to the fear that gripped his heart. He glanced around for Priest Kaaper, who was nowhere to be seen. The priest's headquarters lay close to the King's solar room, and the cleric had, in the past, cleaned the room himself. But as he grew older, he allowed User to assist. The room was cleaned with a sophisticated mix of ingredients known only to the priests and was prepared for the King's visit. Once cleaned and prepared, User would wait for the heavy scent of cinnamon, honey, wine, expensive saffron and other concoctions to spread throughout the temple before settling down on a stone bench outside the priest's sanctuary. Only then would he eat the bread, meat, goat's cheese, drink the water he was provided with and await commands. Rumours were rife amongst the other staff as to what was in the priest's concoction, but whatever it was, the perfume gave off a powerful and seductive aroma. User saw a little of the process once the king entered the room and nothing of the preparation. Priest Kaaper would glare at User if he loitered nearby, which would encourage User to move away.

User, unable to make head nor tail of what was happening in the King's room, especially with the absence of Kaaper to give instructions, decided to search for the priest. He hurried to the priest's room to wake him up, but, not finding him, he hesitated, then dashed back towards the earlier sounds. Fumes were now emanating from the King's room, and User, collecting one of the torches, crept inside. Once inside, the oily scent filled his nostrils as he moved through the gloom created by smoke, and the smell of scent gave way to burning. User gasped as, through the clouds of smoke, he spotted the King's guards dead on the floor, surrounded by a large pool of blood. He recalled his training, which demanded that he restore order and clean the room. User strode further inside the room, extinguished the fire and waited as the air cleared. Something caught his attention in one of the corners. He blinked, thinking that his eyes were playing tricks on him. A giant serpent hovered over the body of Kaaper with the severed head of the priest clamped within its jaws. It turned to face User, and the deep green eyes of the creature locked on him.

User gulped as his heart pounded inside his chest, barely able to look away from the terrifying predator. Broken vessels of rare glass covered the floor of the small room, and liquids of every colour were splashed all over. User was appalled. The room, always spotless, was now defiled not only by the blood and bodies of the dead but also by the precious fluids from countless jars. User was gripped with fear as the serpent dropped the dead priest's head and tugged at something within the throat of the body. He strained to see what it was. It appeared to be a document of some sort.

"You are alive to keep the order and eliminate chaos," he remembered Akila had told him.

The serpent must be the chaos with which she spoke, he reasoned. He must kill the beast.

User looked into the serpent's green eyes and remembered what Akila had taught him over the years.

"When danger looms," she had told him. "Stab the eyes of the serpent and write the words for posterity." She had relentlessly repeated the words to him.

He looked to his left, and his eyes fell on the surgical tools, cleaned and arranged for sacrifices, lying on the table beside the slaughtered priest. User moved through the shards of glass and, never removing his stare from the serpent's penetrating eyes, he snatched up a knife. The serpent, sensing what User intended, slithered across to him. User straddled the beast and stabbed at the creature's eye. He missed, stumbled, fell onto his knees and watched helplessly as the knife slipped from his grasp. He turned as the snake sprang at him, sinking its fangs deep into his throat. User groaned as copious amounts of blood fountained from the severed artery in his neck. He desperately grabbed a shard of glass from the floor, and ignoring the pain as it cut into his hand, he stuck it into the serpent. The beast released its grip on its victim, and using the last remaining bits of strength, User pulled the glass free and struck again and again. The creature threw back its mighty head and hissed at him as blood flowed freely from its body. Its blood began to boil, spraying the priest and burning User. He slumped to the floor, and using the liquid as ink, he scribbled – *Break the sceptre. Find the tablet. Save King and kingdom* – onto the floor before drawing his final breath.

The serpent hissed again, its belly wide open, its entrails hanging from the gaping wound, and with what little strength it had, it tore at User, ripping his limbs from his body and tearing his head from his shoulders. It lifted its head high above the mutilated body of User, barely recognisable as human. The serpent, soaked in its own boiling blood, moved towards the parchment, still wedged within the priest's throat. It had to destroy it, this it knew, but as it neared the headless torso, the snake's strength failed, and it fell to the ground with an almighty crash.

User's Mother – Akila, Heka's Disciple

Gifted in the ways of Heka, a respected deity of magic, Akila received a little of the knowledge the grand sorcerer bestowed upon those he deemed worthy. User's mother instinctively understood the art of balancing herbs in measured amounts to help the women in the village assume some control over their mischievous husbands or lives. Help came in all sorts of ways. Potions subdued uncouth men, giving power to the weakest and the least resourceful. Finding unique skills in Akila, Heka promoted her to chief apprentice of magic in the remote Theban village. Akila expertly developed her own poignant mixtures that sometimes surpassed Heka's recipes. She grasped with enviable speed the finer shortcuts to magic formulae, and, in a land where bartering prevailed, she won many favours for recipes hungrily consumed by desperate villagers. Heka nodded approvingly as he watched with amusement the attempt of a mere mortal to outperform the master. Nevertheless, he coached her in an effort to battle the evil that the deity Seth had left behind.

"Be discreet," he counselled her. "Learn to hide in plain sight."

In time, Akila continued to surprise her coach, modifying some of his methods to better suit the modern times, and she soon became his favourite apprentice at the young age of twenty.

Wise Akila understood that to be accepted as a sorcerer in the small village where she lived, she needed to find a suitable companion to become her husband. The sorceress, not comely and born to poverty, sought a marriage of convenience and set her sights on a handsome farmer called Amsi. A potion was prepared and slipped into his drink, which made him fall in love with Akila and ultimately propose. Amsi came from a wealthy and popular scion which owned swathes of land. Much to the surprise of many young girls who were attracted to him, the couple married in a quiet ceremony without his parents' knowledge.

His mother was shocked when her son arrived home, carrying his young bride across the threshold.

"My dear mother, this is my wife Akila," he told her. "She will love and serve you as much as I do."

Amsi's mother searched her son's eyes, fearing he was either drunk or had lost his senses. "Dearest mother," he pleaded. "I love and respect you, but I cannot live without your approval. Please accept my wife and bless her."

Akila's mother-in-law did not have the heart to upset her son, so she hid her disappointment, embraced the bride and left the next day to her farthest home at the edge of Thebes. Akila had no plans to use her magic on the household to gain acceptance, for abuse of sorcery provoked Heka. The master of magic understood, however, Akila's need to blend in and keep the magic flowing in good faith.

The village grew to love Akila and also the gifts bestowed on the poorer farmers by her wealthy husband. Akila put women a little in charge of the households, and in time, her son, User, her favourite, was born. As he grew, he would sit with her in their home as villagers visited.

"My husband gets drunk all night," one woman complained to Akila. "He sleeps like a pig, and then he blames me for not begetting children."

Women in the village were desperate for children and sometimes had to put their faith in unworthy husbands.

User would sit as quiet as a mouse while watching Akila whenever anyone visited.

"Make yourself useful, my little love," she would say to him. "Fetch bowls and herbs, and I will teach you." Akila spoilt the little boy who watched as she carried out her ministrations.

User was amazed that every time the maidens who visited his mother for help, bore children and could never understand how she succeeded. He would hear the villagers talk in whispers, extolling Akila's magic, but others had doubts about the process. However, the wiser sceptics remained silent in case they required her help for children of their own.

Barren women went into labour, and impotent men became virile. The resourceful woman, using inexplicable methods, always found a way to make the peasants happier. On occasion and in the blackness of certain nights, Akila invited dark and fair men and women who were not from the village to test mysterious spells on them. These strange people who entered her hut came from the sky, thought User. Well, to his young mind, they had to come from somewhere.

After those visitors came and went, the women and the men in the village, who complained they could not have children, delivered healthy babies months later.

At times, Akila allowed User to crush animal horns with a pestle to make a paste, his favourite pastime, and she rubbed the balm on girls. The paste sprang to life on their backs and then disappeared, leaving the girls radiant and confident, blooming with a much stronger physique, especially above the hips. Akila revealed particular artisanship in the preparation of love potions. The small red book, painted with the crimson blood of deer, bound together in papyrus leaves, detailed the mixtures she placed on her clay table. User would give her the parchments coloured in different shades of ink to mark the spells. On that table, hidden under several scrolls in her lab, User glimpsed what might be a wooden slab, shorter than his arm and around two inches thick. He would glance at it daily, curious to know what to make of it.

One day, Akila sat User on her knee and said, "Do you want to know what that slab of wood is?" User grinned, for he loved to hear her stories. "The block of wood," she began, "belongs to the kings of Egypt. Pharaohs wrote their names so the people knew who their kings were. This piece of wood carries the only proof of a dying breed and makes sure that their names are saved for posterity." Akila had found the slab by chance in a field miles away from her village.

One day, she walked along the green bank of the Nile in search of herbs – a practice she diligently embraced – as most sorcerers, good or bad, trained to do. She spoke to the Nile, as she often did, beseeching the river to bring forth the fresh green spices which the river often delivered after the flood seasons. These spices, gifted by the Nile, were remarkable and hugely improved her love formulas.

One day, Heka took the much younger Akila on a trip. "Come. It is time to sharpen your senses. Darkness is moving in."

Akila, wearing her favourite leather sandals, walked along the river through wheat and cotton fields the way Heka had taught her. Heka had sealed a pact with the river deity to watch over her disciples on condition they walked by the Nile and never with their backs to the water.

Gradually, after years of practice, Akila mastered the art of searching for rare roots to put into drinks, balms, or sprays. These she used to heal a variety of illnesses. She told User about these times and called them the days of poetry, smiling as she recounted her carefree life. Alone, armed with a powerful mind and a kind heart, she searched the fields for an ever-increasing array of herbs.

On one of those hunting days, without Heka, Akila crossed the path of echoes opposite the cemetery on the west bank when she heard voices and listened, trying to identify the utterances, enjoying the challenge of new undecipherable magic. She separated the noise made by the wind, leaving the sound of the dead so that the secrets in between could be interpreted – both good and evil. Undistracted by anything else, she patiently waited until the secrets transformed into a chirping bird that guided her through the echoing lane. An ibis waited for her by a muddy puddle in the middle of a wheat field by the Nile, standing apart from the protective colony of ibises. It stared at the sorceress and stomped its long legs as if bidding her to dig at the random spot where it stood.

"The small ibis," Akila said as she recounted the story to User, "a sentinel, most probably wanted me to dig where it stood." User smiled at her. He had heard the story about Akila finding the slab many times but loved to hear it. She continued to tell him how she shovelled earth with her bare hands while the ibis nodded its approval.

"The ibis is my hero because," User said, "he is the guard of the slab."

Akila's mind strayed to that day at dusk as she continued her retelling. The sun had set, and the exhausted Akila sat, but something within the hole she had dug shone. She quickly resumed her digging until she uncovered the silver-white slab, but as she picked it up, it changed colour. She briefly examined it, and unsure what it was made of, she slipped it into her goatskin bag, glanced around to make sure no one was watching, then hurried home. Akila was wary, for she knew that vengeful apparitions could follow her and try to steal the power the slab endowed. She had robbed demons of their magic before and was fearful of their wrath. Though skilled and dedicated to saving the souls of the villagers, she could not save them all. She had lived long enough to realise that one wrong connection with the netherworld, a choice once made, invited a life of horrors.

The day came when Akila decided to teach User a few things about the slab. In her heart, she knew User would not inhabit the earth for long. She loved the boy, but he must deliver an important message in his lifetime. User, a simple boy, had to be taught simple words, obeying the dictates of the able priest Kaaper, who ruled the temple. Kaaper took the boy under his wing and explained what User had to do at the temple. The young disciple understood the chores he had to perform and naively did as he was told. Over the years, however, Akila repeated the words to User like a mantra to make sure he did not forget his mission when the time came for him to deliver the message.

The day Akila found the tablet, she rushed back home with her precious find, with the feeling that she was being watched. When she was nearly home, she encountered a hideous purple frog with sharp teeth which croaked loudly at her when she almost stepped on its head. She had an uneasy feeling that the creature had been transported from another realm. Unfamiliar sounds emanated from the frog, whispering messages from the spirits that lived in the lanes she walked every day. She crossed the footpath and made her way through the fields where lovers often went. She had more visions, but Akila ignored them, closed her eyes and concentrated on the words forming in her mind.

Break the sceptre. Find the tablet. Save King and kingdom, she said to herself. Akila patted the pouch and ran as fast as she could as more of nature's visions appeared.

In her excitement during her run home, she had forgotten to repeat the protective charm, but once inside, Akila shut and locked the door, hid the tablet and cast a spell to make it invisible to anyone but her. She quickly tidied herself up, cleaned the dirt from her clothes, and then bathed in the river. Fortunately, her husband and children were out visiting her mother-in-law. Akila and her husband's mother did not get on. In fact, the ageing matriarch hated her daughter-in-law, suspecting that Akila had used foul play to ensnare her son. Because of this, she rarely visited. The two only ever encountered each other on special occasions such as weddings or funerals.

Akila returned refreshed from the river, prepared a meal of eggs and cheese, washed down with fresh goats' milk, and then went to retrieve the tablet, which sat hidden amongst the herbal potions and other assorted bric-a-brac. Once uncovered, Akila sprinkled the stone with a hurriedly prepared protective oil, cutting connections with any spirits or demons that may be tracking her. Akila hoped that she had applied the spells soon enough, so she squatted and tried to decipher the writing and symbols on the slab. There appeared to be ordinary lists cataloguing the peoples' daily lives and mathematical sums next to these. Akila opened a jar containing a pungent-smelling liquid and sprinkled the tablet with it. More words, concealed beneath the other writing, appeared, and she read it out loud. *Beware the serpent. It hides within the priest. The King is in danger from his own. Beware green eyes. Ma'at – equilibrium and order – is threatened. Find the sceptre, save the King. Beware! The Queen is coming. She must not prevail.*

Akila's Son – User

User sat obediently on his mother's knee, waiting to be told what to do or what to remember. It would be too much to expect him to know what to do with the long message, so Akila kept her sentences short and simple. User had to remember Akila's warnings, but she knew that his life would be on the line. She loved User with all her heart but sadly realised that when the time came, he would be sacrificed for the greater good, a concept beyond his understanding.

"You are a high-ranking disciple of Heka," Heka said. "You must share in saving the realm. User must play his part." Akila nodded her understanding and continued to train her son for the mission. Before dying, Akila organised User's life so that the prophecy could be fulfilled. She helped get him the role at the Theban Temple under the guidance of a young Priest called Kaaper.

"You will be very happy serving Priest Kaaper," she told User. "You will eat the best food."

On her deathbed, Akila cried when she remembered telling User what he had to do.

"But I want to be with you," User had protested. "I have a friend now. He has just moved next to our home. His name is Kai. I don't want to go to the temple. They are old people. I want to play," User said as Akila led him to the temple.

"You will be serving the King," she told him. "It is another life. You will be a great man, and people will treat you with respect. Do you understand?" User nodded, and Akila hugged her son.

Although she hated what she was doing, Akila knew that she did not dare defy Heka. She pushed these thoughts from her mind as they reached the temple.

"I shall take excellent care of your boy," the priest said. He looked at the crying child and handed him a honey and date bar. User smiled, took the bar, and his tears stopped.

Despite Priest Kaaper's skills in the occult, he recognised that Akila's skills far outstripped his. She had assisted him on a couple of occasions with great success. Her magic turning the timid priest into a stronger and more forceful individual, even to the point of speaking with authority to the king. His appearance altered, too. Turning the small, chubby man into a tall, powerful priest who was able to keep the younger priests who battled for his seat at bay.

He recalled trying to learn some of her secrets. "Akila," he said, "how much cinnamon do you add to the persuasive formula? I need the Prince to remain supine so he will lease me the land next to the Nile opposite the temple to build a sacrificial slaughterhouse?" He knew she would never willingly give him the exact formulae, so he tried flattery.

Akila had smiled at him, well aware of what he was doing. "That depends on the amount I am brewing, Priest Kaaper," she said.

At least he succeeded in getting her to hand over the child. In return, he gifted her a valuable blue lotus scent that had hallucinogenic effects – a scent much loved by the pharaohs.

Thoughts swirled around the mind of the ailing Akila. There were many things she wished that she could undo if only she had time before she left the earth.

One time, a strong-willed young man loved a very poor peasant girl, and his mother had pleaded with Akila, crawling on hands and knees, for her help to force the smitten boy to abandon his love. His mother wanted him to marry the wealthy but plain chieftain's daughter, whose family owned large swathes of green land, which took thousands of ropes to measure the size of.

"I wish you would reconsider," Akila told the woman. "I have seen in the smoke that misery will befall your son if you tamper with the love of his life." The woman would not be swayed, and Akila reluctantly handed her the potion, warning her what would happen.

The woman ignored the warnings, and her son married the woman from the wealthy family. Little did Akila know that the jilted girl had become ill with grief after losing her lover and died of a broken heart. Akila knew she might have saved the girl with some of the herbs and probably found her another husband had she known. Alas, she realised that she could not save them all. It was a hard-won lesson and one she never forgot. The sudden death of the young maiden fuelled the anger of the people who knew her.

"Too young to die," her neighbours said. "Her tomb is empty of food and furniture. The maiden cannot transition to the afterlife in a bare grave. Have pity, someone."

Menes, who had only recently settled in the village, became a neighbour of Akila. Settling on the outskirts of the village, Menes had travelled far and wide in the prime of life, procuring cures from the most unlikely of places. A high-ranking priestly official in the King's temple had sent the unknown Menes on a discreet mission to find more potent charms to blunt the growing powers of rival priests. He searched the alleyways in Punt, Nubia and beyond the Cataracts for powers to tighten the King's grip on the land and subvert enemies along the borders.

"The King has expressed his deep distrust of traders to find him the right remedies," the official told Menes. "They are more interested in bartering gold, granite, and leopard hides from southern borders in return for land and entertainment with pretty concubines. Delight the King, and you will be richly rewarded." To the King's and clergy's delight, Mene returned with a treasure trove. An ultimate magic formula to defeat assailants. After coming face to face with some of the meanest creatures in the south and west, Mene survived and was handsomely rewarded by the grateful monarch.

Akila, in the meantime, busied herself with the training of User and forgot about the rejected girl. Heka continued to trouble Akila with more tasks besides protecting the tablet. As Akila grew older, she searched for a wise disciple to carry the flame after she died.

"I can never find an apprentice such as you, Akila," Heka tenderly addressed the ageing disciple, "but the power of magic is fading with each dynasty. Fighting is compromising the super forces in the air."

For a season or more, Akila used her skills to marry User into a well-reputed family. She chose a strong girl who bore him a strong son, Djau, with the help of her magic.

In time, Akila grew older and weaker. User grew stronger in

body, but his mind remained feeble. Until her last breath, she continued to relay the message to him.

Akila left the world and settled in the Field of Reeds, where kind Osiris ruled. Heka put in a good word for her because she had dutifully obeyed the rules.

Yet, before she died, with her guard completely down, Akila's heart pounded with one regret.

"I wish I had left him to play with Kai. Forgive me, my love." Tears fell on her wrinkled cheeks as she spoke unchecked, oblivious to the presence of Heka, who appeared to bid farewell to a faithful pupil.

When Heka heard the blasphemy uttered by his favourite disciple on her death bed, after all the training Akila received, the magic deity held a burning spear and threw it in her direction, binding the tool with a by-spell to imprison her soul in perpetual agony.

"Enough." Osiris hit the spear with a ball of fire and turned it to ash. A few clouds shook as the bolt hit the lance. "The woman has served our cause. She has not changed the boy, but he is on the course that he is meant to take. Her right for remorse is her own."

The King's Room

The priest scrubbed the King's sanctuary room in a time-honoured ritualistic and symbolic manner. User did the heavy work, and sweat dripped onto the floor as he thoroughly cleaned the chamber for the majestic visit. He then went to bathe in the Nile, wrapped himself in linen, and returned to the room to mop with a piece of burlap any contamination on the tiles. The priest entered the chamber to prepare the King's ceremony, which was designed to give strength to the royal and enable him to sit on par with the deities.

Pharaoh Septah strode in, wearing his finest ceremonial clothes. He made his way to a simple chair and waited for the deities to consort with him. The King's sculptor stood close by, ready to chisel the historic union from a massive piece of marble as Guards waited outside the doorway. The arrow whistled across the room, narrowly missing the King and pierced the sculptor's heart. The sculptor groaned and fell to the floor.

The King jumped to his feet and drew his sword. "Put down your weapons immediately," he said. "I am the King."

The Priest Kaaper dropped the vessel he was carrying onto the floor, spilling the King's preparation across the stone. Masked men swarmed into the room armed with knives and bows, smashing their way towards the King. The Priest stood in front of his Monarch and drew a small blade. Fluids and precious powders were scattered everywhere as the King's guards fought the attackers, desperately trying to defend their monarch.

"Stop this madness," the Priest said as one of the attackers slew the remaining guard between himself and the Priest. "The deities will curse you," the Priest screamed, but as he launched himself at the assailant, another took off his head in one swift blow. The headless torso fell across the table while the head bounced across the floor.

Plumes of smoke rose into the air as the powders and potions mixed with the blood of the slain. The King attacked the Priest's killer, quickly cutting him down before despatching two more, but before he could turn to face the final assailant, a dagger was stuck deeply into the back of his neck. The King groaned loudly as his precious royal blood pumped from the gaping wound, and he slumped onto his knees. The knife-wielding man stepped forward, easily parried the weakening King's feeble attempt to defend himself and plunged his sword through the Monarch's stomach.

User, who had trained all his life to be alert and save a king against incoming threats, looked at the King's killer, not truly understanding why one of the King's men had murdered the royal. This man had managed to infiltrate the royal household and assassinate their King.

User watched on as the killer morphed into a huge serpent, coiling its way out of the body of the man. The predator moved across to the substance intended for the King, which lay in a pool on the floor. It licked at the viscous substance and began to grow in size before slithering its way towards User.

Maga's Green-Eyed Serpent

The green-eyed monster thrust its fangs into the dead or dying corpses, saving some of the liquid with its forked tongue and putting what it could into a vessel. Its body could not absorb any more of the spell, and the predator disintegrated. As it died in agony, the serpent hissed its grievances, and a trapped voice deep inside the leathery skin screamed for its tortured spirit to be free.

"I have been promised an audience with the Queen, the usurper," it said. "She has promised to give me back my life."

It had taken Maga's last breath to prepare the serpent for the critical task of seeing through the death of the King and the prevention of the coming of age of the Middle Kingdom – a time meant to correct old mistakes and see the country through to better times.

Maga, now a serpent, was at one time a beautiful maiden who lived next door to Akila. She grew up an orphan but, like most of the girls in the village, strove to work hard until a good man came along. However, when the right man did show up, Akila decided to break their union.

On that fateful day, Maga had already finished her work for the day. After toiling in the fields, weaving fabrics and scrubbing the floor in her home, she readied herself for her meeting with Nour. As she walked a little bit farther beyond the path of echoes, she got lost in thought. The beautiful greenery by the river and the whispering spirits under a full moon filled the scene with the promise of a lifelong romance.

The lovers had agreed to meet under the tree of life, the acacia, a sacred tree from which, along with palm trees, the boat belonging to Ra was built. Along with this, the bark of both trees had been used to construct the boat that carried the sun deity Ra.

Acacia trees also belonged to the goddess of love, Hathor. Maga, captivated by the full moon and the majestic beauty of the tree, waited patiently for her beloved Nour to show up. The lovers had enjoyed many nights in the company of the tree, and as she lay there with a huge smile on her face, Maga drifted off. A slithering creature, waiting patiently in the undergrowth, watched the sleeping girl for a while, slithered over to her, and lay on her lap. Young Maga, deeply asleep by now, did not feel the creature as she dreamed of her beloved and their upcoming nuptials.

The other girls in the village had fashioned a beautiful dress for the bride-to-be, adorning it with golden leaves to mark the festival of the inundation of the Nile River.

Maga woke up hours later and looked upwards at the moon, directly above her, as it shone down on her lap. Where was Nour, she wondered, but when she looked down, she screamed as she looked into the deep green eyes of the serpent. It sank its teeth into her and then vanished into the grass.

By the time Maga collected herself and walked back towards the village, her beautiful skin had shrunk, and her entire face had changed shape. She paused by the river and viewed her features in the still water. Maga gasped at the image that greeted her. Her head had changed into that of a snake, complete with her beautiful green eyes that had captivated the village boys. She looked down at her leg, which, in the time she had spent looking into the water, had fused together and slowly altered into the body of the serpent. Unable to return to the village where she would be reviled, she slithered off into the undergrowth. Her disappearance at first shocked the village people, but gradually, they assumed that she had died of a broken heart. Maga took cover under the shade of the tree, and with her transformation complete, she rested. However, on waking, she realised the snake bite had not only changed her but had also endowed her with abilities. Under a full moon, her fangs would produce a particular venom – a venom which enabled her to cast spells. She could also see into the future with those green eyes that penetrated into the darkest souls of humans, and she became the seer of doom.

The following month, when the full moon prevailed, she crawled into Nour's house and mad with bitterness, she bit her former lover and watched as he writhed in agony and died. But not a quick death, a death that took half the night for him to die – the time she was left abandoned by him under a love tree.

"You have no spine," Maga hissed as he fought for his life.

Nour looked in horror at the eyes as he heard the serpent speak to him. "Maga? Is it you? I…I..." Then, as he drifted into nothing, delirious from the poison, he said, "I will always love you, Maga."

Maga looked down at her dead lover as realisation swept through her. It was Akila's doing. "Akila," she hissed again as she slithered off. "I shall come for you."

Thunder roared as black, ominous clouds covered the sky. Lightning sparked across the heavens, creating vivid red colours that traversed the horizon for the first time in thousands of years. Oh, the pain at what could have been and what could have been salvaged if she postponed the black revenge.

The next day, the wealthy bride lay dead on the floor, her mouth crammed full of jewellery. The remainder of her gems lay scattered around her, and beside the bride, the shrivelled remains of her mother – the blood drained from her shrunken corpse. The horrific murders had weakened Maga, though, and she was forced to rest.

Maga, however, could not control her desire for chaos and longed to wreak vengeance on Akila and her thoughts were dominated by this. The serpent reached Akila's house and ripped off the roof, but even in her fury, she realised that Heka kept Akila safe and that she would not be able to harm her. The serpent smashed her way through the house, destroying everything in her path, and the mayhem she created caused the hidden slab, protected by a spell, to shudder before it vanished. Maga, satisfied with her work, slithered off.

News travelled fast within the village. "Maga, the once sultry young maiden is dead," one of the villagers proclaimed. "She has changed into a python before vanishing."

"That evil cannot be Maga," an older man said. "The girl has been kind to me, bringing me laughter and joy, beer and bread too." He shook his head and wandered off.

The men and women of the village had never seen a python. But they remembered stories from travellers telling tales of giant snakes that lived close to rivers and could squeeze a man to death and eat him whole. The farmers, however, had scoffed at first over such fanciful stories, knowing only of the king cobra with a bite that could kill, but gradually, they began to believe.

Maga settled down in a hole beneath the love tree, and when she came out in the cool breeze, she rested her skin against a rock nearby. Gems collected and placed around the entrance adorned the cave, reminding her of Nour's beautiful face. She had stuck them there with tree sap and watched as they glistened beneath the full moon. How she missed the boy she had killed.

Gradually, Maga's anger subsided, and people would seek her out, especially the vengeful types. One day, Menes arrived at her cave, becoming the first of many followers and a devoted servant.

"I have watched you many nights," he said. "I have seen you transform from a beautiful woman into a serpent and back again. I want to help and to serve you."

She was pleased, and after he swore his allegiance to her, she formulated a plan.

Many days earlier, Menes had watched Maga crawl from Akila's home and into the field behind the hut. He followed and watched. It was then he had decided to side with the snake.

One day, a mysterious older man came to see her. He told her what he could do for her. He could help her to bring about the end of a kingdom – payback for her being cursed – and perhaps restore her former beauty for good if she complied. By now, Maga had embraced the hate that filled her heart and thrived on the wrath she brewed into the potions for her inept customers. She did not care for her former beauty, embracing instead her own ultimate ugliness – a beauty of sorts. Maga accepted tasks which brought the destruction of anything and anyone for free when the clients could not pay. In return, she collected and enslaved people.

The older man who visited her had his own cult, one of a long line of conflicting groups of dissenters. He praised the rise of the sorrowful creature that once lived a simple life with modest ambitions. The breakaway priest, Anhurmose, gave her a knowing smile. Sorcery led him to Maga, and by uniting together, their power would be formidable, he promised her.

"I am one of a group of priests seeking a new order," he said. "You could have a place as a high priestess, a queen, in any province in Egypt, or you could make your realm here by your cave. I can see you have an eye for the arts. Soon, you could have a movement with many followers. I am not from around here, and I have travelled many months to find you." The man spoke softly, and his voice soothed her aching heart. His words, soaked in age-old litanies of spells, calmed the beast within her and kept the creature in check.

Maga, impressed by him, asked what she had to do.

"There are a few conditions," he began. "You have to make sure that a regular stream of grain and slaves make their way to the Libyan borders."

She considered his proposal. Anhurmose's stipulation could be easily managed, she thought, and she could supply the enslaved people easily. The power of her eyes was enough to subjugate even the strongest of people.

He told her about the stone tablet – the one she had seen at Akila's – and the importance of destroying it. The people of Egypt must never know about the tablet of kings, or else, the plan to conquer, build a new kingdom and regain her former beauty would be ruined.

When the time came, Maga was thwarted by User scribbling the words in the blood of the serpent inside the sanctuary. Her chance with the priest was gone, and despite killing User, she could not avoid her own destruction.

User's Message

Despite his limited intelligence, User was still trained by the best in her field – his mother, Akila, the mother of all-time sorcery. The wise, now-dead woman trained her son to perform one last task, and when the time came, he did it to perfection. It took her twenty-five years to coach him to do just that.

When User died, he was a young, strong man of thirty years and married with a few children, but only one that counted. On that fateful day, unbeknown to his father, ten-year-old Djau followed him. The boy, touched by the magic inherited from his grandmother, had the habit of secretly tracking his father. Intelligent beyond his tender years and born with sharp cognitive abilities, he discerned that his father did not act like other men in the village. He watched both his mother and grandmother taking more time to explain simple tasks to User than they did to young Djau or any of the other children. By the time Djau reached ten, he had become adept in following User, mastering techniques that allowed him to travel through the hidden labyrinths used by priests in the Temple of Luxor.

On the night User died, Djau had once again followed him to the temple and, overhearing the commotion in the sanctuary, instinctively waited to see his father's reaction. Djau watched at a distance until the sounds ended before entering the chamber. His eyes were drawn to a long-haired man in a loin cloth lying next to the remains of a huge serpent's head. The man still had breath in him.

"I…I have tried to stop her," Menes said as Djau neared him. "The priest is no good. His promises are lies. I have only wanted to protect her. I will always love her." Djau stared at an ugly gash across the belly of the man, and next to him, the King's sword covered in blood. He looked around and spotted his father through the slowly dispersing clouds of smoke, hurried across to him and knelt beside the corpse. Djau gasped but then caught sight of the message, written in blood that User had scrawled on the base of the wall. The bright boy reasoned that it was his father who had written the words, confirmed both by the blood smeared across User's hand and the familiar style the boy had become accustomed to. Djau did not understand all that was written and how his father even knew the official language reserved for priests and the palace rather than commoners. "Grandma must have shown him," he whispered. Djau studied the writing, and on closer inspection, he noticed that most of the letters were superimposed over others, as if the words had two meanings or some were hidden under others. The boy, clever beyond his years, memorised the letters by repeating them a few times and was about to leave when his eyes fell on the scroll pieces hanging from the priest's mouth. The rest was scattered around amongst the debris, and he carefully collected the pieces. Though heavily damaged, the words stood out on the parchment as if protected by a spell. Djau pushed the pieces inside his belt, gave the room one final look and then fled, hiding within the labyrinth as hell broke loose.

The commotion woke up temple priests and their guards, who quickly made their way to the scene of the carnage. The King was dead, the room soaked in blood and smoke, yet no one alive remained. A few keen-eyed priests whispered to each other as they noticed the remains of the serpent's skin. The ashes remaining reminded the clergy of a type of magic long banned from religious practices. But all eyes looked at the message that stood out.

"She is coming," a senior priest cried. "It is her time. Osiris must be alerted."

Another stepped forward. "Kaaper has been the best among us to understand the dark literature and the means of protection. His books may help."

"Time is of the essence," the senior priest said.

"Then we get started right away," one of the others said, "we have a kingdom to save. With counsel from others, we can reach another learned colleague." The priests dispersed to ready for the council and prepared the names of priests who could help.

"Look!" cried one of the priests, pointing to the lower base of the walls on one side of the sanctuary room. Broken vessels of clay and glass littered the sanctuary chamber in the wake of the tragedy, and above on the wall were the words that User had written.

"User must have written them," the Priest said.

The priests understood the signs and had heard about Akila's powers.

"Have them decrypted straight away," the Priest said. "And burn the wicked beyond recognition so their souls will suffer for eternity." A hurriedly erected pyre was constructed, and the assailants burnt.

Amunet

The beautiful village girl Amunet worked the field daily at her usual place at the same time at dawn. Ten years had passed since Djau lost the tablet. On that day, Amunet, another gullible messenger, unknowingly led the way to the find, which could be instrumental in changing the course of history. When Djau saw her acting weirdly, her eyes alight with a strange colour, a brightness that lasted for as long as it took a drop of water to fall into the bucket of time, he knew.

The pretty maiden grew up near the Temple of Abydos, a place of worship no less significant than the temples at Thebes. Those times saw kings growing weaker while priests became stronger and more manipulative. Rumours had spread since then of a vicious queen, Nitocris, about to ascend the throne in Abydos, ushering court conspiracies, new cults and religions.

In those days, Abydos stood tall and majestic like Thebes but was inclined to invite black rather than white sorcery. The people in Abydos lived in fear, worrying over inexplicable happenings, and were not as calm and confident as the Thebans. They talked of a black cult ruled by a phantom chief, unknown to most, and some reported encounters with a spirited ephemeral from a particular necropolis.

"I am telling you," one person said, "I have seen the Queen kill a cow and drink its blood. She will bring doom."

Being an only daughter, Amunet's parents decided to move to a safer place in the south, Thebes.

"It is a place like home," her father said to his wife. "Amunet will enjoy the festivals."

Choosing an early boat to travel on, the parents took their young daughter with as many possessions as they could carry and boarded. They hoped to attract as little attention as possible but feared that one of the dark apparitions might follow them.

Abydos had changed of late. The evil that always pervaded had given way to something even more sinister. This unruly magic distressed the natives greatly, and terror within the community increased. The simple people feared that demons were living amongst them, controlling their lives and reporting to cruel beings.

The family of three set sail before dawn, but on their way to the big city, another boat attacked their vessel. Men with daggers boarded the boat, beat Amunet's father and took the little belongings that the family had. The crew was quickly slain, and as it looked like Amunet and her parents would go the same way, they were saved by a tall black man who appeared from nowhere and, using his bow, killed the attackers. Amunet's father managed to steer the boat to shore and helped his family onto the bank. The man dressed in a linen cloth carrying an arrow sling bag over his muscular shoulders joined them and squatted beside Amnunet's father.

"You will need donkeys to carry you to Thebes," he said. "I will take you to the border." Although curious as to why the Nubian archer was helping them, he readily accepted the assistance.

The archer returned to the vessel and searched the skiff, returning with cheese, bread and beer. The four sat by the Nile, eating hungrily and drinking the beer. Once the beer containers were empty, they filled the flasks with water from the Nile to take with them on the journey.

Amunet's father thanked the man and asked where he had come from.

"I have taken leave of absence from the general to go to Nubia to visit my ailing father, but my betrothed lives in Thebes. I have spent time with a mission to the Assyrians in the west to save an Egyptian base from an army approaching from the farthest east."

The archer went on to explain a little more but decided against telling the family the real reason he crossed paths with them. He had dreamt that the temple of Thebes had come under attack, which prompted him to travel where he encountered the distressed family.

At the boundary of the Theban city, Amunet's family rode on, and the warrior bid farewell and quietly vanished. Once in Thebes, Amunet's family settled into a farming village along the Nile and set to work in the fields alongside a distant cousin.

The beautiful Amunet was readily accepted, and her good

nature earned her many friends. She wisely reasoned that she needed friends in the unfamiliar town but worried that some of the other girls might feel threatened by her looks, so she never flaunted them.

In her new habitat, Amunet still yearned for the festival of Osiris, which took place every year in Abydos. Thebes was grand and civilised, with impressive temples, but lacked the friendliness of her hometown. Amunet wanted to play as she did in Abydos when she gave full reign to her beauty, especially during the celebrated Osirian festivals. Back home, she made her own fashion in coloured overlapping linen skirts. Wealthy and admiring scions gifted her with headdresses, and she walked with grace after the priests' procession to celebrate the resurrection of the deity of the dead.

"I miss those festivities and the magical nights when Osiris appears in clouds and fire," she complained to her mother. "It is not the same in Thebes. It is for old people and priests."

Unbeknownst to her, Osiris had chosen Amunet as the one to find the slab on one of those festive nights in Abydos. The deity himself had noted the blooming beauty, nodding approvingly at the unassuming girl. She shivered, just as she did when she held Nieth's baby in Thebes and earlier when she stepped on the location of the slab. She never understood these feelings. No one did except for the watching Djau.

Amunet's father had no way of knowing that a demonic courier had intercepted Osiris's beckoning to the child, let alone knowing that Osiris had his eyes on Amunet in the first place. If Amunet's parents knew of the workings of the cosmos, they might have remained in the hometown of Abydos, seeking, at most, help from a priest or sorcerer to break their daughter's objectionable mystical connections. Amunet's mother, an excellent homemaker, could have bribed helpers with wheat pies, dates and pomegranate juices, baked ducks and perhaps, with any luck, venison from a game animal to offer at the temple. Sending food and costumed clothes to priests and sorcerers secured protective amulets. The wife gained fame and connections among the women in Abydos for a sense of unmatched baking. She also understood how to fashion linen skirts for eager young villagers and gained recognition among some nobles for making wonderful cotton dresses.

The passing days and years saw Amunet grow into a young woman desired by many, and on that fateful day Amunet had broken the charm which protected the tablet, exposing its position. Had he known his daughter's future, the girl's father might well have stayed put in Abydos. Unbeknown to anyone, his daughter's goodness had attracted a demon who tracked Osirian gifts to followers and diverted the tablet to the dark side. The doors to hell might be opening soon unless…

The Cult

Djau learned of the cult from his mentor, Apep. He travelled a few times in the dead of night in the company of his teacher to meet their chief Assim in Abydos when the village slept. Apep, accompanied by Djau, took the long journey through the desert, river and field to meet with the elders in a sanctuary in Abydos. The last days of Pepi II, who was frail, brought discontent among all classes.

Apep desperately needed to meet with one formidable priest, Assim, at the Temple of Abydos after Djau had brought a message of him to the sorcerer's doorstep. The arrival of the tablet heralded the coming of a stronger king whose face could be decrypted in night clouds on a full moon. Dark forces were at work, and Apep and Djau were looking to bring an end to the reign of the tablet. In the meantime, Apep continued to tutor the boy on how to establish this darkness, little knowing that his apprentice would end his life.

Assim worked hard to build a safe haven for the loyalists of the dark order under holy grounds at the Temple of Abydos. An intelligent priest, he had joined the educated class of clerics who studied magic and writing. He later joined the order of priests in Thebes and became well-versed in the rules of the afterlife and their connections with the stars. He soon stood out as the smartest disciple at the temple and won over the chief priest.

"I shall keep you informed, my liege," Assim told the chief priest. "Some of the esteemed priests have been seen consorting directly with the King and his ladies." The chief priest nodded sagely. His faith in the younger man was absolute.

Assim travelled to Abydos with a lotus parchment extolling his undivided loyalty to the chief priest. In no time, the priests of Abydos put him to work – despite his undoubtedly questionable past. No one asked where he had come from, but because of his dark complexion, it was assumed he was from the south, below the Cataracts.

Suffice it to say that he proved himself indispensable, and the priests welcomed him in, happy to make use of an extra pair of hands and his obvious intelligence. The fastidious apprentice rapidly learned about the power potions and used his own unique ingredients. He quickly improved on the old methods. Eventually, the most powerful priests agreed to allow Assim to take additional classes, a privilege which was rarely granted.

In his mind, Assim believed that magic, letters and the cosmos complimented each other, although he kept his ideas to himself. He abstained from much of what life had to offer, except for his love of music and put his time to better use than socialising. Assim calculated a complicated formula that allowed him to foretell the future and used hieroglyphic writing to decipher the messages. Although the star signs told him little, it was enough for him to foresee the turbulent times ahead and how to interact with kings and sway them.

Assim's exceptional human talent at reading stars bent the priests to his will and surrounding himself with loyal disciples – he helped in return for favours – his power grew. The newcomer, a mathematical genius, could solve even the most complex cosmic riddles, enabling his reputation to increase further until no one dared to cross him. By turning the priests into loyal assistants and finding out their weaknesses, Assim's power and influence knew no bounds.

However, some within the temple grew concerned over Assim's increasing influence. "Eminence," one of them said to the high priest, "Assim is becoming more capable with magic and the reading of stars than some of the seniors in the temple. His calculations have helped him become unassailable. This is a dangerous precedent for someone we know little about."

The high priest waved aside the protestations, for Assim had helped to solve the most complex of the riddles much quicker than even the wisest clergy at the temple. He gently silenced the priest. "Perhaps," he told him, "you can learn from Assim instead of complaining about his progress. Don't you agree?"

With those biting remarks, the priest bowed and kept his fears to himself.

Assim continued his evolution from beginner to expert and worked tirelessly to conjure the perfect ruler to do his bidding. But what the stars did not tell him was vitally important. Would Nitocris, the coming queen, yield to such a man as he?

Assim based his cult on a simple rule. He commanded his followers to believe in his own depictions of the language of stars. His demons monitored cult members, and in return, the spirits were reborn and pardoned from burning into ashes. If his calculations proved conclusive, he might rule the Kingdom of Egypt, and the demons could carry his dictates throughout the land. The short-sighted demons only wanted chaos, but Assim sought eternal domination.

To complete his cover, Assim decided to use Nitocris as his puppet queen to reign over his cosmos while allowing believers to practice his tenet. If ever Osiris arraigned the evil spells, stopping the uprising, Nitocris would face the backlash. Assim picked the vicious queen from the darkest part of history to become the face of his new order, believing that he knew how to manipulate her spirit.

Meanwhile, to retain his current position and put his plan in motion, the wily sorcerer recruited enslaved people within the palace walls to report back about the current ruler until he could clinch full authority over his own temple in his beloved Abydos.

The limping Apep accompanied Djau to an audience with the ultimate magician, the soon-to-be cult leader Assim. Despite his impediment, Apep often travelled to Thebes' eastern bank to keep the books, never letting his leg get in the way of his movements. However, his journeys came at a cost, for the sorcerer inadvertently became addicted to ever-increasing dosages of cactus, wild mushrooms and opium in his beer to calm the sting of pain in his leg. Apep extracted the drug from resin in hemp and kept an ample supply in a clay pot beside the bed. Some of his clients, who travelled from beyond Nubia, often brought him purer and more potent forms of the drug that dramatically relieved the pain. He learnt to cultivate cannabis and mixed it with mushrooms, which also helped in his pain relief, but his increasing reliance on the fatal drug would be his undoing. Initially, wary of the size of doses he allowed himself, he grew not to care.

Over time, Apep traded favours with one senior priest to get his hands on a specific kind of mushroom, which was reserved for the highest class of royal figures. In return, he would have one of his men follow the King's favourite concubine, who lived on palatial grounds, into town. The King's mistress enjoyed her escapades, disguised as a common mistress. Apep reported that these adventures of that particular consort were harmless. The King, of course, authorised these trips and loved to hear unadulterated stories about his subjects relayed by her. The pharaoh smiled on many occasions as his favourite confidante whispered how his people lived in towns, on the road and sometimes, in their own beds.

Sorcerer Assim saw great potential in Djau when he met him. "Apep," Assim said, "you have done well to nurture this young man, for he is hungry indeed." Assim smiled and nodded approval at Apep as he spoke about Djau but secretly wondered what Djau was actually hungry for.

Other clever recruits climbed up the echelon of the cult with rewards of silver and land, for the time came close to declaring the existence of the cult and encouraging the people of Egypt to join the dark forces quartered in the heart of Abydos. Assim stationed loyal servants throughout Egypt to protect his tenet, and elderly disciples taught gullible recruits below the arched coves in Abydos within the walls of the demonic construct. Youths embraced the new doctrine delivered by the master of sorcery without blinking, and Djau enrolled followers from Thebes and Memphis. Word spread about Assim, his new army and the abilities of the clan, and as his prominence rose, he promised believers everything, becoming the uncrowned ruler of chaos.

Both Thebes in the south and Memphis to the north were worthy adversaries of Abydos, so Assim sent his most loyal soldiers, coached in the cruellest arts, into those cities. With black magic cultivated over thousands of years within the rooms and tunnels under the majestic temple, Abydos fought and then fell.

Assim had spent years hunting down the rarest of herbs, exceptional animals, and the finest specimens of humankind. He pursued the wickedest samples of all things, even finding the blackest of flowers that sickened the foliage, poisoned bees and harmed the humans who thought they'd swallowed the most notorious elixirs in beer and wine.

He travelled to oases, east and north of Abydos, searching expanses which were dry as bones but ripe with spilt blood and legacies of the fiercest of witches. He crossed dreary deserts, untouched by man, inhabited by the strangest-looking creatures who dabbled in darkness in his pursuit of the dark arts. He brought back the behemoths to rule the empty lands, igniting their dormant abilities to rise again and quench their thirst for the deepest, most rotten desires with a bit of help from Assim's forged elixir.

In earlier times, the arid land harboured unbelievable beasts who dived into deep waters, searching for the vilest potions and coaxing mountains to smoke out the ultimate scorpions, crawlers and all things bestial. The soulless creatures ably combined the worst of undetectable poison made of hemlock and wolf bane with their sophisticated amounts of opium in precise measurements.

A priest once walked in on Assim, who was offering a drink to a servant in the temple. The priest was horrified by what he saw. The shrivelled servant grew tails, each of which grew into a small cobra and then disappeared underground. The servant, however, remained in a dried-up state for months until he died.

"Sire, I am telling you," the startled priest told his superior, "Assim is giving dark potions to helpers within the temple. The black art is forbidden and has been since the birth of the kingdom. The man has no scruples." The superior ignored the Priest's warnings, and it was then that the Priest realised Assim had planted a demon inside his superior.

Once the demon had been discovered, it fled, leaving the Priest's superior free again. "What is this you are saying?" he said.

"I think we have to remove that man," the Priest said.

"Forgive me," the superior said, "I think it is time to wake the deities. The matter is grave. The demons have come, and they will wake the usurper."

In the end, Assim always got the best and most evil of disciples. He developed an insignia for his followers to recognise each other – a simple sceptre engraved at the back of the left thumb, soaked in litanies of black magic. He adopted the red sceptre and ordered a local blacksmith, who owed him plenty, to carve several branding irons. Then, handpicking dissenting priestesses in Nomes, he entrusted them with the irons. The priestesses who shunned the goddess of love, Hathor, opted for envy and hate, marking followers with the chosen sceptre, just as Assim ordered. The dissenting priestesses, however, cunningly devised less painful methods than the scary iron brand, tattooing maidens with the symbol of the fallen sceptre instead and reading the words that brought the etched symbols to life. This submitted the souls of the fallen into the web of the cult. As the new order grew, so did the number of boats they owned, each with the recognisable sceptre painted near the bow to mark the growing fleet, which, when spotted on skiff or thumb, made it easier among dissenters to foment a discipline of chaos.

Whether Assim truly believed in the tenet dictated by the cult he orchestrated was questionable, but for now, he carried on and readied himself for the storm. The people, however, mired in the ravages of intra-wars forged by weak leadership within palace walls, craved false hope. Since the death of King Pepi II, locals became marionettes in a system marred by short-term nomarchs across the country.

"You are destined for greatness in the next life," Assim told them. "The faith that will steer you to happiness lies within the tablet. Bring it to me when you find it. Your coffers will be rewarded, and so will your soul in the afterlife." Assim and a few other experts could decipher the tablet to conjure a new and able queen.

Dissenters drank Assim's poisonous elixir made from the blood of crocodiles, asp venom and running Nile water prepared under specific star alignments. The drink bound the followers to their leader, and they readily accepted his commands.

Occasionally, Assim performed ritual killings to further cement their loyalty, calling it a celebration of the cult. One time, he tied a man over a sanctuary board, spoke a litany of magic chants and sprinkled the poison over the victim. As the men and women watched, a phantom spiralled out of the living body on the stretcher while the poor man's skin turned to ash. Assim opened a cell made of glass, ushered in the ghost and locked the door. He left the spirit to become acquainted with its surroundings and then opened the cage door. The ghost, searching for its host, blended with the dust on the ground and wandered off into the ether, howling and making horrible cackling noises as if lamenting the end of someone it used to know. Assim then ordered the spirit to reconnect with the man's ashes. The result was a morphed atrocity blending man and demon. In complete control of the apparition, he ordered it back into the cage to await his instruction. The ghost complied, and the watchers were subdued.

The members of the cult came from towns and villages and were tasked with tilling the fields and constructing temples, promising their allegiance out of fear of damnation. Faced with the new reality under the power of the sceptre, the gatherers sent word of what they saw. "They call him Assim," they said. "He has the power to make us better or worse."

Assim did not disclose an important secret to his closest followers. During a pharaoh's coronation, a magical ritual had to be conducted to rejuvenate the King and give him strength enhanced by sorcery. Sometimes, the King could be reborn, appearing in his younger form. In the case of Pepi II, pushing ninety, his younger form would have looked completely different. Assim had sinister plans to replace the King altogether with his own puppet, opening up the King and putting his viscera in a jar to make sure that the actual King never woke up.

Assim still needed the tablet, which foretold the date of the King's death, and the alignment of stars to make it work. His potion had to be prepared when the soul left the body of the monarch, and the charm, which the sorcerer had put together, sketched the features of the new queen in the clouds. He had a good idea that Queen Nitocris would be the eternal ruler. Tailoring a queen and aligning her with his plan was not easy. He now had to travel paths to find the necessary recipes to seal the queen according to his vision for the future.

He left Abydos after creating circles of followers to protect the laborious work in the tunnel. The believers expanded, and the gold and silver coffers brimmed with precious metals. His spells would endure until his return.

Assim took paths among fields full of crops and fruit, ate their harvest and hid in the foliage. He travelled quickly and only rested for a few hours at a time. Living on figs, dates, and wheat, he drank from the river. He travelled hundreds of miles within weeks while continuing to live off the land. He continued on to Thebes, Nubia, and then to Memphis in the north. When he arrived at the Queen's necropolis for her extraction and later her crowning ceremony, he had his potions ready to subdue her before the reincarnation. Otherwise, she could eat him alive. They were ideally suited for the Queen to remain among the vilest of usurpers. According to the registry, Nitocris killed her brother Nemtyamsaf II, son of Pepi II, and took the throne for a while before she committed suicide. She ruled in her short life from Memphis in the north – a rich, strong nome. In all probability, the queen was buried without ceremony, having desecrated all religious vows by taking her own life. She, therefore, had not prepared herself at all for the afterlife. She chose her burial in Saqqara, and before dying, she performed the magical ritual by herself to make sure her spirit lived on. She evolved into a shapeshifter – an ethereal being surviving on blood potions. She had to connect her apparition to her body in order to rule from a palace and sit on her rightful throne. On her tomb, she wrote down the spells that had to be cast every full moon by the faithful to rise again. In return, she did the same for the followers who persevered, bringing them back to life with riches until such time they were sucked into a prospering eternity. If they failed her, they risked a painful death, destroying their passage to the thereafter.

On the eve of her demise, Nitocris gathered some Memphite followers and made them promise, under penalty of being cursed alongside their families from beyond the grave, to always keep a flame burning, clear the path to and from her tomb, and make sure to recruit loyal disciples from their own line of descendants. The resourceful Queen secured her eventual return.

The Queen made sure to keep another empty grave in Abydos, and her disciples embalmed her viscera and took them for burial in Abydos during a long secret procession that marched from Saqqara to Abydos. The journey lasted a month. Fearing bandits or the

King's guards in pursuit of her fledgling followers, the disciples undertook their journey in the dead of night. Eventually, the Queen's suicide was recorded in her secret tomb, tightly shut with binding magic to terminate the life of any intruder – be it a wandering hyena or a wayward disciple curious for more royal privileges.

When Assim came across her tomb, he discovered a rare magic kit left by her, which was to prepare a secret tomb in Abydos for her rebirth. He recovered her viscera and heart and kept them at the Temple of Abydos. He discovered the perfect building site for a cult temple right below the incomparable Temple. He avoided a location that could be discovered by Osiris, to whom the seven sanctuaries were dedicated, but, at the same time, the magic had to be stored below the formidable temple from which a path must be forged for the potions to flow. He tried his best to build the demonic temple under the sanctuary of Osiris, the only sacred room with one entrance from where the secrets of deities and kings unfolded, the intersection where rulers were made or broken. When priests became stronger, kings reasoned they had to work closely with priests rather than challenge their authority. Eventually, temples became more formidable, and the coffers of priests remained full, so the power of kings continued.

In the chaotic days when opportunists like Assim fought for power, the lines between politics and religion blurred. Assim found the perfect spot to hide the Queen's vital organs at the far end of the inner sanctuary of Osiris. Inside the sanctuary, he removed a canopy, exposing a niche. He pressed a little wooden lid and pulled out a linen cloth. He placed the preserved viscera of the dead queen on a shelf inside the niche and covered the sealed contents with the linen cloth. The entrails, kept inside a jar, would remain until her grand tomb was built within the new temple walls. From around his waist, he opened a pouch and drew out the parchment which Djau had given him, on which were scribbled stark warnings against his sect.

The night King Pepi II was murdered in the Temple of Luxor, Djau took the parchment, which he covered with a torn piece of the priest's garment. He had no idea he was being followed by Assim that night. Assim, who vaporised in a plume of smoke on the night of blood and sorcery in the Temple of Luxor, had spotted the young Djau snatching the parchment. Assim, a quick thinker, knew he had to escape the temple and follow the child. Before Assim left the crime scene, which he masterminded, he saw the scribbled text.

Assim had to get out of the room. He had run out of potions, and his only chance to save his plan was to follow the boy. He remained at a distance, like a ghost in the fields, watching the boy running into his tiny mud brick home. The leader of the cult had no way of looking into the roofed-in centre room with high and small windows. He waited by a tree, watching the boy running towards the river and returning cleaner. Assim waited in the distance until the boy left with the villagers to bury his father – the only chance he had to walk into the now-empty house and search for the parchment. Pulling the document from below the cot was a simple task, and he returned to Abydos, only stopping on the way to visit a few Nomes to consult with senior followers.

Back at the temple, Assim was satisfied as he examined the parchment, which was littered with spells only Nitocris could undo to help herself out of the obstructive charms that kept her in her tomb. Assim stared at the parchment. In his Abydos hideout, he had time to think about User's death. He worried about the way the simple guard died. Perhaps Assim had missed something about User's role in saving the dynasty, which began after the simple-minded man knew he was about to die. The trigger for completing his task was knowing he had little time to write down the most complicated text. Despite his limited mental ability, he spelt the letters in a particular format on the ground in a most professional way to preserve the magic. He must have been expertly coached, Assim reasoned, coached by the best to carry out the mission he died for. Assim's eyes widened with anger, for he deduced that User was under the tutelage of yet another sorcerer, and he had not been made aware of Akila's long-standing training of her grandson. The Queen should have known what to do. Assim would call on her apparition, knowing he could only consult with her ethereal version for a very short interval or risk imperilling her spirit. She needed to rest to rise again, in a fit state to rule.

Against his better judgment, he decided to exorcise the Queen's spirit. He picked up the jar where her viscera was kept and picked up the organs with tremendous care. He read a few chants and summoned her. In all her splendour, the ghost of the Queen appeared. She looked towards the now-illumined scroll that presaged her coming. The words were double-layered, and her vision was still impaired as she was summoned before completing the reincarnation ritual. Her remains had to be close to the viscera when the time was right to expedite her return in a solid form. She did, however, agree to be beckoned by her obedient retainer for urgent consultations. The fact that their plot might be detected putting her army in jeopardy, called for her immediate attention.

"The most I can do in my ephemeral shape is to sharpen the efficacy of my wizards," she said. "But that comes at the expense of my abilities. Don't call me again until you can give my shape its full form. This meeting will soon be over. Work fast and read the scroll below the words, between the lines, or better still, burn it once it tells you where to find the tablet of Kings. I am growing weak. I have to unite with my remains."

The Queen left to merge with the rest of her physical form in the necropolis. Assim, head lowered, waited for her to leave, fearing her enchantment if he looked directly at her.

Djau

Apep looked at the young Djau. "The Theban Trinity turns lands into holy grounds by their footsteps," Apep explained. "Right here, deities of creation touched that insignificant patch on their way to self-rejuvenate and take their place across the Nile at the Temple of Luxor. The spirits of the dark know of the marked lands and that a deity's touch turns inconsequential footprints into holy lands. Those spirits evoke curses on some of the spots the divine trio steps on, sucking in the deities' breath from under the soles of their feet where they crossed paths."

Thebans paraded strength, magic, and continuity in boats at the Opet festival once a year. The curse of Nitocris passed on to her demons cleared the tablet from protective spells to locate and capture. That very spot, touched by Osiris, his wife and son, stepped on by an innocent, caused the shivers in the beauty Amunet, unveiling the place where mythically powerful Thebans lay hidden and forgotten for a long time. The beautiful Amunet unknowingly became the vessel that delivered the era of Nitocris and whose imminent rise defiled the Osirian footholds on the sacred earth.

Apep told the attentive Djau about Osiris during their lessons together when the ageing sorcerer drank too much beer and resorted to his potent drugs. "When Osiris walked," he said, "the earth breathed under his feet. That breath called on all royal beings, without discrimination, including Nitocris, to know he once ruled the earth."

"Soon," Djau said to himself, "my queen will rise from her hole in the ground to reconnect with her entrails. In full regalia, she would breathe life into the tablet, transforming the words into an ode to Seth, the dark deity of the netherworlds, gifted with unmatched power." Djau imagined the might he could inherit if he could keep the Queen forever in need of his help.

Djau could not believe his luck. Under the watchful sky, he started digging. The Osirian footsteps on the ground had led to the tablet. The designated space began to burn in small detectable flames, pointing a path to the holy list below. The scent grew stronger as Djau moved carefully and closer towards his find, digging quickly, sweating out of fear and excitement until he eventually unearthed his prize. He deposited it inside his pouch, looked around at the ominous sky, which seemed to disapprove of him finding the tablet, and hurried away. Assim, his father's killer, would be proud.

Nitocris

Assim's tools were now on the table at the far end of the Temple of Abydos. He placed the breath of deities, the viscera of his queen, and the original parchment down and began. He opened his book of chants and started reciting the words. Djau stood proudly by Assim, who faithfully called on his queen. The ground shook. From high windows, the sky grimaced with portending doom. Clouds collided, and thunder thumped, alerting only the pious to the dawn of damned days.

After a litany of words, the ground shook again. Outside, at a distance, a man swimming in the Nile gave out a terrorised scream. The guileless man was enjoying his refined water strokes when a seven-metre-long crocodile ate him up. A friend watched him die and lived to tell the story to bystanders.

In halting words, he told the crowd what he saw, "I had been chewing on warm bread by the water when my friend decided to swim." The man then said an enormous crocodile sprinted suddenly at the swimmer, with eyes shining bright red and looked more like a man than a beast. "A beast of a man," he explained. "It devoured my friend."

The crowd assumed that the man was in shock because his friend drowned and dismissed the story as fanciful. But the earth shook, and the thunder roared as if ready to feed on the people below. Only then did bystanders believe and run away in terror. They remembered their elders' stories about the shaking earth regurgitating a wicked queen in Abydos. Running from what and from whom, the natives did not know, but they were catching up on their bedtime stories, the myths about the shaking ground giving way to a terrible queen, once obliterated from the Kings' list and from the pleasures of the afterlife, doomed to roam in the abyss of realms. They should have listened. Assim, Djau and the cult of a re-birthed queen could have supported the testament of the bread-eating man who saw the fiendish killer crocodile.

Beasts and men shared dismal times ruled by a misfit queen, and the death of the swimmer was the first in a long line of random sacrifices to an undesired queen. The usurper had returned.

Nitocris made a formidable entrance into a time of chaos. Assim opened a secret drawer below the little niche that held the Queen's entrails and put them on a gold platter. He was prepared. He held out a golden threaded cloak decorated with lapis lazuli stones and a silver necklace inlaid with gold. He dressed his queen, and she rewarded him with a ghost of a smile. She took her entrails in one hand, and with the other, she knifed open her belly with the long sharp nail on her index finger and replaced her entrails. She blew her breath at the wound to close it, and the two men watched on in awe as the wound disappeared.

The death of an innocent unleashed a reign of terror by Nitocris. Her powerful telepathy guided Djau to the time and place where Neith's child and the beautiful Amunet lived. In honesty, the Queen looked enviously at the maiden's natural beauty, thinking how best to dispose of the girl with braided black hair, for the Queen missed how she used to be before her soul was defiled.

"Too much sorcery has ruined my looks, and I have to live with that, but what shall I do with you?" she said.

The queen continued her reverie while Assim and Djau waited. The pair knew only too well that their mistress was considering potions to capture the girl's beauty and youth.

When the Queen was not fighting to rule, she studied spells to quench her insatiable appetite for beauty, the type that stopped men in their tracks, like poor Amunet. How Nitocris desired those looks now, wasted on a poor girl without a future. Her wicked lips curled as she frowned. Nitocris reached out in her trance and studied the girl who only had a life on the lowest rung of a ladder ahead of her. The Queen followed the easy birth of Nieth's baby by the Temple of Luxor and passed by the waterwheel into the field.

Assim had seen the Queen's look before, in another life, perhaps. That same calculating sneer, the curl of the lip, with her brows drawn together into a venomous snake-like shape. The Queen smiled as she remembered long ago when she laughed sweetly with her brother, the King. She had poured beer made of barley into slim alabaster bowls while joking and gossiping to the amused King. He had dismissed his entourage as he continued to enjoy the company of his sibling. Unbeknown to him, however, she deftly added the venom to his drink and laughed innocently as she handed him his death sentence.

Her brother slumped to the ground after the merest of sips, although his eyes remained open long enough to see the mask fall from his sister's face. The last question on his mind as his crown was tossed away and he struggled for his life was why he hadn't seen his sister's face change from angel to demon, from order to chaos? Fool, he thought, he should have seen that coming, and then he was dead. Assim was there when she murdered her rightful king and brother. He witnessed the look on the King's face before he breathed his last. Nitocris's head was already on matters of the kingdom before the King had fallen off his throne, stabbed again and again in case he did not die of the venom. Assim, besotted by the beautiful woman without a heart, fell in love that day, swearing to serve her in this life and all the realms. In a single coup, the Queen had assuaged Sobek, the crocodile deity, revering it by shoring her perfect body with a crocodile's tail. She blended the tail with her body and killed an innocent man with a predator. No doubt, the deity promised her fertility and the support of the River Nile. In her trance, Assim watched cruelty defined on her face, portending death, and he wondered whose.

Nitocris, about to suck the beauty of young Amunet, stopped as if she had an afterthought. Amunet's guilelessness might be helpful to the Queen in that rising chaos of a world. Nitocris's interest changed course suddenly, deciding instead to suck the life out of young Nieth as the latter lay on a mat on the mud-tiled floor, suckling the child. When the two men studied the Queen, she somehow looked a little more radiant and perhaps temporarily satiated. Perhaps the Queen wisely thought it too soon to upset Osiris, who still had eyes for clueless Amunet. Another time, perhaps.

Battle For Power – Nitocris

The construction of a palace under the Temple of Abydos by cult loyalists continued. Assim supervised the architecture, giving Nitocris surroundings that befitted her expansive ambitions. She was well aware of her need to be close to her sorcery, without which she remained a dispensable apparition. Her strategy took her beyond reason to beguile the chief architect and treasurer of the late King Pepi, Ikhernofret.

"I want you to build me a palace," she said. "It must be simple on the outside to avoid attention." She glared at the terrified architect, who knew he could not object. She would later cast protective spells to protect her from surprise attacks or betrayal. Meanwhile, Assim arranged a meeting with treasurer Ikhernofret, who did not stand a chance when he took one look at the Queen. He was mesmerised by her. She continued to bark her orders for potions of every type and ordered niches to be constructed on the upper tier to house them. They were everywhere and lay on either side of the walls on her walk to the throne.

At dawn, Ikhernofret hurried to the Queen and showed her the plans on the proposed map for the underground layout. The Queen smiled and was so impressed by what she had seen that she stamped the parchment with the sceptre insignia in the right-hand corner. Unbeknown to anyone else, within the stamp, Nitocris had placed wicked eternal spells intended to enchant and bewitch all eyes that fell on the map, drawing them to the cult. She also threaded the path to her ornate throne with more spells and potions to further protect her movements throughout the palace.

Ikhernofret fulfilled every whim of the Queen, and no expense was spared. Enchanted limestone carvings and reliefs were added along the halls to further puzzle would-be attackers. Figures of Sobek and Osiris also adorned the rooms, but the image of a falcon, a representation of Queen Isis seducing Osiris, was omitted. Nitocris did not care nor fear the wrath of the original queen or her son Horus.

Ikhernofret was given just a month to complete the palace,

which he did, adding torches and copper, inlaid with turquoise, incense holders close to each niche so that the Queen would not lose her way through the palatial maze or waste precious seconds searching for favoured potions brought in by ships from the southern land of Punt all the way by the Red Sea.

Nitocris And Her Mother

Nitocris's mother gave birth to her in the deserts of Sinai, the eager baby arriving before her mother felt any pain as if the infant knew of her destiny and had no time to waste. Her mother had gone into labour in the shadow of a beautiful mountain littered with turquoise, and in gratitude, Nitocris's mother adorned her child with the similar-coloured stone at all times.

Nitocris's mother, Bastet, descended from an ancient family well-versed in old-styled, simplistic witchcraft and dressed themselves in hyena skin. However, Nitocris, as she grew, soon outshone her mother in style and beauty as she moved like a serpent, lithe and sultry. When Nitocris reached adulthood, her mother sent her to Memphis to charm the King. The young woman's reputation having travelled far beyond her homeland.

Nitocris glided with confidence beyond her years and carried a pouch with a sand viper inside to remind her to walk in a way that would entrance kings. Her mother had a small pendant fashioned, which the snake had worn around its neck since the birth of Nitocris and that had subsequently burnt a mark into the creature's skin.

Bastet, despite coaching her daughter on the rules of seduction, omitted to tell her about a small indiscretion in her life. The event had happened years ago and led to a chance meeting that positioned the sceptre as an insignia for the uprising which her wily daughter would set in motion. Bastet and Seth had once met, and the two of them, feeding on their individual depravities, instantly fell in love.

Seth had been chased away from the lands of Egypt, mercilessly hunted by the natives who recognised the darkness within his soul. Osiris had removed Seth from the Temple of Abydos and forced his treacherous brother to wander into the deserts, provoking sandstorms and inciting violent conflicts among all those who encountered him. Bastet, who sought knowledge of the dark side, met the deity when Seth appeared to her in the guise of a Cretan, who arrived from the Aegean islands by sea, thereby escaping the prying eyes of his brother Osiris.

"I can help you," Seth said to her when they met. He had

disguised himself as a sailor from across the Mediterranean and lured Bastet with a bit of magic. Bastet spotted the mark of a sceptre on his arm, which revealed his true nature, and she dropped onto her knees, begging to be taught.

"There is one caveat," Seth said. "I want you to help me."

She readily agreed, and the pair travelled to Memphis, where he taught her how to appear before the King and to become a chief concubine or even a queen. In return, Seth impregnated her.

The King, charmed by the beautiful maiden, fell in love with Bastet and declared her the most favoured one at the palace while Seth's seed grew within her. However, it happened too fast, and Seth's child had been conceived long before the King made his move. As Bastet's belly grew, whispers reached the ears of the King about her suspected infidelity. Despite this, however, the couple married, so besotted was the King with her.

"My liege," she said, "I suggest I travel to Sinai to deliver the child in rough terrain to instil strength into our offspring. But I will leave the decision to my mighty husband."

But as she neared the end of her pregnancy, the much older King began to lose interest in his one-time favourite. Her enchantments, bestowed by Seth, were losing their potency, and he was quickly becoming tired of her, especially when his eyes sighted a newer and younger woman.

He wished Bastet well and ordered a safe escort to take her wherever it pleased her. The court breathed a collective sigh of relief and made offerings at the temple, hoping that she would not return.

During her stay in the desert, Seth appeared to his pregnant lover many times, decorating the mountain she sheltered under with turquoise. After her delivery, Bastet journeyed back to Memphis with young Nitocris and their entourage, opting to settle on the outskirts of the great city rather than return to the palace grounds where she knew she would be no longer welcomed.

Rumours spread about her infidelity with Osiris's chief nemesis, Seth, and fearing for her life and that of the child, Bastet decided to kill her entire cortege in case any of them gave away her whereabouts. She waited until her attendants brought her an evening meal of grilled lamb, grapes, bread and butter and invited them to drink with her. Unbeknownst to her servants, she had laced the drink with poison and gleefully watched on as they all succumbed.

Nitocris blossomed into a seductress, and her mother decided that it was time to throw her daughter to the wolves. Initially, Bastet had planned to visit the palace with Nitocris when she was still a baby but wisely concluded that the King had a short memory, especially when it came to his women, and her presence would be unwelcome. She, therefore, waited until her daughter blossomed into a rare beauty that few men could resist.

Nitocris had been taught well by her mother and proved to be a formidable enchantress. She arrived with very little beyond her confidence and, after tricking her way inside, murdered the King. Despite warnings from his most trusted advisers, the King had chosen to ignore their advice that a female usurper would claim his throne and that he should name his eldest son as his heir.

"My liege, forgive me," his sorcerer had pleaded. "The stars and the charms are spelling out the name of a daughter. I am grieved to say that one of your women, Bastet, whom you have taken to bed in good faith, has carried a child of Seth and is expected any time into the palace coming from the eastern desert with potent venom. You must name an heir."

The tired, ailing monarch, his kingdom weakened by wars, droughts and the growing powers of the nomarchs, agreed. Yet no one imagined that the beautiful and enchanting Nitocris was the toxin that the sorcerer spoke of, and his undoing would come at the hand of a daughter of the deity of the nether world.

Assim

Assim summoned his followers and uttered his spells into the air and the running river as Ibises, carrying the scent of his breath, alerted the loyalists to gather. Bees, fish, ducks and birds carried the call over the winding river and told believers to converge in Abydos. In a matter of days, his disciples marched towards their temple, hidden beneath the Temple of Abydos.

NITOCRIS – In Abydos, the sprawling, demonic structure underneath the temple of Osiris buzzed with activity. The Queen, who had found a home among the caves, waited and watched from near her huge bathtub as quartzite rock was brought from a quarry at Gabal Ahmar in the Nile Delta up north to line her circular cistern. A copper spout was built into the wall adjoining the bath from which Nile water poured. The architect had ensured that a fireplace built below the water flowing into the cistern would provide the Queen with as much hot water as she liked. Immersing herself in the hot liquid, the usurper celebrated the retrieval of her human form. Satisfied that her building of the temple beneath Osiris's had gone unnoticed, she lay back in the honey, cinnamon, ground cloves and salt-infused water.

"If only my father could see me now," she whispered. In her mind, Nitocris imagined herself in the Osirian white robe, holding the insignia of the sceptre of Seth instead of his crook and flail, ruling the south as queen and deity, the rising sun falling on her face once every year. A bluish smoke billowed from the special bath concoction, lulling the witch into a sleep, but just as quickly, her sharp ears picked up the sound of subtle footsteps approaching.

"It is time to talk," a voice said as a shudder ran through Nitocris at the sight of her nemesis.

"You have come," Nitocris hissed, not looking to where the voice came from. Her arched brows merged into a sinister web on her forehead. Slowly, Nitocris turned to look at the wrinkled woman.

Akila

Akila timed each of the life spans gifted to her by the deity of darkness, Ptah. The potions kept the woman alive and functioning for a hundred years at a time, but she ran out of lives and still had one final task to complete.

Akila and Nitocris had known one another as children. As a young girl, Akila had a knack for healing, randomly picking seeds and blending them with stones, reading incantations, and treating ailing villagers. Her skilful hands, touched by a higher echelon of spirits, mixed earthly crops in measured amounts to soothe the pain of others, but not always successfully. In alien worlds across realms and on this earth, she became known as the fixer whose knowledge of the power of seeds invited people in the east, west and south to visit the benevolent sorceress. And sometimes, Akila travelled to strange lands north of the sea in search of more potent ingredients. The magic, though, had its limits, soon to wither and die like Akila.

Standing as firmly as she could, Akila, carrying a sack over her shoulder, looked down at Nitocris. Inside the sack lay the ingredients she hoped would help her defeat her one-time friend. Nitocris viewed her through serpent eyes and coiled herself in the tub as her crocodile tail grew in size. Slowly, her body transformed into a reptile, and her head became that of a cobra. Akila pulled the bag from her shoulder, but before she could open it, the creature attacked. Akila, now a very old woman, with her abilities faltering, was unable to do anything as it sank its teeth into her. Akila collapsed and lay on the floor as her mind wandered back to when they were children.

Nitocris giggled. "Did you see how the scribe devoured Mama's dates?"

Akila laughed. "Yes, and he drank two flasks of beer and ate the entire loaf of bread. His belly grows each lesson."

The scribe taught hieroglyphics, and the girls secretly made fun of the chubby man when he took breaks to relieve himself. He had an insatiable appetite, and the girls waited for his belly to burst.

Akila and Nitocris had met when they were both young.

Bastet, Nitocris's mother, hid in the desert on the borders of Memphis and carried the infant to a nearby temple. "I want my daughter to learn to sing, dance and read the forbidden language," she told the priest. "In return, I am at your service, my lord and servant of the gods."

The priest looked into the eyes of Bastet, and he held his stare like a tiger sizing up its prey. Yet there was something about her that worried him. Behind those eyes lay something dark.

Nitocris first met Akila at the temple after a kind scribe recommended that both of them become companions to a princess in court. This would ensure that the girls would get a good education, something usually reserved for boys.

In the palace, no one recognised Nitocris nor asked about her family as long as she kept the princess amused. In return for the scribe's favour, the girls had to work fields and learn to weave from the servants in court. They made the princess laugh and fitted in perfectly.

One cloudy day, Nitocris wandered off into the palace garden, searching for the princess's leather ball made from the skin of a hyena. It had been missing for days, and the princess was inconsolable at the loss of her most favoured possession. Nitocris hurried past the protective palm trees, stumbling over a granite stone. Nitocris thought that if she ran fast enough, she could find the ball before Akila, thereby becoming the princess's favourite. The granite stone concealed a lair of a cobra, a follower of the dark recruited by Seth to subjugate loyalists for an ominous future ahead. On that day, Nitocris fell to the ground and found herself staring into the eyes of the creature. She was unafraid and captivated by the yellowish orbs, tinged with blue, peeping out from under the granite stone. They were the most beautiful eyes she had ever seen, and as she continued to stare, she fell in love. The creature slid from the hole, revealing a green cobra head attached to the body of a lion.

"My slave," spoke the creature as it held the ball between its fangs, "go back to the princess and wait for the call."

"Yes, master," she said.

When Nitocris made her way back, a thought entered her mind. The creature had spared her from a life of servitude, not to fetch a ball but to summon an army and rule the kingdom of Egypt down to the Cataracts in the south. She looked at her hand as a stinging sensation shot through it, and there next to her thumb was a sceptre.

Nitocris ran back with the ball and handed it to the delighted princess. As Akila studied her friend. "Where did you find the ball?" Akila said, continuing to scrutinise the face she thought she knew.

"I was lucky," she replied.

The memory came to Nitocris as if there was a connection between herself and her one-time friend. She looked down at Akila. She had expected more of a fight from her adversary and hovered over the stricken woman. Akila, unseen by Nitocris, withdrew the small pouch from her bag and threw the powder at the Queen. Nitocris, paralysed, stepped back and fell into the tub.

It had taken Akila years to prepare the spell, and she slowly got to her feet and studied the beautiful face of Nitocris.

"Where are your demons now, witch?" Akila's said.

Nitocris attempted to rise. "You are dying, old woman," she said. "Where is your Isis now? Your goddess is gone. We can rule from Thebes together. I shall make you minister." Nitocris groaned, too weak to summon her followers, her brain befuddled by the spell. The foolish old woman had sacrificed her last vestige of power to stop me, she thought.

Akila had stalled the inevitable attack on Thebes. If Thebes fell, Egyptians would live in darkness until such times when destiny forcefully intervened or when the Nile rose to battle with flood or drought. Akila stood by the bath, protected with spells woven into the linen wraps around her diminishing form.

Akila's faithful vigilantes waited outside in the shadows along the River Nile for the signal to storm the underworld of the Queen. "Look over there!" one of the elders said as a faint plume of smoke rose from the hidden fortress.

Akila dropped to the floor, watching as the paralysed Queen fought for her life. Nitocris, her hands shaking, reached for a nearby bowl.

Outside, the elder studied the sky as the smoke slowly dispersed. "Akila has failed," he said as he and the other followers withdrew.

The Queen picked up the contents of the bowl and dropped them into the water. The miraculous blend breathed life into her as the disfigured but fast-healing creature slithered from the bathtub.

She laughed. She had envisioned this attack by her enemy and had prepared her own preparation in advance. The usurping Queen had perfected the sinister arts.

By the time the Horus sun rose, Abydos was fired up in bright orange colours. A good day, thought the Queen. Trained falcons spread the word for the marches to begin as a trickle of followers assembled at the back of the temple. People came from the south, from as far as Punt, beyond the Cataracts, from the lands of gold, silver and incense, driven by hope to become whole in this life, their sins as light as a feather when beckoned by jurors to pass through the gates into eternity.

Riva

Riva's movies about the occult and the ancient world continued to skyrocket her to even greater career heights, especially after her outstanding performance in a second franchise. However, Riva had remained out of touch with her muse, the princess, for two years. Perhaps she settled back home between Memphis and neighbouring Libya, thought Riva, and she was now in need of a new story.

"Let's take the crew south to Abydos on a Nile cruise, gear and all," Riva said to the director. Despite the estrangement from the princess, she was experiencing vivid and recurring dreams. She had dreamt of a woman wearing a white cloak walking towards her, which she could not explain, and she felt compelled to visit the South. The apparition held a sceptre, which she seemed to be communicating with, calling on her subjects to attack and take over the kingdom. Despite the beauty of the Queen, she dragged a crocodile tail behind her.

The cruising boat docked at the Temple of Abydos, the passengers disembarked, and the entourage headed to the temple. Riva hurried with the film crew and other actors following in her wake. No one asked her anything, knowing from experience that it was never good to interrupt her in her quest. For them, Riva's grim face meant another franchise in the making, but it also implied sordid visions coming in parallel with actual bloody encounters.

Riva strode into the temple and headed to the chapel of Osiris. *Osiris is troubled,* a voice in her head seemed to say.

She headed to the back of the temple and, ignoring the other sanctuaries, into the chapel of Osiris. Riva was momentarily disorientated and attempted to leave through the door she had entered by, but she could not. It was as if she was now imprisoned within the sanctuary's walls, held there by an invisible force which gently nudged her into one of the corners. She sat as multi-dimensional war pictures assailed her. People with spears and horse-drawn chariots, heavily armed with various weapons, were deployed for an imminent battle. The woman in the white impersonated Osiris, carrying a sceptre instead of a crook and flail. The picture in her head seemed to vibrate with force from within the carvings on the wall dedicated to age-old Osiris.

Riva stared at a large frame before her, with Nitocris standing fearlessly in the black and white Osirian colours after she deposed the deity. In previous dreams, the plots described were relatable to ordinary issues. Even crime stories flowed without too much complication, but these disturbing images at the Temple of Abydos were different somehow.

Riva's mind drifted back to years ago when an ancient urn she was carrying smashed in her hands. The actress had learnt a valuable lesson. She had managed to salvage some of the ashes the urn contained and put them inside a small pouch. She knew, not really understanding why, that these ashes were important. It was only later that the notion arrived that they offered her some protection.

Her chaotic trance ended, and Riva, gripping the pouch tightly, headed across to a sketch on the far side of the room. She took some of the ash from her pouch and blew it at the wall, not realising how dangerous this was. Her action left her vulnerable to ancient spells she knew little about. Another vision appeared. This time, the phantom of the Queen jumped from the painting and appeared to be rallying her absent followers to barricade the temple and occupy it. She ordered strikes at fellow Egyptians while their attention was diverted towards the flood season. Riva gasped. This Queen had the power to raise long-dead loyal subjects around Abydos, further south towards the Cataracts and in Memphis to the north, promising eternal life to those who remained loyal.

Riva, engrossed in the visions of a coup against a kingdom, did not see the shapeshifter, Assim, appear wielding a club. Before she had a chance to turn, she was struck by him and crumpled into a heap onto the dusty floor. Assim changed shape, and within seconds, he had transformed into a modern-day detective called Fayed.

Assim

Assim, the crown prince of darkness and assistant to Queen Nitocris, had watched the police precinct looking for one of the officers who mostly resembled him. He had shifted across many realms, exploiting thousands of demons over countless years, which he trained to help him reach the future after receiving news that sorcerers in the modern world were working together to destroy his cult. Their ultimate goal was to save the tablet and destroy the Queen to the point that return would be impossible. Most of the demons had been consumed in flames and destroyed while travelling through time. Those who survived the exhaustive journey proved too weak to exist for long. Despite their loss, Assim was able to glean important information and serve as a bridge, allowing those who followed to move a little further forward on the rungs of time to locate Riva in Abydos and retrieve the legitimate list of kings. The wizard of darkness considered the demons expendable but was concerned about the length of time it took to recruit and train more of them.

He could not continue to fail indefinitely, and Assim recognised that he was running out of time to achieve his goal of immortality. Assim focused on finding demons who were able to withstand the arduous journey and searched long and hard for them. Assim studied the modern kingdom of Egypt and discovered a land with formidable warriors who fought like no others with weapons he had never seen before.

He found himself at the barracks, which settlers of that realm called a police station, and watched the guards who tended the grounds of Thebes, or Luxor, as it became known. From there, he could make his way across the temples of his people in Abydos. Stunned, he found that most of the members of the police force, if not all, looked very much like him, and he could fit himself well enough in any of them. He chose Fayed, the hard-working detective credited with being above suspicion, as opposed to himself, who revelled in the title of self-proclaimed sorcerer supreme of the dark cult.

In Abydos, Assim dressed into his original garb and looked ominously at the young woman. No one should meddle with the past, he thought as she carelessly threw her ash spells against the wall and left herself vulnerable to spiritual attacks. According to Assim's instant evaluation, the girl had acted foolishly. He curled his lips into a bitter smile, remembering how he had instantly picked up her scent and finding her was easy.

A few tourists wandered into the sanctuary, barely noticing the strange individual dressed in a linen robe, sandals, and eyes lined with black kohl, presuming his presence in the temple was part of the tour, although impressed by the murderous gaze he gave them. Assim became a person of interest among casual tourists but wasted no time on onlookers unless they came too close to him. He quickly understood that he was from a different world and had to embrace the quirks of alien realms up to a point.

In any event, Riva was his target, and while she was off guard and the other members of the film crew were preoccupied with the temple, he pounced, throwing his cloak over her and dragging her away.

Fayed – The Detective

Detective Fayed hailed from Fayyum, northwest of Thebes and much closer to the fertile land in the Delta. Drilled by his grandmother in the cult's old ways, Fayed learnt that his roots could be traced back to the dark cult. The little boy loved visiting his grandmother's house in the early morning, welcomed by the smell of freshly baked bread out of the oven. Her tender and toothless smile often greeted him as she ushered him inside her kitchen, where her wonderful homemade bread, sweetened with dates, awaited him.

When he arrived at lunchtime, she would prepare boiled lentils and roasted vegetables rolled in garlic and, for his sweet tooth, leftover bread coated in honey. The young Fayed would devour the lot. He adored her and listened intently to his grandmother as he ate, and she explained how her recipes had been handed down over the years from ancestors who had built temples and pyramids. She told him of Nitocris, a beautiful queen and the real founder, how the Queen rose and what it meant for the ancient world and Fayed.

"What if she does not rise, Grandma?" he said. "What will happen to us?" the young Fayed, who possessed an enquiring mind, would ask.

She smiled at her grandson. "Oh, but she must rule and shine above all." She explained that the Queen protected Fayed's family and its fortune, so he had to help her to retake the throne. The time for the Queen approached and Fayed would be the hero who brought her back. Her time to rule coincided with Fayed's grown-up years on Earth. "Wait for the dawn to come and watch the alignments of the stars," the grandma kept telling the young man. "Learn to recognise the brilliance of the shapely suns in the image of Seth, of a crocodile's tail or a sceptre, my little hero." The old woman continued to instruct Fayed on how to read the ominous signals when predators attacked homes and took over the place of children. He did not really understand what she meant then, and she did not elaborate. Perhaps, Fayed mused, that she feared she would scare him. As he grew up, he welcomed the meaning of her stories about the beasts of prey driving families to flee and the shape of stars. Just like her, he grew to welcome the terror that came.

Fayed continued to prove his loyalty to the cult of Nitocris and obeyed the dictates of the chief priest Assim, who continued to exist in the present times. Some of the followers were reincarnated like Assim, and others lived double lives, while some remained dormant and underground to avoid unwarranted attention. These unworldly believers still had temples, hidden since forgotten dawns, in total darkness, in labyrinths right under famous temples of mighty pharaohs, etching indelible names of the heretic Queen in symbols. The temples of Nitocris, built below the surface of the earth, fossilised from lack of attention, gradually buried deeper, had remained uncovered through modern times. The deafening sounds of the increasing number of tourists, fake cult seekers, or battles that ruined the cities and displaced people away from the location of the evil sanctuaries underground. Other things kept the demonic sanctuary hidden. The hundreds of followers of the cult of Nitocris branded a sceptre forged in spells on members of the cult who found their way to the doomed area by means of spirits who led the path upon recognising the familiar charms. Assim, the modern Fayed, had masterminded the device much to the pleasure of the mistress of the movement.

One fateful day, Fayed visited his beloved temple in the vicinity of Fayyum, as he usually did as a boy, a sheltered cove by the ancient lake shrouded in witchcraft and fashioned with the blackest of tools. The temple, hidden under the famous Temple of Medinat Madi, was dedicated to the crocodile deity Sobek, a predator very much admired by followers of the darkness.

Along with everything else, his grandmother drilled into him how he should worship at the Nitocris Temple. The priest at the temple ordered the young Fayed to tattoo his thigh with the sceptre and instruct followers to tattoo the sceptre on a prominent spot on the hand, close to the thumb.

Fayed, who came from an ancient stock of loyalists, had to be initiated differently from other followers as he was now considered amongst the elite sect of priests. However, during his tattooing, something went wrong, and Fayed bled profusely, which caused his genitals to shrink to virtually nothing. The priest continued, holding him down as his grandmother stood by, emotionless with serpent-like eyes.

"Stay strong, for you are destined for greatness," she whispered to the boy.

The priest managed to stop the blood, bandaged the wound and wrapped it with charms made of a layer of ground jasper, adding an ancient amulet to the bandages to make sure the boy survived. The moment the charms touched the wound, fumes erupted, and a smell of burning filled the air, leaving Fayed screaming in pain. The priest lifted a small bottle to the boy's nose, and Fayed instantly fell asleep before the priest placed the remaining mixture into the boy's hand.

The process successfully saved Fayed's life, but without fully functioning sexual organs, he couldn't reproduce followers to the cause.

"It really does not matter much," the priest explained to Fayed when he awoke. "Your ... inadequacy will gain you access into other domains, otherwise impossible for the well-endowed to enter." The young Fayed did not fully understand what the priest had told him but smiled politely. It was years later that he realised the enormity of what had happened and the irony that it happened in a temple dedicated to Sobek, a deity of fertility.

Detective Fayed possessed a talent for tracking relics, especially jewellery and working for the police department gave him entry to places that others could only dream about. Imbued with a power bestowed by his grandmother, his search for powerful stones, potions, ointments, vapours and human organs, as well as blood from the most unique predators, gave him a decisive advantage over others.

The arcane recipes, left behind by ancestors, ensured that more people were lured into the fold, which in turn maintained a powerful cult for the rule of the Queen. She, in return, promised a life for her people in the present and future – or so the followers of the cult believed.

On days away from the precinct, Fayed dedicated his time to locating the tablet and completing the Queen's sanctuary below the

Temple of Abydos. He scoured his hometown in Fayyoum, uncovering troves of precious stones, some of which belonged to a princess, Sit-Hathor-Iunit, hidden in a cache in a huge sack where skeletal remains of two people, along with ceremonial daggers, lay close. He learnt that earlier dynasties bribed their way into eternal life, securing their passage with stolen gems. This was a concept he understood well, for he descended from a long line of criminals, murderers, and sorcerers who dabbled in the blackest of magic and who obstinately never repented in the belief that the Queen could heal their tortured souls. Fayed left the treasure in a cove with plans to transport as much as he could back to Abydos for the insatiable queen. The find assured him that he had come close to a much more significant discovery, and he decided to resume his search. After almost fainting from fatigue and running out of useful potions, he eventually found a shaft. Excavating further, he uncovered the most spectacular structured tomb of Princess Sit, complete with jewels and the bodies of dead grave robbers. The more Fayed dug, the more treasures he found, leading to the biggest hoard of all. He unearthed pillars, corridors and parts of a long-forgotten temple. By the end of his three-day dig, driven on by curiosity and greed, he pushed forward to a centre which opened up to the palatial grounds of a great king.

As the sun rose on the fourth day in the desert, he heard echoes all around. The echoes turned into the savage howling of an incoming storm that transformed into a mighty twister. The whirlwind, as if driven with a soul of its own, headed towards him in measured movements until, close enough, it swept him off his feet and embraced him inside its powerful force. The whole scenario lasted only a few seconds, and then the unworldly storm ended, dropping him heavily onto the ground. Fayed brushed himself down and checked himself for injury. He was unscathed, and he felt stronger. His mind spun with a chaotic energy he had never before experienced, as if a temporary force possessed him and wanted Fayed to do its bidding. From that moment, Fayed completely changed, travelling east for thousands of miles on foot, ravaging cemeteries of kings in Saqqara, searching tombs for stones, silver and gold. His search always proved fruitful, as if he knew where to look.

He trekked east to ancient Memphis, once the jewel of the ancient world, until the rising power of Osiris lured kings down south to Thebes and Abydos. He sacked tombs and unscrupulously robbed farmers as they picked their crops. He stuffed the many sacks he stole or found littering alleys with the treasures he picked on his way. He snatched amulets from dead noblemen as they lay in their tombs and robbed the women lying in their sarcophagi. He pocketed antique carnelians, feldspars and antiquities sitting beside their mummies. With his newfound energy, he hid his cache at locations near Saqqara – he still had miles to travel between Fayyum, Memphis and back to Saqqara, where he hid his plundered loot with the others.

By the time he collected his treasure for the rebellion of Nitocris, the power and foresight he had gained left him as quickly as it arrived. It was time to find help from a follower of the sceptre and go back to the Queen at Abydos with his treasure trove. Fayed made up his mind to leave Saqqara for Memphis but first made sure that the cache could not be found by archaeologists, wandering tourists, or tomb raiders.

In Memphis, he had to blend in until he found a believer with the tattooed sceptre near his thumb. Many of his family lived there, and he was confident he would find someone he could trust.

He remembered the words of his grandmother, "You will find plenty of your bloodline beyond Fayyum and all over Egypt."

Fayed washed himself in a spring near Saqqara and tidied himself for the trip to Mit Rahina, which had thrived as much as ancient Memphis thousands of years ago. He found a driver willing to make the trip and set off, finally reaching a sprawling village to the south. He searched for a place to eat in the bustling district, found a coffee shop and sat in a corner, fantasising about his ancestors who served around the Memphite market where enslaved people and vendors tended rich folk in similar eating spots.

In the early and quiet morning, he remembered he had barely eaten while hoarding treasures, so he ordered several breakfast plates of fava beans, hot bread and soft, unsalted white cheese, boiled eggs and green salad with onions, vinegar, garlic and olive oil, washing down the food with minted tea and mineral water.

He gave a generous tip to the owner, remembering the time he worked undercover as a baker searching for followers like him. He remembered proofing bread for a few hours after adding yeast, salt and flour, and as he ate his meal, his mind drifted back. He had become an accomplished baker, and people would visit from miles away to get their hands on his rosemary-infused bread.

He woke himself up from his reverie, gave a handsome tip to the smiling waiter and readied himself to leave.

"Do you know of a good place where I can rest for a few days?" he asked the waiter. "I shall come every day for my breakfast. The food here is divine."

"Lotus," the waiter said, pointing to a small motel painted white, pink and purple.

Fayed walked a short distance to the hotel and entered the reception area. Fayed mused as he waited to be seen. Perhaps the waiter could be trusted enough to locate loyalists to his cause. He was finally served, handed a key, made his way to his room, undressed and fell into a deep sleep.

In his dreams, Fayed saw the Queen biting at him. She was searching for her white cloak and sceptre, and in her anger, she became a twister, a falcon, and a massive python with fangs that oozed poisonous fluids into a cup. His nightmares continued as he viewed the Queen as she tried to pour a thickened drink down the throat of the legitimate ruler of the kingdom.

Fayed woke up drenched in sweat. He showered and returned to the café from the day before and was met by the same waiter. He ordered humus with tahini, lemon, and olive oil, which he mixed with the white cheese, tomatoes and dill. The waiter, pleased to see such a generous tipper return, had made a special dish for him, too. He had obtained a beautiful piece of lamb's liver from a nearby butcher, which he pan-fried, adding spices and herbs before presenting it to Fayed.

Fayed glanced around and waved the waiter closer. "My wife," he began, "has fertility issues. Doctors are doing all they can, and I have a relative who believes Mit Rahina can solve such issues with a different type of local medicine." Fayed pulled a few notes from his pocket and held them up to the waiter. "Of course, you will be richly rewarded if you can point me in the right direction."

The waiter's eyes glinted as he looked at the money. "On the outskirts of town is an order that is said to be of great use in such matters." He nodded across the road to a coffee shop. "That coffee shop is run by people who have a tattoo here …" he pointed to the side of his thumb. "They may be able to help."

The detective waved the waiter even closer. "I would try anything to help my wife," Fayed said. He pulled some more money from his pocket and handed it to the waiter.

The waiter smiled and secreted the notes inside his pocket. "They have a tattoo of a staff like the one we see in temples," he began. "The cafe is run with great discipline, not like this place at all. The owners look like they come from outer space and do not belong. I must admit, I am a little afraid of them." The waiter glanced around again, and happy he was not being watched or listened to, he continued. "One day, my supervisor went over there to complain about them poaching our customers. You know what happened to him …? He could not talk for a week. Since then, word spread that these people should be treated with courtesy. The village heard of miracle babies after visits in the middle of the night through a side entrance to the Sawlagan by women and men known to be impotent."

Fayed listened intently as the waiter went on to explain that there was a scary man with a tattoo on his thumb who dabbled in dark matters. Fayed, always a generous tipper, pulled some more money from his pocket, thanked the waiter for his help and stood. "I may require another favour from you," he said. The waiter nodded his understanding. "There will be a good bonus for you." With that, he left as the grinning waiter snatched up the cash.

There was an undeniable aura of magic in the air at the coffee shop, the Sawlagan. Men and women were fitted in pyjama-styled uniforms made of an off-white linen fabric. Around their necks, they had a necklace of Horus's eye. Fayed briefly studied them. Not a single person the world over, except for himself, would suspect that the symbols were crafted of genuine stones, thousands of years old, dug from ancient quarries near the Temple of Osiris. Every single amulet worn was not from the present day. Wearing the eye in the upright position protected the wearer from Seth. Fayed sneered. Clearly, the workers, who moved like robots when unobserved, wore their amulets upside down out of disrespect for the son of Osiris. They clearly had loyalty to Seth, Horus's worst enemy and killer of his father. The eye, made of lapis lazuli lined with silver, matched the braided silver-plated gold chain that held the lopsided gem around their necks. Cult members were obviously growing bolder, he thought, defying Osiris in plain sight. Openly proclaiming their belief in the order of chaos, refusing the protection of Horus and preparing to die for anarchy and Seth. As long as Horus was not united with his other eye, the north and south of Egypt could never be united, or so they believed. On their feet, they wore sandals made of palm leaves. With a bit of imagination, one might conclude that pharaohs operated the diner.

A waiter glanced at the sceptre on Fayed's thumb and waved a young man across. Fayed had no time for pleasantries, nor did they. "This is Kyky," the waiter said. "He will assist you with everything you need."

"I need someone to drive me to Abydos," Fayed said.

Kyky beckoned Fayed to follow him as he made his way outside to a truck. "Wait here," Fayed said and made his way back to the coffee shop. He persuaded the waiter, who was ending his shift, to accompany him to Saqqara. The waiter readily agreed. Clearly, the prospect of more money from the generous Fayed was too much to turn down.

The three men set off, and on reaching Saqqara, they loaded the sacks of looted treasure into the back, filled the top of each sack with flour to escape detection if they were stopped, and headed to Sawlagan. Kyky loaded provisions of water and food.

The waiter made excuses to the coffee shop owner that he would be away for a couple of days as one of his relatives had died in Abydos. The waiter hurriedly placed more provisions of fruits, cheese and bread along with a small kerosene heater. Mint, tea and sugar were added to the consignment, and happy that they had all they needed, the three men set off.

The truck, when in sight of Saqqara, changed direction as Fayed steered the vehicle towards the pyramid area, which was closed at this hour. Fayed had left a second cache of treasures close by.

"Where are we going?" asked the waiter.

"I have found some gems near the Step pyramid. If you know someone who can authenticate these stones, you will become a wealthy man. But of course, you are free to go back to the coffee shop if you wish."

The waiter rubbed his chin. "I will help," he said.

They waited until nightfall before making their way across to where Fayed had hidden the sacks of jewels and gems. The loading took quite a while, and as before, flour was placed on the top of the sacks to disguise what lay inside. Fayed handed the waiter a small bar of gold. "This is for you," Fayed said.

The waiter, wide-eyed, viewed the treasure, but as he studied the object, which was worth more than many years pay, Fayed pulled a knife from his pocket and slit his throat. The dead waiter, who barely had time to covet his reward, was pushed inside the empty hole where the treasure was stored and covered by sand and rocks.

Osira

In modern times, tourists visited the necropolis in Saqqara, which housed ancient kings and noblemen. Fayed and his cult companion had to find a place to rest near ancient Memphis before a long drive south to the Queen in Abydos. They could not go back to Mit Rahina just yet in case someone remembered Fayed and his dealings with the waiter. The two men agreed to stay close to the cemetery, as they already covered a lot of ground and the minutes counted.

The light could be seen from a considerable distance as the two men neared King Zoser's third dynasty pyramid outside the cemetery. They continued on, drawn towards the light, before stopping nearby at a small inn with an air of familiar history, a replica of an ancient Pharaonic diner.

The old inn catered for a specific clientele, those who preferred a more ancient-looking setting rather than some of the more modern places. The owners had spent a great deal of time on the building, which offered up a pharaonic ambience, giving the impression of being transported back in time. The innkeeper, a slave to routine, only left the household three times each year on business. His wife, Osira, whose eyes were narrowed and black as coal with lashes to die for, held tell-tale signs of alien ancestry. Some believed she descended from the Hyksos, who had invaded Egypt from the east.

Her father, Hong, who descended from a family of warriors from the farthest east, was a short but powerfully built, quiet man, and her mother, Aida, inherited the inn.

Aida and Hong dropped by to see their daughter and son-in-law late one day, when the moon was full, for something to eat. This tactic was inherited by earlier foreigners from ancient times, who wanted to learn more about the locals and report back to their chiefs.

Hong had initially intended to uncover treasures and spells and learn about the weaknesses of their hosts to discover where the more precious treasure lay. Hong's cover depended on marrying a native, settling down with children, and learning the language and the customs of the people. To achieve what was required of him, he needed full integration into Egyptian life. Aida had stayed on to look after her family-run inn after the rest of her family moved to pastures new. Despite her comely looks, she had lived alone since their departure, and as she grew older, her prospects of marriage shrank.

Hong's arrival and subsequent courtship with Aida served two purposes. It removed the loneliness she had felt since her family left and also meant that she could continue to run her beloved inn. She easily succumbed to Hong's charms but recognised that she would have to utilise her ability in witchcraft if she was ever to bear children. Aida knew that her falling pregnant at her age would arouse suspicions where she lived. However, it was not unheard of that someone as old as her could conceive.

She remembered the daughter of an incense vendor in Aida's neighbourhood who had implored a priest from Mit Rihana to help her. The cleric did not have the heart to refuse the middle-aged woman as she often supplied the church with various goods. The woman explained to the priest that she wanted a child to support her into old age and could not bear the thought of growing old alone. Sure enough, nine months later, she gave birth to an unruly and mischievous daughter who had to be kept in a cage due to the problems she would cause. The daughter's wrath knew no bounds, and other villages shunned the frightening child.

A rumour persisted that the priest had fathered the uncontrollable girl, but Aida kept up the pretence and denied it. Hong's arrival from his northeastern homeland and his help in running the inn proved a cover for gathering information. He reasoned that if he returned to his homeland, he would have comprehensive information with which to regale the rulers. Both Hong and Aida agreed to a marriage of convenience out of mutual interest, and this union gave birth to the present innkeeper's wife, Osira. Aida, Hong and their daughter Osira lived quietly on the outskirts of the village.

"It will be best to build our living quarters on the ground floor at the back of the inn," Aida told her husband. "Don't you agree?

We will soon be too old to use the staircase." Hong was indifferent and never expressed an opinion, allowing his wife to make such choices.

The family's business soon thrived. Serving food and drink to villagers and passing travellers, the arrangement became as convenient as their marriage. The family served beer and wine, and, in return, they collected not only money but also information and were particularly interested in collecting news about the stability of the state, of provinces from beyond the Cataracts in the south, or south-east by the seas beyond Punt and the known world, and up north-west towards the Aegean Sea.

As word spread about the delightful inn, their clientele expanded, enticing guests from all directions, even as far as Hong's homeland. Husband and wife had managed to position themselves the perfect hideout in plain sight.

Osira learnt much from her father, the warrior, teaching her how to use a spear, arrows and how to wrestle. Hong talked to his daughter about the world beyond Egypt in the northeast, the rivers, and the fabulous architecture, regaling her with stories about his ancestral home. He explained to her how his people would fight off floods, building walls to ward off the mighty waters. How his people fashioned stilts that they would wear, allowing them to wade through the deepest inundation while the others, less wise, were engulfed along with their homes. The waters, he explained, had invincible powers and would never let up, it appeared, until all the water in the world was drained.

He gave his daughter bronze coins that he had brought with him, engraved with the faces of his own deities. Osira treasured these and studied the faces with big eyes, large noses, and painted eyebrows.

Osira's mother, who kept her husband content and well-fed, taught her much about herbs and magic formulae. The daughter quickly learnt how to keep people like the detective well served and, in the process, gained knowledge about the turbulent affairs of the state.

When Fayed and Kyky first walked into the inn, the family instantly recognised that their impressive-looking guests were the tomb raiders and demonic worshippers that people had mentioned. Rather than slip a potion to loosen the tongues of the men into their drinks, the innkeepers adopted a more acceptable approach.

"Let us know if you need help transporting the cargo," Osira's mother said. "We have been here a long time, and my husband has many business interests. We would be happy to assist you."

In time, Osira's husband became known as the innkeeper, taking over the hard labour from her parents, who had grown old and hardly left the upper floor of the building. Osira, meanwhile, helped to serve the travellers who arrived and took care of her parents. At the same time, Osira's mother polished her magic skills and took regular doses of obsidian and rosemary potions to stay radiant and younger, leaving her husband smitten. His expressionless face, a trait he learnt from his wife, with help from herbs, became a fixture he carried with ease, making it impossible for the detective to discern his true feelings.

Meanwhile, Fayed, tired, impotent, and running out of time, needed to get the loot to Abydos and decided that he would have to learn more about the family another time. "We should go," he said to Kyky.

"But if the innkeepers are offering to help us," Kyky said as he followed Fayad outside. "Shouldn't we take it?"

The detective paused and glanced back at the inn. "We could do with someone to help with our baggage." Fayad stroked his chin. "The inn is in a good position to help recruit more into our cult. It is the isolation that makes it ideal."

"Indeed," Kyky said.

The two men went back inside. "I need someone to help on the long drive to Abydos," Fayed said as he looked at Osira and her husband.

The innkeeper exchanged glances with his wife and smiled. "Tell me what you need. I will accompany you, and my wife will take charge until I come back."

The innkeeper travelled three times a year for a reason. He rode once beyond the eastern sea and the rivers to the ancestral home of his father-in-law with letters in strange writings that only Osira and her father understood. He travelled twice more to buy stock for the inn, returning with gifts for fellow vendors and cheese, wheat and barley for clients and the frequent visitors. The innkeeper also took the opportunity to meet up with friends along the way to pass on additional information when he couldn't. However, he decided to keep these details to himself and not tell Fayed.

For centuries, the information sought by spy rings did not change much, except that interest diverted from focus on the power of priests in the past to religious power play in general. Ironically, the innkeeper kept the hawk-like enemies on the borders informed even after his father-in-law became a drunk and too fat to care. Aida had already taken what she needed from her foreign husband and kept him around to cover her real interests. Perhaps she, too, did not notice that her ageing warrior husband did not entirely succumb to the wine, as he would like her and others to believe, and stayed in contact with his own units stationed around there.

Aida kept her magic under wraps and sought customers beyond the few empty-headed village girls. Her clients came from across lands where her husband grew up. She traded secrets with sorcerers from the Far East, becoming one of the first witches to organise magical conventions to gain access to treasures of dead pharaohs, amulets, and formulae that kept queens empowered and concubines beautiful and smart. She kept her senses sharp, enslaving guards and queens along ancient and modern palaces across time zones, getting rid of them when they became too needy, too greedy, or committed their fatal mistake of threatening her with exposure. When her sources attempted blackmail, she would put on a vulnerable smile and acted scared out of her wits. Then, she would offer potions to lift their status, a repetitive lie they all wanted to believe. The moment they touched the potion, they were doomed and quickly died, turning to ashes in front of her, which Aida collected. She would add these to her potions, thereby increasing their potency.

Aida's brain still worked like the sundial despite her growing old – she was a hundred by then – and she understood that Fayed and Kyky were taking the treasure to the Queen whom she served. Even after all these years, she could not truly trust her husband, the warrior, to join her cult, but she kept him from leaving, assuaging his pride with invented secrets about the borders of her kingdom. Maybe one day she would set him loose, but not yet.

Aida encouraged her son-in-law, the innkeeper, to go with the men. He was a compliant man who loved her daughter with or without spells. The innkeeper obliged. He had hesitated at first because it was a deviation from his patterned schedules, but he finally agreed. He did not ask where they were going or why. Aida, whom he regarded as his mother for he never had one, spoke to him in the language he understood. "When the Queen rises, you will be richly rewarded," she told him.

At speed, it would typically have taken a day to drive to Abydos, but Fayed decided to travel slower and occasionally stop for rests, allowing two of them to sleep while the other watched over the treasure.

On their second day, a fellow driver approached the parked vehicle while they rested near an abandoned petrol station and spoke to Kyky, who was guarding the treasure. Seeing just the young boy in the back of the truck while his colleagues slept in the front, he curiously looked inside.

"What are you carrying?" he asked the startled Kyky.

Kyky did not answer and pulled the sheet covering the loot further across the load.

The driver stepped closer and narrowed his eyes. "Did you not hear me?" he said. "Are you afraid I'll steal your load, boy?"

Fayed, woken from his slumber, jumped from the cab and made his way around to the rear of the truck. He took out a cigarette and offered one to the stranger. "Are there any cheap rooms to rent nearby?' Fayed asked him. "Our employer doesn't pay us enough to stay in a nice hotel."

The stranger pointed across the other side of the filling station. "There's a nice parking area over there," he said. "You can rent a fold-up bed cheaply. It's much better than paying the ridiculous prices the inns want."

"That is not a bad idea," Fayed said. "Can you show me where it is?"

"Certainly," said the man. He and Fayed strolled across the deserted petrol station as Kyky and the innkeeper followed at a distance. When Fayed and the man reached an isolated spot, out of sight from the road, Fayed pulled an obsidian stone, a lapis lazuli, a garnet from his pocket and showed them to the man. The driver eyed the objects and grinned as Kyky put a cord around the man's neck and, assisted by Fayed, they strangled him. The two men rolled the body into a ditch and covered it with pebbles, stones and branches from the vegetation scattered around. The innkeeper's stone face did not twitch as he watched on.

Once they reached the Abydos Temple, the innkeeper proved invaluable. Although the owners of the inn did not carry the mark of the sceptre, there was something mysterious about them. Fayed, who would normally have killed anyone who had outlived their usefulness, decided to allow the innkeeper to live and promised himself to look into the origin of the man and his wife.

"In truth, I shall not be surprised if the inn folds on itself and returns from whence it came," Fayed told Kyky as they watched the mechanical method of the innkeeper as he shifted the loot into the temple, turned around, got into the truck and drove home without a word.

Assim patiently waited until all the treasure had been loaded into the Temple of Nitocris before he stepped free of Fayed's body and struck. As Fayed looked about, momentarily confused by his surroundings, Assim hit him with a club, killing the detective instantly. Kyky watched on, having been warned by his brothers that another murder should occur and in which he could not take part.

However, unbeknown to Assim, Fayed came from an ancient tribe that served Nitocris in her quest for power.

When Assim borrowed Fayed's body to blend in with the present, he did not count on the fact that Fayed could not be vaporised. The detective came from a line of loyal followers, versed in protective amulets for thousands of years. Assim, who could not stay in one realm, was compromised.

Riva

Unseen hands shook Riva. "Wake up, Riva. Wake up, or you are going to die on temple grounds," the female voice said in an effort to wake her up. Riva groaned and put a hand up to her aching head as a lightning bolt of pain shot across it. The amorphous form stood above her, clearly speaking, yet Riva could hear no sound.

"Assim has taken over Fayed's body," the Princess said. "He is stronger in that body. He has set to work rallying followers behind the Queen."

Riva groaned again. She enjoyed the success that the Princess brought about with help from the spirit world, but she did not want to deal with murders and political turmoil.

"I need you to wake up," the Princess insisted. "You must stop the Queen's army, or you will cease to exist." The Princess carried on talking, but Riva, who lay on the ground, ignored her, the pain in her head so intense nothing else mattered. She remembered being struck by someone. Was it Assim?

"Stand up and look into the eyes of the people," the Princess persisted. "They have been taken over by demons. Stand up and look."

Riva sat and glanced at the people inside the temple. She clambered to her feet and climbed on the base of a pillar to gain a better view. She saw the waters of the Nile roiling as if in anger, creating huge waves that smashed against each other as the unworldly currents pulled boats to the bottom of the riverbed and clouds blackened the sky.

"The drought is coming," the Princess said. "The Nile will halt the flow despite Sirius the star urging on the river."

Riva gasped as massive crocodiles invaded the temple, and a man outside the sanctuary screamed as one of the beasts neared. "Help!" he shouted. "Help me, please."

A hippopotamus galloped towards a crowd of people near the Nile bank. Men, women and children were crushed beneath the animal's feet, and others were swallowed up by its enormous mouth.

"What is happening?" someone screamed.

Riva walked out of the temple, watching the puzzled expressions of the natives. Over the next few days, unusual events continued.

The people of Egypt who toiled and worked looked on in confusion at what was happening around them. They fled the danger and called for help.

"The elders can help us," one of them shouted. "They go back to the old days and have been taught the signs. They can tell us how to save ourselves."

A group of people gathered around an old man who sat with his back against a pylon in the Temple of Luxor, his amulets laid out on a table in front of him. "It is the banished queen. She has come to wreak evil. Her demons are upsetting the River Nile, interfering with the rich flow of silt."

The people stopped and listened to him as he continued. "Demons have stopped the water. The lands will be parched."

As Riva's vision continued, she watched on helplessly as the priests, using their most potent potions, attempted to calm the Nile while the wealthy gave offerings of gold and lapis lazuli to ward off the evil. Meanwhile, vegetation wilted in the fields, and as frogs rained down from the skies, a storm of locusts stripped the wheat bare.

Riva, her head still aching, met Steven and John Abel in the adjoining room of the Luxor Hotel. "The Kingdom needs our help," she began. Her face was pale and drawn. Steven and Abel glanced at her and each other.

At first, the writer thought she had devised a new plan for the upcoming franchise. Then he worried that a person, perhaps an ancient politician, possessed her and did not wish to leave. "Riva, are you still in there?" Abel asked. He glanced at Steven when she did not respond. "She appears to be living in two separate worlds at the same time," Abel said to the director as he took hold of the actress. "Riva, you have to come back."

"You will have your story," Riva said, turning to face him. "We have to stop the detective from supplying Nitocris with an army. Then we will have the story.”

John Abel frowned. “That is beyond my job description. Which detective are we talking about?” The writer took hold of her shoulders and stared into her eyes. Riva said nothing, her eyes fixed on something he could not see. He stepped away from her and shook his head. “We have had a good run, but I cannot be part of this charade.”

Riva sighed and turned away from the two puzzled men. Clearly, she had to face the upcoming events on her own.

When the police came knocking at her door the next day, she opened it and stared at the two uniformed officers accompanied by Detective Abanoud. She waved them inside and slumped onto a chair, already knowing what they were going to tell her.

John Abel had been found dead in bed at his hotel. His suitcase had been packed in readiness for him to leave, and he had informed the receptionist the night before to set a wake-up call for his checkout in the morning. But when the receptionist did not receive an answer, she sent the assistant manager to wake him up. There, the hotel employee discovered the body, and the police were summoned.

The offices were confused about the manner of Abel’s death. The weapon could not be found, but next to the body was a sketch. Riva examined the drawing. “It is an ancient sceptre, probably stolen from Memphis.”

Detective Abanoub, who had sat silently while his colleagues questioned Riva, studied her, trying to deduce what she knew. Someone had selected this girl to fix part of the past, and he could not be sure if her life was also in danger.

Rahim

After the police left, Riva dressed and made her way over to the historian Rahim's office. She glanced outside her taxi as it headed through the streets past sprawling temples. As she journeyed, she imagined the ancient Luxor, the people and the sounds.

On reaching Rahim's, she knocked, and the smiling doctor ushered her inside. He listened grimly as Riva recounted what had happened. Rahim had never spirited himself into the ancient realms but had helped those realms from the present time. Greatly respected among many elders in the ancient world, especially those who sought his help, Rahim had spoken to those from the past when they appeared in the present day or spoke to him through dreams, like the great architect Imhotep.

He remembered that one time, the Chief Minister of Cheops, Hemiunu, had appeared and spoken to him in the office, but the spirit did not appear in full regalia, so urgent was the matter that it demanded Rahim's intervention. Hemiunu was deeply trusted by Cheops, to the extent that the mighty pharaoh allowed the minister and confidante to be buried next to him and to enjoy the luxury of the afterlife next to the King.

On another occasion, Rahim had crossed over to the west bank in Luxor to visit the twin Memnon statues and attempted to interpret the harrowing sounds they made when the wind echoed. Deciphering the wind's words was not easy as he stood among the tourists as if taking notes from the guide when, in fact, he was secretly decrypting messages. With the help of Rahim, the ancients aborted harmful interventions within power cycles, thereby maintaining the equilibrium.

"What you are saying," Rahim said to Riva, "is that an invisible wall must be built at the entrance to one of the sanctuaries in Abydos, probably the Osirian chapel." Riva nodded her understanding as Rahim continued. "A barrier which is made of sorcery at the sanctuary of the imposing Temple of Osiris at Abydos will choke the Queen, arresting her movement after we kill her and throw her back. Her spirit must be burnt, and the remains drowned in seawater." The historian smiled as he hung onto his words as if in one of his classrooms.

The Princess appeared, and Riva smiled. "Princess, can your highness bring me some items from Memphis cemetery? We have to work fast. There is only one magic spell that may finish off the Queen and burn her soul. Her remains must never reach the River Nile, or else the freshwater of the ancient river will bring her back to life to trouble the universe."

The Princess's eyes glinted, and she nodded as Riva listed the ingredients required. "I will go immediately," the Princess said.

Egotha – King Of Cobras

That night, the Princess came to Riva in the hotel room in Luxor, bringing a trusted friend. Her husband's sister came from a large family from cities along the Egyptian borders. Egotha, who was almost inseparable from the Princess back in their own world, had come all the way from Nubia to escort the Princess.

The pair had enjoyed many clandestine journeys in time as ethereal beings without the knowledge of their families. Sometimes, they had even possessed the bodies of innocents to run short errands in other worlds. However, these poor innocents who became disoriented when possessed by both the princess and her companion Egotha were generously compensated. The Princess, after releasing herself from the unsuspecting victim, would slip a little gem or a gold piece into the victim's pocket in return for sharing their body, and life returned to normal.

The Princess came to know that gold had a calming effect in the present world to the extent that she enjoyed the furtive looks the innocents gave once they saw the metal tugging at their frail pockets. The Princess would smile, easing her conscience whenever she mischievously borrowed a person's body and soul.

Years previously, Egotha's father had ventured into Nubia on one of his many travels and chanced upon the most beautiful woman he had ever met – a beauty who outshone all others. The dark Nubian woman instantly stole his heart as she fished in the river. He watched as she threw her net again and again until her boat was full of fish. Egotha's father, a warrior from beyond the eastern sea who was tired and hungry, watched as she made her way ashore. She was even more beautiful than Queen Tiye. She did not appear real to him as she glided across the sand once back on land, and he vowed that he would marry her. He introduced himself to her and despite her initial reluctance to have anything to do with the young and handsome soldier, he persisted. Eventually, she succumbed. They married, and within a year, a daughter was born.

Egotha, a pretty little bundle, quickly grew into a strong, young maiden, as pretty as her mother, who loved to adorn herself with make-up. Her eyes shone like two deep pools of water, hypnotically entrancing everyone.

Years earlier, before Egotha was born, a cobra slid inside Egotha's mother's room and bit her. The snake, captivated by the woman, spoke to her through her mind. "You look as if you have blossomed out of a rare flower and are living on the land in the guise of a woman," the snake said. "I can gift you my powers rather than end your life here and now." The snake had never before witnessed such beauty and feeling guilty for what it had done, allowed her to live, imbuing her with unique gifts. Egotha's mother survived, passing on her abilities to her child, and as Egotha matured into a woman, her powers grew.

The Snake Had No Way Of Knowing

The cobra had not always been a snake. In another life, it was a cruel king who came from mountainous terrain in the Far East and served evil spirits of the underworld. His brother, learning of his sibling's dark secret, overthrew him and banished him from court. The King, badly beaten, was thrown out of the palace into the Tigris River and believed dead. The gentle currents of the river carried the unconscious king downstream and into a colony of snakes, where a huge cobra bit him. However, he did not die, and slowly, over time, he changed from a man into a snake. The king-turned-cobra slithered away and found refuge in a cave where it avariciously gathered trophies from tribes it raided. It travelled far and wide, crossing countries and high mountains in eastern regions, before finally settling in the Nubian south.

The fearsome reptile, armed with strength and magic, returned to the palace after its banishment. It found a hard-working builder within the palace walls, etching images on the facades. The angry cobra despised the new designs of his palace commissioned by the usurping brother, who brought in fabled artists to refurbish the court with his own icons. The venomous predator whispered words to the artist and guided the craftsman to carve reliefs of snakes on the palace walls instead.

"What have you done?" the new king said as he entered the pillared hall. The artist, hypnotised and enchanted by the Cobra King, vomited an evil spell over the King, turning him into a lowly grass snake. The horrified guards struck down the artist as the grass snake slithered off. The King cobra, who had been loitering nearby, followed his brother and devoured the usurper.

The Cobra King, relishing its vengeance, moved on through the lands of Phoenicia and Palestine, bidding goodbye to the borders he protected in another life and travelled to Sinai. From the mountains of the land, it crawled to the sea, slid into boats and visited many lands before arriving and settling in Nubia. The people, especially the women, were a sight for sore eyes and the incense to die for. For a while, the cobra scared the natives and helped mercenaries win wars. The predator hypnotised men to do his bidding and ordered the building of a cave adorned with spoils from petty battles, and taught witches hate potions with coiled strings of hair tied in the most unusual knots and adorned with irresistible stones, charmed with ornaments made of braided fur plucked from black coated panthers in the deep south beyond the four Cataracts.

"That complicated charm," the cobra told the witches, "will keep the love goddess Hathor away and your coffers full."

He trained the sorcerers to summon a mob of rogue warriors by telling them to draw unusual tattoos stamped with courage spells on the arms and backs of mercenaries and strong men. Mesmerised, the men fell to their knees and swore allegiance only to him and fought the conflicts the predator itself fomented.

But over time, its potions lost their strength, and the snake renounced its bloody life and commanded the growing mob to distribute their wealth and return to their homes.

The cobra, having outgrown its lust for revenge, deserted the cave and left behind the spoils for the men and the women.

It slithered north, passing a temple built by a pharaoh out of love for his first wife in a village called Abu Simbel. "Love!" sneered the beast.

It slithered to Luxor, a good four hundred kilometres from where it had come until it reached the Temple of Luxor. It arrived on a fateful day, whether by chance or by charms – a day that marked a historic event. A rehearsal took place for the deification of a king, during which a priest was symbolically cleaning the small sacred room along with his servant User.

The snake entered the chamber and was met with a bloody sight. Priest Kaaper, spread on a table, was very nearly dead, and other men lay everywhere, torn or cut to pieces. The King Cobra recognised the remains of a fellow snake, for he understood anger all too well. He looked into the eyes of Priest Kaaper. As they remained like that for a few seconds, the priest recognised the pained expression of the man imprisoned within the cobra. The dying priest, benevolent to the end, read a charm to extract the King from the belly of the beast before his blood drained onto the stone board in the sanctuary room. Kaaper had salvaged the soul of the banished king, giving him back his human form.

The King, humbled by Kaaper's good deed, vowed to do only good. He quickly dressed in the cleanest clothes he could find and left the temple, leaving the dead priest and User, as well as the rest of the congregation, swimming in blood. He could hear the commotion as he made his escape, but he had been given a second chance and did not intend to waste it. Making his way to a skiff moored by the riverbank, where the crew were eating a midmorning break, he paused. The captain of the vessel smiled at this unusual stranger and invited him to eat with them.

Still becoming accustomed to his human form, he joined the men and gratefully accepted their hospitality.

"We are going to Memphis," one of the men said. "If you assist on board, we will give you free passage." He nodded and joined the others when they set sail. In Memphis, the former king and cobra, now just a humbled man, met with Aida. She became his wife and mother of his child, the handsome baby girl Osira.

Riva

Riva's room hosted the strangest ethereal couple, a princess in the accompaniment of Egotha with her hypnotic eyes.

"My powers are not enough to overcome Nitocris," Egotha told the Princess and Riva. "The Queen has more powerful spells and collects and steals from older kingdoms. I need not remind you of the army and the followers she has."

"What if Egotha hypnotises the man who hit me in the temple?" Riva asked. "I have seen him before with the officers. I have had time to see him before my collapse on the temple ground. I think he is possessed by someone close to the Queen. You two, with luck, might be able to overturn the orders given to Fayed by the Queen before he came into contact with her."

"That is possible," Egotha said. "I may have time to hypnotise the detective before he comes in contact with the Queen and order him to enact a spell from one of Rahim's powerful potions to kill her. However, it is not without risk."

The Detective

Over the years, the Queen's dedicated loyalists committed to a resilient system of digging and excavating. Centuries of shovelling rock from a hole in the ground and depositing it outside had resulted in a mile-long cave where the Queen rested. The cave had been further expanded, and a dark city grew to enormous proportions underground. Loyalists met with dissident priests to extol the life they would enjoy when the Queen came to power and settlement grew, annexing a training ground for a dissident army.

In time, the city below became more intricate, replete with military battalions, brigades and divisions. The Queen's followers multiplied, as did her battleground in the labyrinths below the grand Temple of Abydos. She still kept her private quarters and her bath, where she rejuvenated herself and rekindled her waning potions. The bath under the temple was connected with fresh water from the Nile, and the size of her shrine expanded to reach south below the Love Temple in Abu Simbel.

It took hundreds of years to build the city. Nitocris insisted that water springs be dug below the Temple of Abydos, with access to the same fountain from which legitimate kings above received their protective charms. She developed ill feelings towards Ramsis II, who had an unfettered love for the Queen.

She had plans for Abu Simbel and made sure her army remained strongest below the Love Temple. Men in her life admired her ambitious drive for the throne, and some even suggested that she would be a better monarch than a man if they had given her a chance. She promised herself to drown the temple of love that Ramsis built to honour his queen and bring in crawling crocodiles, gigantic and hungry, into the temple grounds to maul builders, priests and anyone who dared approach the temple to serve its king. She looked many times with a broken heart at the indelible details etched with undying love in the temple at Abu Simbel. Even the sun caressed the Queen and her curves on the walls from all directions, greeting worshippers inside the temple walls. The sun would not look at the beautiful Nitocris.

Over the years, Nitocris used the common decorative styles applied in the majestic temples above to beautify her own. Making minor changes, the Queen had the labyrinths covered in sceptres, challenging the beliefs of all kings and deities and placing the emblems of royalty at the bottom of pillars. On temple floors, she carved the faces of kings who shunned her, along with their Apis bulls, the most revered symbol of fertility and strength, to be stepped on by her followers. She enjoyed seeing the filthy faces of ancestors under the feet of commoners while she emerged clean and unblemished from her bath with potent charms. Even the articulated lapidary-styled writing, much revered by the ancients in ceremonial shrines, was re-crafted from left to right, not right to left, to distort the old ways and insult the forefathers. She went further, disrespectfully using hieratic writing in making her own family list, discarding the approved kings' list in the formal hieroglyphic scripts. Her childish acts temporarily dampened her lust for revenge against order and ancestral crafts. She declared war on the beginning of life in the figure of the first deity, Ptah, planner of the universe, plucking the deity's beard and painting him distorted on the temple floor. She ruled in darkness. Her bathing room became her throne. Her washroom overlooked fresh cascading waters from the Nile. She protected herself with potions, giving her false hopes of fertility and an illusory sense of legitimacy. Cursed to be impotent with no claim to the throne, despite all she worked for, she cried herself to sleep.

Fayed saw her cry once in her material form when she transported herself to the present realm to plan a coup against the past. The Queen seethed with rage that he saw her at her weakest point, a mere commoner. She retaliated with such a temper that she threw a sceptre that caught him on his thigh beside his already absent genitals, scarring him gravely across his leg. He still loved and believed in her. Ever since Assim set eyes on Fayed's body to dwell in, thinking he could throw out the original inhabitant, he became a prisoner in that body. Assim failed to cast out Fayed, and now, both were imprisoned. With all the learning he amassed, Assim had picked the wrong body to reckon with.

The Dungeon

A few feet away from the Queen's temple, styled in reverse order from the sanctuaries above, Nitocris ordered the construction of a dungeon, more of a giant cage, with solid metal bars without a gate. Entry was achieved through a hole with two metal handles on top of the cage. Two strong individuals were required to open the cage or an elaborate spell recited by Nitocris to gain access. Inside, the Queen held hideous monsters with plans to unleash the beasts when the stars aligned and the march to the Theban palace under the banner of the sceptre took place.

The usurper's palace had everything needed for her to seize power – a vast array of weapons, prepared potions, and trained soldiers.

"Add a dungeon for my enemies," she ordered. "Use my purple potion to strengthen the sides so no one can escape its walls."

The guards came in many forms. Usually, the younger and weaker ones cooked the most potent potions, making up for their physical inadequacy by preparing the spells to cure, paralyse or encourage the more stubborn of prisoners to tell everything they knew. Other soldiers, the strongest and most imposing, were given additional rations to maintain their physical strength and were even allowed to marry and raise families. A final batch of soldiers – the smartest amongst her army, guarded the grounds and entrance to the temple or gathered information outside.

The city below had expanded to enormous proportions, becoming the nemesis of the good souls who lived above. As rumours of the Queen grew, an increasing number of people were drawn to her, enticed by promises of a secure destiny and riches in the hereafter.

"I shall live in the fortress for now," the Queen said to Assim. "But soon, I shall have it more fortified than the sanctuary of Osiris. I shall take his place and throw his pieces back to the dogs."

Assim stared at her as her eyes, like two pools of blackness, sent a shiver through him. He bowed. "Yes, my Queen."

The Jewels

Fayed moved the jewels, silver, gems and gold into the sanctuary at night to avoid too much attention. The innkeeper and Kyky had stacked the treasures in a store in the sanctuary, close to the Queen's quarters, as Fayed conducted more trips back and forth across Egypt. He started the looting in Saqqara and proceeded to pillage temples along the Nile after Assim separated from Fayed. This seemed to sharpen the senses of the two men, allowing them to detect even the rarest and most difficult to find gems, gold and silverware objects.

Black magic often protected the rarer treasures they found, but despite this, the pair, although often lucky, escaped with their lives. Sometimes, predators would chase the men from the caves, and only the Queen's sophisticated charms saved them.

On another occasion, Fayed was saved by the innkeeper when an invisible being began choking him. The hands had relinquished their hold only when Osira's husband had appeared.

Assim initiated other helpers to catalogue the stolen fortunes and branded the boxes which held them with sceptres to foil any attempt to rob the Queen of her treasure. As the riches arrived, so did the followers, as wealth fed the greed of the newcomers. Assim had his helpers branded with a small sceptre near to their thumbs. A painful procedure which was assuaged by a balm that Fayed administered.

One of the females who carried out the branding and who was popular amongst the village girls approached Assim. "Sire," she said, appealing to his vanity. "The procedure is painful and disfiguring. The village girls love adorning their bodies with tattoos inked with copper. Perhaps this would be better."

Assim smiled, amused by the bold woman. "What are you suggesting?"

"Maybe a tattoo of the sceptre would be more acceptable. It would appeal to their vanity and stop them feeling like cattle, branded by their owners."

Assim agreed and eyed the pretty girl. "What is your name?" he asked.

"Anat," she said.

"Your idea is a good one. I shall reward your wisdom by making you chief marker."

The tattooed design also weaved in magic spells. Its intricate appearance, created with dainty copper tools, greatly appealed to the younger generations, who loved such things without fully understanding the new cult. The lives of the young passed peacefully as long as they ran errands for the cult. On a few occasions, when they caused any delay or if anyone tried to remove the tattoo, the punishment came swiftly. Such kids were found in ditches, hardly recognisable, and the image of the sceptre they tried to remove was indelibly printed all over their poor bodies.

Guards suffered a worse fate if they failed to carry out their duties efficiently. The Queen's wrath became legendary if angered or displeased and she had to be indulged in all aspects of the court life.

Fayed made an example of one of the guards who openly showed dissent. "We have chosen the cult out of our own free will," the Guard said. "I demand less stringent measures. Why do children have to die if the errand takes a little more time? Inform the Queen of our demands." The strongly built man came from the newest batch of followers in Abydos. "I have vowed my commitment to the Queen," he continued, "but I am troubled by doubts."

Assim, who was inwardly seething, remained outwardly calm, entranced the man, burnt incense and read chants as he stared at the doubter. The man collapsed as his body crumbled, and precious fluids poured from him until he finally turned to ash. Only a little red worm remained, which Fayed crushed underfoot. Then, he burnt the worm to make sure it never found its way to the afterlife. On hearing what had happened to their friend and colleague, the others bowed their heads to the new order, sealing their fate.

The innkeeper, always stone-faced, watched on impassively as the horrific punishments were meted out. But these random acts of violence had the desired effect, sending a strong message to the Queen's followers that once committed, they could not have a change of heart.

Nitocris continued to gain ground as her dark powers increased, yet she still had to wait. To rule, she had to destroy the tablet of kings, which did not include her name. Then, one day, she had an idea. "Perhaps," she said to Assim, "I can bribe my way through the priests of Osiris and become a deity rather than a queen?" She grinned, and Assim studied his Queen, whose eyes resembled those of a demon.

Fayed finally completed the transfer of goods after six months. However, on his journey from Memphis to Abydos, he still found time to plunder more cemeteries in Memphis and Amarna, where even more exquisite finds were located, ably assisted by his tireless assistants, who travelled back and forth many times. In the process, he acquired further helpers who he trained to loot and rob the innocents. He rewarded the newcomers with gold, a tattoo featuring a sceptre and a promise to meet the Queen. "She alone can gain you higher positions in the afterlife," he told them.

As more and more treasure made its way back to the Queen's palace, an increasing number of rooms were built to house it all. The dungeon expanded, too, with wickedness, crooked beings, potions, demons, protesters and all things bestial. The dark city braced itself against famine with silos to keep grain in one section in case of an imminent attack by the King's army. Under the Queen's orders, Fayed built a safe beside her bath, which lay right behind the throne room, to keep the most treasured spoils of dead royalty stolen from graves over many years.

The Queen used every method at her disposal to gain information. Her informants, in past days, adopted cunning techniques to gain access to palace grounds, even returning a trinket or two of what they had stolen to the palace's chief treasurer. But some fell foul of this when the jewels they had stolen were recognised.

"Kill the slave and make an example of him," the chief treasurer said. When the executioner finished off the servant, the trinket was returned to the happy nobleman. However, despite setbacks, the cult continued to gain information about kings and their armies flowing all the way to Abydos.

At times, the cult member who infiltrated the palace would form a relationship with servant girls to gather information. Assim insisted, however, on specific rules that informants must not be allowed to engage in any courting unless necessary.

"Majesty," he said to the Queen, "we have to be careful to whom we assign the methods of courting. If we are going to gather ever more valuable information, we must seek to have our people form relationships with the princesses."

"Aren't you Seth personified, Assim," the Queen said.

"Mistress," he said. "Our officers have to act as if their devotion is devoid of any motive and seek nothing in return. In a way, they are not lying, for they seek only words to topple their king and put you in charge." The Queen nodded her understanding, and Assim continued. "I shall put a class of trained lovers on a higher plain than the brute guards who we ordered to marry and father loyalists to Your Majesty. That way, no information will be beyond us."

The Queen listened to her apprentice and lowered her head. "If I was genuinely loved for myself, I may have spared the kingdom." The Queen screamed and looked skywards, then fell to the ground weeping.

Assim ran to the Queen but stopped short because she did not care for the love he had for her. His love would never be good enough. He hopelessly desired the Queen, who despised what he had become – an Assim, Fayed hybrid.

She waved him away, recognising the lust within his eyes. "I have no need for you," she said. "You are an abomination. I will dispense with you without batting an eye when you outlive your purpose, should I desire. Never let me catch you looking my way again." She stood and turned away from him. "You must know your place."

Osira

If the innkeeper had learned anything that mattered from his wife, it would have been the art of survival, and he would have been able to convince Fayed that he would be helpful in the future. For his part, the detective knew where the innkeeper and his family lived. The innkeeper feared for his wife, whom he doted on, but Osira, a fighter and sorcerer, knew how to take care of herself.

Osira lived between two separate realms just like her parents, a secret she had not yet divulged to her husband. In the other realm, she picked up a position at a temple but preferred working in the kitchen. The cooking area provided the resourceful Osira with an ideal place to try out potions. Once inside, she controlled almost everyone except perhaps the senior priests, who were cleverer. But then, magicians recognised one another and might need each other on occasion. She, too, had plans for her little kingdom. She might decide to build a realm from falling stars and an entourage of beings, a type of kingdom in the south along the banks of the Nile. After all, Osira descended from a warrior king-turned-cobra.

Riva

Rahim laboured with books and potions to find the key to end the era of Nitocris as Riva waited in his office for a breakthrough.

"I have to visit the Queen's original birthplace to discover her weak spot," Rahim said.

"You are on a first-name basis with Hemiunu," she said. "He gifts you priceless relics, and you have helped him on many occasions. It is time you pull in a favour. Don't you agree?" Riva stood.

Rahim studied the young woman. She was right. The Queen's origins were missing from all historical documents. "Perhaps you are right," he said as he opened the book of spells. "I will call on the chief vizier. My friend, Nitocris, is coming with an army of young recruits versed in spells to take over both past and present. She has to be stopped. I beseech you to seek an audience with King Pepi about the dangers facing his son."

As an advisor to Cheops, Hemiunu was the only one permitted to confer with King Pepi in an ethereal setting outside their body forms. Kings, advisors and a few retainers met across the ether when any of the realms came under attack. Hemiunu might be the only politician whom Pepi would listen to. But Hemiunu was growing weak. Travelling across realms to settle scores and help keep the peace was having a massive cost to his health. Cautious rulers refused to meet on the borderline realms to preserve their own strengths, delegating instead their most trustworthy assistants to go on these exhaustive voyages. Time travel weakened their powers, making it impossible for some to enjoy the fruits of the afterlife, but Hemiunu consented to sacrifice his strength for the good of the realm. However, by now, he had grown too weak to oblige Rahim.

"My spirit is tired, my friend," he said, "I can no longer make the journeys across nor stop ethereal demons from disrupting our crucial gatherings." Hemiunu, dying, confided in Rahim that he no longer powered the gatherings. "The meetings scared the dark forces, bonding minds and souls, a union of practice, history and legitimate rights to the lands in the forty-two Nomes of Egypt."

"I beg you," Rahim pleaded. "Is there someone you will pass the torch to? Nitocris is scared of the union of kings across time zones. Those kings and queens are connected by blood and trade routes and bounded by the tablet of kings. If no one helps, we are spelling disaster into the present."

Hemiunu sighed. "I shall send a trusted disciple to confer with an advisor to Pepi, both in ethereal forms. The damage of Nitocris may be contained, but blood will spill. It is written. Visit the sanctuary of Pepi in Memphis up north. You have the key. I shall be there, one way or another. Trust your find, my friend, for you will have the key in the ashes."

Hemiunu had offered Rahim a clue to be found in Memphis, but his ominous words left Rahim with a heavy heart. The historian packed a small bag with potions and one ancient book of spells and headed to the pyramid of Pepi in Memphis with Riva.

In Memphis

Rahim and Riva took a plane to Cairo, the capital of Egypt. From there, they rode to the necropolis in Saqqara, where King Pepi I lay in state.

"I am not interested in the pyramid of Pepi I," he said to her.

Using a magnet and a compass, he directed himself towards a now non-existent path which extended in ancient times from the pyramid via a causeway to the Nile. "This is the same path that Nitocris once used to escape. She hid inside a priest's robe, a disciple of hers, after stabbing the legitimate King Pepi II. She then assumed the throne in the powerful capital, Memphis, some three kilometres from the tomb of Pepi I."

Riva listened intently as she followed Rahim, guided by his trusty magnet and compass, which he had inherited from his adoptive parents. "The Queen has become drunk with the power. She may let her guard down, but we may only have one chance."

Nitocris, by now, had covered her body in sceptre-styled tattoos. Each tattoo had drawn blood from her silky skin, and each line had opened a pore into which Nitocris uttered protective chants that kept her invisible to foes. Before she had murdered the King, Nitocris had approached him to seek his counsel on the matter of her marriage. His guards allowed her safe passage to his throne after the King had granted permission. She was, after all, his daughter. She strolled towards the throne, carrying a cloak over one arm which concealed the weapon beneath. Then, as she neared him, she charged and plunged it into his heart.

The personal guards had instantly risen with their spears raised high to kill her, but she disappeared. Nitocris had blocked their passage with an invisible marble slab against which they crashed and fell. This was time enough for her to make her escape by the way she came. In the commotion, she pulled the cloak on to disguise herself and hurried away. A disciple who was waiting for her shielded her with his body and led her through a walkway to the King's pyramidal tomb. By the time the spell broke and the marble slab vaporised, Nitocris was gone. Once free of the palace, the disciple won her more time as he fought the guards until he was cut down and lay dying in a massive pool of his own blood.

Nitocris made her way to the mortuary temple prepared for the stately burial of the King upon his death and hid there, plotting her next move.

While King Pepi II's body was embalmed and made ready for the ceremonial burial, Nitocris and a few of her acolytes made a temporary home by the Nile, close to the causeway that led from the burial ground to the river. She cleaned and anointed herself and waited, ready to move back to the palace to assume power.

In her rapturous lust for power, Nitocris made a mistake that cost her the crown. She failed to realise that her absence from the palace after the murder marked an error in judgment. She left the palace vacant long enough for the nomarchs to grab power of Memphis. Nitocris closed her small window of opportunity, opening the gates of hell on a kingdom devastated by drought, famine and power struggles. The news came to Nitocris as she rose in style from her bath by the river. The ceremonial march that carried King Pepi II to his temporary resting place had taken place and petty officials assumed command of the royal palace while Nitocris was still soaking in her bath. Once dressed, she was hurriedly briefed by her guards as she stood by the dressing table with all her potions. She had been named as a traitor and would be annulled from the historical list of the kingdom.

That night, furious, Nitocris screamed and smashed her entire assortment of alabaster jars. One, containing a flammable substance, quickly engulfed her room, and unable to escape, Nitocris was burned beyond recognition. Her screams resounded around the building as her guards fought to put out the flames. The murder of the King had been avenged.

Rahim sat back and looked at Riva as he finished recounting the story.

"Nitocris came close to completing the waiting cycle to rebuild her destroyed soul and body," he said. "The respite has lasted thousands of years until now. While burning to death, she vowed in her screams to return and to remain for eternity." He stopped and searched for the spot where the Queen burnt, for signs of any gem attached to her body at the time. He tracked the same route Nitocris took with a few mercenaries and renegade priests leading to the river. "She took this way," he said to Riva, "because she wanted to hide but still remain close to the temple.

The pair moved slowly, guided by the instruments in Rahim's pouch. He reasoned that there should be pot shards leftover from cooking vessels or alabaster vases that carried some of the Queen's potions too potent to be in fragile glass jars. Some potions were known to be stored in obsidian vessels or even gold to protect the contents within.

"We must rest," Rhaim said. "I am not as young as I once was. We will eat." They sat and stretched out a piece of cloth where cheese, bread and fruit were lain.

"No reason to take chances," Rahim said. "It is too early to find clues to the whereabouts of the Queen. Unless your friend, our friendly Princess, comes to the rescue."

Riva shook her head. "She is not here. Maybe she will come."

Rahim nodded and removed a potion from his bag. "This will blur the vision of the guards or demons should we need to hide."

The Memphis Find

An hour remained before sunset when visitors at the mortuary temple trickled out of the royal tombs, fatigued and nourished by the information from the past. Rahim enjoyed the time before the sunset as he ate his cheese, drank his Turkish coffee and stretched his legs. He turned sharply as the magnet shook and the compass fluctuated madly – the needle spinning wildly in circles as pebbles nearby jumped. The ground rumbled, and the sky darkened into the sort of night that welcomes unpleasant forces. Rahim came from Luxor and was not accustomed to colder nights, so he pulled the collar of his jacket up high and strode off. Riva followed him, searching around for signs of the Princess or Egotha as she struggled to keep up.

An elderly security guard waited impatiently for the tourists to exit as Rahim and Riva slowed and lagged behind the leaving throng. The watchman grumbled to himself, eager to get home to his wife's hot rice mix of fried eggplants soaked in tomatoes and onions, swimming in butter and minced meat – a dish he adored. As the others left, he approached Rahim and Riva and waved them on. "Come on, you two," he said. "I have a home to go to even if you haven't."

Rahim smiled as he spotted a blue stone on the ground. "Sorry, we'll be on our way now." The lapis lazuli lay nearby, and Rahim allowed his bag to drop from his grasp. As the guard looked towards the exit as the tourists jostled with one another, Rahim scooped up the gem and slipped it inside his pocket.

"It is very peaceful in the old city," Rahim said to the guard. "We shall return tomorrow to continue the tour. Have a good night."

The watchman closed the door as the couple left and locked it. He smiled. The older man was a sorcerer. He had inherited a little knowledge of determining real magicians from his parents. He frowned as he trudged back to his office, remembering how he had almost lost a son to bad magic and vowed ever since to stay away from the lives of ancestors, especially those resting in Sakkara.

However, he had recognised the goodness in Rahim and had no plans to stand in his way. Whatever he was up to.

Back at the hotel, Riva and Rahim met for dinner to discuss their next move. Rahim showed her the stone he had found. It looked like any other blue lapis lazuli from any gem store. However, this one trembled when exposed to the magnet and the compass. After finishing their meal, they left the restaurant and made their way to Riva's annexed living quarters in case the Princess decided to show up.

Within minutes, the Princess appeared. "I see you have found the stone," she said. The other two jumped. "You are very close to finding pieces of the renegade queen," she continued.

"She is running out of lives," Rahim said. "This is my interpretation of the tremors in Saqqara. Some of the stones trembled, but others sank into the desert. She died and was interred for many years. Magic has its limitations. The usurper may be waging her final battle to win eternity."

"I believe," the Princess said, "that the lapis lazuli was the last of the pieces left behind by Nitocris when she escaped the King's guards. She settled in Abydos and regrouped her army all over Egypt with Fayed's help."

Rahim nodded. I believe she could be cornered in her barracks and defeated." Rahim stood. "We need to get back to the mortuary temple at dawn before anyone turns up." He smiled at the Princess. "Perhaps your Highness could give me cover."

The Princess returned his smile. She enjoyed the courteous manner of the historian, which he exhibited at all times. "Yes," she said.

Before dawn, the Princess, Rahim, and Riva made their way through a backway to the necropolis, which was revealed to them by the Princess. Rahim took note of the route, being all too familiar with the efforts of pharaohs to hide their treasures and not wanting to get lost. "If the Queen is building an empire underground," he said to Riva, "the best and simplest plan will be to seal all openings leading to the city below with a lid of eternal magic and bury her there."

Riva frowned. "Can you do that?"

The Princess, on the other hand, understood. "Egotha can fetch the potion of the cobra which her father has used."

Rahim paused. "I will call Hemiunu. He can send me the rosemary seeds of goodness with one of his trusted apprentices."

The historian carried on again before stopping abruptly. In front of the three of them was a small pebble mound, likely man-made. As the sun rose higher, casting rays across the mound, Rahim cleared away the pebbles, revealing a tunnel beneath. With Riva and the Princess following closely, they made their way along the passage, which opened into a bunker.

"Search for anything belonging to the Queen," he said. "We must hurry. It is not long before the gates to the temple open.

Rahim felt the ground tremble. Clearly, there was still evil lurking under its sands, posing a threat to his secret plan to attack the Queen in her headquarters. The earth was reacting to the magnet and compass in his bag. "We must be quick," he said. "She may know what we plan."

For Rahim, each delay to end the Queen's reign brought the forces of Nitocris closer to the throne as their numbers increased like rats inside her bunkers. Her sunken, rancid dungeons and hidden stairways behind fake doors in Abydos threatened to overhaul the seat of power in Thebes and the stalwart efforts of many pharaohs.

Once he had found what they were looking for, a charred remnant from a silver sceptre, he held it aloft. "I have what we require," he said. "We must go now."

Only one hour remained before the sun fully rose, giving them away. They had to escape back from where they had come, but as they headed towards the tunnel leading to the surface, the ground beneath Rahim's feet cracked, and he fell. Riva dashed forward and grasped his hand as he slipped into the crevice. She pulled, attempting to get Rahim clear before he was lost. Someone appeared in front of her, and Riva almost allowed him to drop. It was a beautiful woman with the cruellest eyes Riva had ever seen. The apparition held a sceptre in her hand, but as quickly as it materialised, it was gone. Rahim was slipping, and Riva winced as she held on. The security guard appeared and gripped Rahim's arm, and along with Riva, they pulled Rahim free. Rahim and Riva sat on the ground, panting from their exertions.

"How did you know we would be here?" Riva said to the guard.

He nodded towards Rahim. "I read it in that man's eyes," he said. "You are looking for something. So, naturally, you will come back."

"How did you know about the secret entrance?" Rahim said.

The guard smiled. "I know every entrance and exit inside the temple." He studied the pair and thought, what were they thinking? Of course, he had access to the back door, one of the many hidden entrances his family had made a fortune from over the years. Centuries ago, his tribe had found and sold relics, a crime they paid for in curses that took away their first child in each of their extended families ever since. He had decided, after going home to eat, to see his five children and his caring wife, that he would return. He had assessed that Rahim and Riva would have to show up early to search. He woke at five, headed to the necropolis, and stationed himself unseen with binoculars by the pyramid of Seti II. He felt the ground tremble before Rahim did and ran as fast as he could.

"I must open," he said, and with that, he left them, assured that he had made the right choice.

Rahim and Riva raced back to the hotel, gathered their clothes and hurried to the airport, back to Luxor, and Rahim's office. The find required immediate attention before it vaporised. The sceptre had something on it. "Look," Rahim said, holding the sceptre up. "I think some of the Queen's scorched skin is attached to it."

"To salvage a relic after one thousand years is a miracle," Riva said. "Let alone intact after a fire."

Rahim studied the relic, too engrossed to notice the Princess and Egotha appear. When he looked up, he smiled. "Could you examine this," he said, handing the Princess the blue gem he had found in the cemetery.

Egotha took the object from the Princess, bowed and placed it down on the desk as Rahim, and the Princess exchanged glances. Egotha scrutinised the find.

"We will leave you to it," Rahim said. "Riva and I have not eaten. We will return soon."

Riva followed Rahim as she thought about her next movie. With John Abel dead, the studio would have to assign another writer. Steven was waiting patiently for her return. But how long would he wait?

Rahim took Riva to a traditional and popular restaurant on the banks of the Nile, enjoying a delicious meal of grilled minced meat, lamb chops, stuffed entrails, breaded sheep brain fried in oil, salad with onions and vinegar, minted rice cooked in meat oil and freshly baked Egyptian brown bread. By the time they headed back, the pair were fully sated.

Egotha sat at the table, waiting for the results of the potions. She arranged the potions based on their efficacy, much to Rahim's dismay, who preferred to work haphazardly. His parents desperately tried to mend his ways, but he could not work except when all potions across time spans filled his desk.

"I dislike all this order," he had told his parents. "The untidiness confuses thieves."

His mother laughed. "Any thief will feel sorry for you, my dear son. They may even tidy up for free."

Egotha looked up at Rahim and Riva as they stood nearby.

"I have prepared this mixture of ground coral and fresh rosemary leaves among other demon-repellant potions," she said. She handed Rahim a small linen purse with writings on it. "I have decayed ancient skin and a lapis lazuli gem, which my father found in the cemetery in Saqqara," she continued. "In order for Nitocris to vaporise for good, the contents inside the pouch, along with the little remains I have extracted, must be washed in the sacred Theban Lake at the back of Karnak Temple. Once the water touches the recipe, burn it in a crucible, purse, and all, collect the cleansed potion and throw it at the Queen. If any of it touches the ethereal or physical form that has the misfortune to be occupied by the Queen, it will destroy her."

"Where can we find the Queen inside the labyrinth?" Riva said.

"How can we get close enough to her?"

"Finding her is the easy part," Egotha explained, addressing Rahim most of the time. "The potion I have cooked will guide you to her presence, and your magnet, compass and lens will do the rest." She sighed. "The difficult part is getting close. The Princess can do that because her royal blood gives her certain privileges. The usurper cannot easily hurt her because she comes from a legitimate line of rulers." Egotha thought for a moment before adding, "If the Princess is at risk, send word to her father through chief architect Hemiunu when it is time. He will help."

Rahim nodded his understanding and looked down at the table which Egotha had rearranged. He was impressed but said nothing. She had sorted the jars according to the severity of the demonic issues and historical relevance. Rahim was jolted from his musings as the Princess stiffened and the desk shook, causing jars to crash onto the floor. A small fire erupted, which the Princess quickly extinguished.

"I shall need to bring Nitocris to the surface," Rahim said. "Not too much, just enough to choke her with my own additives."

Egotha nodded approvingly. "Then sweep the ashes of Nitocris below the manhole, sealing her fate eternally underground."

"But what if the manhole is found?" Riva said. "Will the Queen be free again?"

"The entire presence of temple and lid will cease to exist once the Queen is locked below and touched by my spell," he said. "Like any medicine, I shall have to heal the earth around the manhole for a few years with potent herbs to make sure the evil never returns. The difficult part is to lure the Queen above ground, at least her head. It is always the head that settles the war. We have to move." Rahim snatched up his pouch, put it in his pocket and walked to the door.

The Battle For History

Riva and Rahim made their way to the Temple of Karnak, as the Princess and Egotha followed close by and waited until nightfall. Rahim removed his prepared potion and soaked it in the sacred water at the back of Karnak.

As Nitocris's army readied themselves in Abydos, her undercover loyalists, who were deployed everywhere, waited to show their true colours.

Riva stared over at the lake as she remembered the monster. Rahim, sensing her discomfort, placed a reassuring hand on her arm. "Not to worry," he said. "I have brought the beast's favourite meal to calm its spirit." He opened his backpack and showed her the cooked sweet potatoes and carrots drenched in honey and oil.

Rahim summoned the monster, using himself as bait. The monster emerged from the water and slowly crept towards Rahim, waiting with a potion in one hand and a food bundle in the other. The monster took the food and then disappeared back into the water.

Riva watched in awe as the enormous creature slid beneath the surface. Rahim took the small pouch containing the spell from Egotha, dipped it several times into the lake, and then administered his own potion. "We will not be bothered by the creature now," he said. He took the pouch, emptied the wet contents into a crucible, and set fire to it. The ingredients burned, leaving a small blue mass, which Rahim scooped up and put into a clean linen purse similar to Egotha's original one. "We must hurry," he said, and the four of them headed out of the temple the same way they had come.

Riva and Rahim dined at the hotel and agreed to meet early to catch the bus to Abydos, thereby avoiding movements that might alert spirits when they neared the battle scene.

Riva had fallen into a deep sleep when she was awoken by heavy pounding on the door to her bedroom. She sleepily opened the door, and Rahim strode inside. Riva glanced at the clock. It was midnight. "What's up?" she said, yawning.

"I have a brilliant idea, and I cannot wait until tomorrow."

"I'm listening."

Rahim sat. "I have figured out a method of approaching the Queen through the manhole. The potion must touch the usurper in her material form. The Queen, as vile as she is, has total disregard for human life. She probably lives in the body of an unassuming victim." He opened his bag and pulled out a canvas roll, which he lay on the table and unrolled. Inside were several glass tubes with a sharp point. "Each of these," he said, pointing at the tubes, "has enough potion to kill the Queen. This is how we'll administer it."

Riva picked up one of the makeshift darts, and Rahim took it from her. "Be careful," he said.

"How can you be sure that the glass darts will pierce the Queen's body?" she said. "What if she escapes when she senses the danger and finds another victim?"

"The glass will self-destruct on impact," he said. "The potion coming into contact with her body will be enough. I will take steps to dull the Queen's sense of danger." Rahim reopened his bag and drew out a model of the crown of King Menes, who united Egypt. "When the Queen sees this powerful emblem, she will want it for herself. We will be ready with the darts when she appears. I have brought a sceptre, too." He reached inside his bag again and pulled out the sceptre. "Together, they will be irresistible to her."

Riva frowned. "Are you sure this will work?"

"We are taking a great risk," he said. "I cannot say for certain that it will work, but we have no choice." Rahim stood. "I am sorry I disturbed you. I will see you in the morning." Rahim patted Riva's arm, then left.

Riva was comforted by Rahim's conviction to triumph over evil. If only she could make a script to profit from her wild adventure. She smiled.

Fayed's Jewels

Egotha stared at Rahim as he slept. She and the Princess knew that Rahim had borrowed the ancient Egyptian crown and sceptre from Fayed. Rahim, who knew Fayed, his weaknesses, and his family, took a deep breath and gambled on winning over the detective's already broken soul.

Fayed had found the Queen's sceptre in the cemetery at Saqqara during his first trip to rob tombs and collect a fortune at the Queen's behest. Around that time, Assim scoured the precinct to take over the body of an already broken man, going about his task in both realms. In the past, he served the Queen, and in the present, the precinct until finally, it was only the Queen he served. Assim, being the master of wizards, had inhabited Fayed throughout the treasure hunt. He acted spontaneously, tore a piece of his shirt and covered the sceptre to disguise what he had found. The Queen, in anger, had hurt him in his thigh when he witnessed her crying. As the pain in his leg increased and the wound festered, he decided to visit his childhood friend Rahim, who he hoped would heal it with his masterful compounds. While Kyky and the innkeeper were hauling the treasure in the truck to Abydos, he detoured. "Drop me off in Luxor," Fayed said. "I have to run an errand for the Queen." He instructed his helpers to go to the temple at Abydos. "They will do the rest," he said to Kyky and the innkeeper. "Then come back to pick me up, and we shall continue to move the remaining items. Both of you will be richly rewarded."

They left him close to the river near Luxor and continued on to Abydos. Frail and hardly able to stand upright, Fayed travelled by boat to his old friend's house. The boatman suspiciously eyed the cloth-covered sceptre in Fayed's hands. "Are you all right, Detective?" he asked.

Fayed, well known in the vicinity as an able police officer, did not look his usual self to the rower but more like a thief escaping punishment.

"Yes, yes," Fayed said. "I'm fine."

As they continued on, Fayed drifted off and inadvertently

allowed the boatman to see what he was concealing. The boatman looked on greedily at the glimmering gold object encrusted with jewels. A large wave splashing against the side of the boat woke Fayed from his slumber. Seeing the boatman eyeing his treasure, he quickly re-wrapped it in the cloth and stood. "We are almost here," he said as the boat neared the jetty.

Fayed understood greed, and as the boatman manoeuvred his vessel, he waited. "Thank you," he said to the boatman as he joined him. "You have been very kind, my friend," Fayed said, handing the boatman several notes. "Can you dock the boat in the shade beside the sycamore tree over there, brother? I must wait, and the sun is killing me."

"Of course," the boatman said as Fayed closed his eyes. His hands gripped tightly onto the sceptre.

The two men waited until night fell and Fayed asked the boatman to take the boat across to the other bank. He turned and was unfastening the boat when Fayed brought the sceptre down on his head. He slumped to the floor dead as a pool of blood formed around him. Fayed acted quickly. Although hampered by his injury, he wrapped the body in a large quarry sack, added heavy stones and dropped the dead man over the side. He then rowed the boat further down the strait and hid the vessel amongst trees. That should buy me some time, he thought. He clambered from the boat and limped his way from the dock. Still clutching the sceptre, he made his way to Rahim's.

"You do not have much time, Fayed," Rahim told his friend when he saw his injury.

The detective, once the best at his job, understood that Nitocris would have no use for him in his present condition. Fayed handed the sceptre to Rahim, who placed it on his desk and began treating the injured man.

Once finished, Rahim looked at his friend. "I have done all I can," Rahim said. "I have administered a death balm to chase out the spirit that inhabits you."

Fayed nodded wearily. "Thank you, my friend."

Assim's soul gave life to the dying detective and took from his own. Fayed might have lost his way to darkness, but he lived yet to atone.

Trip To Abydos

When Riva stepped off the bus to Abydos, unseen hands grabbed her and knocked her to the ground. Rahim and several passers-by ran to her aid, but the assailants could not be found. Rahim took her by the arm and led her away from the bemused onlookers. "Clearly," Rahim said to her, "the Queen has sent her messengers to stop us." Rahim paused and looked directly at Riva. "Are you all right?" he said. Riva nodded, and they walked across the sandy path to the magnificent construct, where they slipped into the shadows and waited.

When darkness arrived, Rahim and Riva hurried into the temple. The guards were still on duty and ignored the pair. A few shook their heads as if they knew the challenge that awaited them.

"Nothing remains a secret along the banks of the Nile," Rahim said.

"They know why we are here?" Riva said.

"Yes," he said. "Most of the guards will have witnessed strange occurrences within the temple walls. They will have heard incomprehensible sounds at night, particularly during a full moon. They know not to meddle in such things."

As they continued on, other guards helped them as much as they dared. Some opened doors and allowed them unhindered passage. In truth, most of them owed him favours for helping relatives touched by dark forces. Rahim smiled as he passed one particular young guard at the gate of the temple of Abydos. He remembered healing his mother's injured face. Years ago, Rahim arrived at the humble dwelling when the guard was still a boy. Using one of his special ointments, Rahim was able to remove her facial scar. The guard's mother, hideously scarred – one of many victims hurt by the dark forces – just for being good. But it was the name of Nitocris, the fatal charmer who bent people to her will, which struck fear into all of them.

The young guard guided Rahim and Riva inside the Temple of Abydos and to the sanctuary. "Good luck," he said to Rahim and handed him a bag. "I have brought you cheese, fresh bread, some grapes, and water." He pulled a thermos from the bag and gave it to Riva. "Mint tea," he said. "With plenty of sugar. The way you like it. Drink it while it is still hot." He wished them well again and then hurried away.

Smoking Out The Queen

The war came to Abydos as natives of the ancient cities along the Nile bank whose families went way back nodded in silence. Migrants could not understand as the ground shook beneath them, heralding the coming of the Queen.

Abydos, the pantheon of deities, replaced in power by Thebes, had a special place in the heart of Riva. She had always enjoyed filming her scenes in the temple's courtyards. As night crept in, Rahim and Riva sat on a bench beside the remnants of food and the empty thermos, readying themselves for the inevitable. The moon shed its brightest light on the manhole lying at the centre of the open courtyard facing the internal sanctuary, and silence reigned except for the subtle subterranean waters rippling gently beneath in tunnelled caves.

Rahim glanced down at the crown of Menes and the sceptre he had brought along and gathered them up before securing the items to his hips with a thick leather strip made of cobra skin. The makeshift belt, which had been sprinkled with aromatic herbs and spice, with a bright copper tip and buckle, glistened.

While waiting, Rahim had read a few chants from the Book of the Dead over the belt that now held the relics to slow the Queen's attack and keep the trophies out of her reach.

Rahim and Riva looked up as a small twister, as high as an average person and coloured gold and blue, moved towards the bench where they sat, raising pebbles off the ground and breaking the silence with a hissing sound sending the mortals off the bench along with the thermos.

Rahim struggled to his feet. "Nitocris," he said as Riva joined him. "She is trying to replace King Seti I at his coronation while receiving his vows from the deity of writing, Thoth, and register her name instead."

Riva gasped. "What will happen?"

"If she succeeds," he said, "it will be impossible to eliminate her name from the tablet of kings, and she will be legitimate."

"Why are you only telling me this piece of news now?" she said. "We could have changed tactics and searched for the tablet and kept the book safely away from her. That would have been much easier than facing a monster with dark sorcery."

Rahim sighed. "How can I explain?" He picked up the Book of the Dead and opened it. "I found out when I read from the Book of the Dead and sprinkled incense to reveal messages beneath. It is challenging to get into the thoughts of a dead person, a wizard desperate for power. Nitocris is aware of the potion we have, and she is asking spirits to find a legitimate path to eternity other than the tablet of kings. We shall prevail. I will stick to the plan." He smiled at Riva and patted her arm. "You have done enough. You have to leave." Rahim closed the Book of the Dead and readied himself.

Riva shook her head. "I will not leave you to face her alone."

Rahim made sure the belt he wore was wrapped tightly around his waist and the spell of Egotha was still in his pocket. "Very well," he said. "I believe I have created my most dangerous potion yet," he said, patting the pocket that held the poison darts.

As the pair headed off, the sky changed colour, giving way to a cloud formation of Nitocris's face as the moon took on a reddish hue. Whirlwinds swirled around Rahim and Riva, forcing them onto the ground. Sandstorms were whipped up around them, filling the hall with a sea of sand. At the centre of the melee, a woman in a white robe appeared, accompanied by guards cramming the hall. Despite the storm, the ethereal images stood their ground behind the Queen, and the sceptre fell from Rahim's grasp. Guards moved towards the stricken figure as he desperately felt for the poison darts. Riva took refuge from the onslaught behind a pillar and watched on desperately as Rahim gripped his darts.

Nitocris caught sight of the sceptre on the ground, and her hand transformed into fangs, moving towards her prize. Rahim watched through partially closed eyes as the sand whipped up by the storm assaulted them. At least he had managed to lure the Queen from her redoubt, which was more than he had hoped for. Nitocris moved forward, reptilian tail swishing behind her. Rahim fired a dart and then another, both of which found their mark piercing the

Queen. She roared as she realised what had happened and lashed out at her assailant with her tail. The Queen halted and screamed in agony as she looked at her slowly disappearing form. Her shrieks were ear-piercing as the clouds above returned to normal and the moon turned white again. Nitocris's fangs closed around Rahim's neck as he fired another dart, but then, as she remembered the sceptre, she loosened her grasp on the historian and reached for it again. But as she stretched a claw-like hand, the sceptre shot forward and embedded itself in her chest – the tip of which pierced her heart. The Queen briefly glowed red before collapsing into a pile of ash.

When the dust settled, Riva, who had watched the era of Nitocris coming to an end from her hiding place, ran to Rahim. He lay on the ground, ice-cold, with a bluish vapour coming from his mouth. Riva picked up a torch hanging on the walls and tried to warm the stricken man. From nowhere, images of ancient priests appeared, marching towards Rahim carrying pouches.

The unearthly congregation, led by a senior Priest, Yuf, hurried to the side of the fallen historian, giving him their undivided attention. The priest gently moved Riva aside and beckoned to one of the assistants to collect the torches and build fires in crucibles to warm the historian. He ordered the burner on the desk to be close to him as he burned the stones they had brought to heal Rahim in mind and soul. Yuf created a magnetic field that chased away the demons who surrounded Rahim. For what seemed like an eternity to Riva, the Priest and his helpers worked to revive Rahim, applying balms and ointments until he was breathing normally. They stepped back, and Rahim opened his eyes.

Yuf then turned his attention to the fate of Nitocris, ordering his helpers to gather up the ash from the defeated Queen. In a corner of the hall, the Princess appeared, lying dead on the floor where Nitocris had died.

"Our young Princess has given her life to save the realms," Yuf said. "She valiantly stabbed the Queen with the sceptre, dying from the venom erupting from the mouth of the usurper." The priest shook his head sadly for the loss of the young Princess. "We must honour her," he said.

Before departing, Yuf removed a lid from a jar and allowed a vapour to emerge. This he blew towards Rahim to make sure that the friend of Hemiunu continued to heal. Rahim climbed to his feet, and the ethereal priests vanished from whence they came into the past, except for the priest, Yuf and his most loyal assistant. The priest moved towards the Princess, recited some words to help her soul cross over into the afterlife, and then ordered the assistant to carry her body and join the rest of the assembly.

Riva watched the events unfold before assisting Rahim towards the exit. He smiled at her. He had lived through such trials before, but never one this dangerous. The chief minister, Hemiunu, had sent the priests just in time to save his emissary. Hemiunu obviously needed Rahim to stay alive for more errands to come. However, it would soon be time for the ageing historian to be replaced by someone younger and stronger. For thousands of years, Hemiunu recruited loyal mortals to assist him in his battle with the dark side. Rahim had done all that Hemiunu had asked.

Back at the hotel, it did not take much time for Riva to conclude that she had to keep what she had seen to herself to protect Rahim and some of those who had helped them along the way. Rahim reminded her that not all incidents had to be fought with bloody outcomes.

"In some cases," he told her, "it is more effective to be subtle. One time, King Ramsis II came under threat from Seth, the master of chaos. Seth committed the unthinkable by trying to kidnap the King's beloved wife, Nefertari, for whom Ramsis II built the famous Love Temple at Abu Simbel." He went on to tell Riva how Seth stormed the palatial bedroom one night while Ramsis II courted his wife and almost succeeded in vaporising the King had it not been for the wise intervention of the scribal deity Thoth, who had insisted on inscribing protective amulets all over the marital bed. The charms made so much noise that Ramsis stopped his lovemaking and paid attention to the noise, only to find Seth with a spear in his hand pointed at his heart. Seth's other arm pulled at the Queen, trying to pull her away from her husband. Worried that Ramsis might report him to Osiris, Seth immediately retreated. Ramsis, however, wisely let it pass, and Seth never tried to attack him or his wife again. The wise Ramsis, from then on, made offerings to Seth in an effort to assuage the deity who decided against taking Nefertari for himself, settling instead for the most beautiful girl in the whole of Egypt, a Theban villager.

Rahim predicted the attack on Ramsis II's bedroom. He saw the commotion in his vine leaves and potions. He alerted Hemiunu, who reacted fast, sending an army of spirits to future descendants in the New Kingdom, inspiring Thoth to make the charms over the bed of the great king. Despite the roles he played, Rahim remained as humble as ever. Hemiunu appreciated Rahim's humility. In return, he gave many favours to the modern sorcerer.

Assim and Fayed, still weak and living in the same body, neither alive nor dead, finally separated. Fayed claimed the soul of Assim and spirited himself away to the ancient realms, leaving his rotten body to die along with the dark sorcerer. He had much to atone for. The detective, however, retreated courteously to the ancient realm and remained in Abydos, joining a retinue of priests as if nothing had happened.

Going Back

Back at the temple, Riva watched a retinue of clerics covering their tracks and recording the death of the usurper. As she continued to watch, she noticed that one of the ethereal priests had a sceptre tattoo near his thumb. She gasped, and the priest turned to look at her. The young man, who she had never seen before, glared at her.

Kyky, the young fanatic cult member, turned away from the actress and moved towards her. If she had noticed him, he reasoned, maybe others had had too. He fell on Riva like a cobra with the strength and determination of a predator and blew ash recovered from Nitocris into her face. Riva was mesmerised and unable to move, but then a grin appeared on her face. The priest Yuf, who was standing nearby and had witnessed everything, hurried across to the pair and attacked Kiky with an amulet, burning him to ashes. He helped Riva to her feet, and she thanked him.

Riva flew back to the capital with a fiery twinkle in her eye – a glint that belonged to someone else. Someone who now lived within her. Floating at a distance from the actress, Egotha recognised the look in Riva's eyes and pondered. She might have to decide soon enough which path she preferred to take.

Epilogue

Osira – It had been a long time since Osira had gone hunting for food. She hunted people for body pieces, carefully inspecting their livers, which she needed the most for her procedures. Her mother, a formidable sorceress in her prime, had inspired the promising sorceress to a point. The rest of the path Osira was forging on her own. In time, she became one of the most sought-after exponents of her art in her day and thereafter. Her name travelled far and wide as she became a magical force to be reckoned with across many time portals with her particular skills.

In search of potions and more effective remedies, she travelled to the east and south. Since her ageing mother depended on her to obtain cures, the girl had mastered travelling across time portals. Osira bribed the sentinels who guarded the time gates with money or love potions and caught stowaway travellers who sought passage across realms without permission. Those time guards had the authority to eliminate robbers at portals using any method at their disposal. The guards were only too happy to give the bodies of the slain to Osira so that she could harvest their body parts for her potions. The potions satiated them long enough until she returned, handing over just enough to keep them coming back for more and to ensure they sneaked her back into the realm when her task was completed.

As time passed, she became ever more familiar with the occult. These times were marked by much wizardry, mainly ancestral but not sophisticated. Much of the magic went unchecked and which, when applied, had total disregard for tradition or expertise in later generations. Dabblers in magic were growing in number without proper education in the dangerous arts. However, these fake magicians were mainly weak and mostly ineffective. None of these charlatans bothered to study their art correctly and relied on their clients' ignorance, who were desperate to be cured. Osira had her own vision of the world of magic. Growing up, she habitually inspected old Memphis, which was a powerhouse and maker of kings. Osira painstakingly tested her potions and carefully checked their efficacy before using them on her clients. She learnt the hard way that magic had a soul of its own, losing a lover to its power. She came to know that magic was an untamed and mercurial creature that would gladly bite her when she was not looking. She was wise beyond her years and thoroughly believed that magic could turn against its dabbler, growing into a crooked life of its own on occasion. It was thus she developed her own counter charms and became a Queen of Queens in the dabbling arts.

It had been a year since Osira travelled northeast to Mesopotamia in search of exotic poisons and more potent healing herbs. She connected with old relatives who inhabited the land and lived in semi-seclusion. Most of the girl's family lived by the River Euphrates in Lagash, a city that prospered during the days of the Akkadians. The Gutians came, took over the city, and impoverished its people. Osira's tribe, however, were well-versed in survival. They, unlike others, prospered. They bought land and worked with other people. Using their magic, they enslaved the needy and the mighty alike. People, in the dead of night, flocked to their sprawling lands, hoping for an upturn in fortunes. The desperate citizens of the once-rich nation in crops and gold turned to magic for solace.

It was a family tradition to strive for the perfect magic formulae. Driven by a lust for knowledge, she became the uncrowned high sorceress. She left the motel her parents ran in Memphis by the pyramid of Saqqara in ancient Egypt and moved on in search of more progressive herbs in distant lands along more enchanted rivers. Her parents understood. The three members of the small family had incredible pasts, and since apples do not fall far from trees, they understood Osira's search for more. Her future would soon become as enticing as the lives of her parents. It took Osira one month by road to get to the Asian lands. The land was immense. It was fortified by mountains and a high wall built over many centuries. Her mother, the famous wizard, a descendant of a long list of sorcerers that cursed thousands of humans over limitless centuries, had retold a prophecy to her daughter. She explained that one of her ancestors told all forthcoming descendants about a secret to longevity – an elixir that rewarded its holder with eternal life. The drug lay hidden in the first-ever library in Mesopotamia. A great-grandson of the ruler, Sargon II, Ashurbanipal, and the very last ruler of Assyria, had built the first library in the ancient world. It was said that his father, Esarhaddon, had gone on a looting spree in Ethiopia and Egypt. One of Esarhaddon's generals had found a sceptre, or, more likely, the sceptre had found him. The general discovered a shiny object in the ancient Egyptian capital, Memphis. He absent-mindedly sheathed it to inspect for later. Back at his home in Assyria, the honest general headed straight to his king to show him the find. The general was shocked to find that his king had gone on a killing spree. It seemed his liege was afraid that others might seize his reign, so he massacred most of his advisors. The general wisely masked his feelings and bowed to the King for further orders. He did not disclose his find. The general was later told that the King suffered heightened paranoia that everyone was turning against him, so he slaughtered his entire line of councillors. The general, in fear of his life, followed the King's orders diligently but kept the sceptre secret.

One day, weighed down by news of the death of his son in battle and missing his daughter, he decided to head home. Rather than take the sceptre with him, he visited his friend the keeper of the King's vault and secreted his find inside a huge book made of papyrus leaves. The book had many cavities to keep the leaves breathing as they slept for thousands of years. The general, who by now realised that the sceptre had a life of its own, had found him. The sceptre embraced the pages and lay within the book as if it had found its home. The general sighed with relief, as if a huge weight had been lifted off him, closed the book and hid it with great care behind a heap of relics while the keeper was absent.

Years passed, and the son of the paranoid emperor, Ashurbanipal, built the first-ever library in Nineveh, Iraq. The sceptre, which had remained hidden, along with many of the books and writings in the vault, were moved to the library. The general travelled back to his homeland and never gave the sceptre another thought. Osira, on the other hand, having become aware of the sceptre's existence, was to find it.

When Osira set foot in Nineveh in the ancient Assyrian city of Mesopotamia, she was aware that the land was filled with more evil spirits than she cared to count. Her journey to pick up the sceptre was not going to be easy. The python was resting facing her. Its large eyes appeared to look straight at her from behind its hood. Osira did not move much. It was approaching sunset, and her snake would want to eat. It was difficult to tell who was afraid of whom. She had been training the snake ever since she killed its mother in Saqqara. Using her body temperature, she had trained the python to communicate with her. If she was too warm, it meant she wanted it to pounce on whatever creature, man or beast, she happened to be next to. Osira knew the snake was impatient and sought to prowl in the darkness for something to eat. Osira had given it several beatings of late when it moved without permission. She had even sliced off a piece of its new skin when it had just shed its old colours. The new skin had deep green and purple hues that shone in the dark. That never stopped Osira from chopping off the tail along with the skin. The pain was excruciating, but the python accepted its punishment. From that time, the python would not so much as look her way when it needed to stretch its twenty-metre-long body and about a metre in girth. Osira still had one mission for the massive predator and then would probably kill it and use its body parts for fertility potions.

She was in a hurry and could not let the python choose its own prey as she already had her eye on some birds nearby. With great agility, she adjusted her bow and arrow, killing two ducks in the stream. She had used her magic seeds to paralyse the python and placed the ducks before her gigantic pet.

The Old Man – He was washing his aching muscles and tired old face in the stream next to his shackled hut – his white hair pushed behind his ears. The old man had served, many years ago, at the gates of an emperor in China and lived within the palace walls of a benevolent but impotent emperor. The palace was home to hundreds of concubines and thousands of guards. It was located on an island, at one time connected to the nearby mountain that overlooked the Yellow River. The river was abundant, and the birth of a prosperous ancient China was witnessed. Those were good times with plentiful harvests. The prosperity gave birth to magnificent architecture that towered over the landscape. The old man, a warrior in his day, undertook his daily chores and went home to his rudimentary shack to sleep and get ready for another day. A simple black-and-white life based on hard work, hunting for game by the river, or one of the huge fish that lived in the waters, angled from the river. He had few complaints. Many of the junior army officers who knew of his past eyed him politely with a questioning look as to why he would subject himself to such a rigorous life. He explained to anyone who enquired that such a life kept him vigilant. He was always careful to live by his own example, telling the eager boys from the villages that they must beware of lazy habits. It opened doors to sleepless enemies. He should have reminded himself of that rule when his life was changed forever by an inadvertent lapse.

He lived by a warrior's code, steeped in dedication to the emperor. The latter was incapable of carrying out his marital duties, a fact that threatened the continuity of his bloodline and endangered the prosperous and united empire to the lurking danger within and beyond the palace walls. His wife had done her part to secure the rich, sprawling lands. The waters of the rivers and the abundant rains had given rise to crops that fed the country. Much to the dismay of the now-aged guard, he had walked one night into the empress's chamber to summon her to tend to her husband. It was that night of all nights that, unassuming, the guard came across one of the most repulsive scenes yet within the forbidden walls of the kingdom. The Queen was standing over the head she had just separated from the body of her lover. He was the emperor's gardener, a young, handsome man of nineteen. The women within the walls had swooned over the boy, but he never appeared interested until he was approached one night by the empress herself. She was a clever, vicious woman who knew she had to bring offspring into the world by whatever means. The wise guard understood the scene he encountered. The empress was obviously done with her lover, made sure she was with child and put an end to the life of the one man who would give her away. The guard looked down and immediately understood what he had to do. He asked the Queen to kindly go to her husband and that he would take care of the mess. The woman left, eyeing the guard with apparent gratitude, giving him orders to wait in his room for her to summon him while she tended to her liege. He disposed of the body, cleaned the blood and called on the servants to tend to the room. By the time the Queen returned from her husband, the incense candles burned, and the guard was gone.

Swordsmen were summoned and feverishly searched for him. *No loose ends* was the Queen's motto. Thankfully, the guard, who recognised and understood the Queen's ruthlessness, had already packed what belongings he could carry and left. He had climbed from the bedroom window so he would not be spotted, saddled his loyal horse, and headed south and then west like the wind, always staying close to the river paths. He never looked back.

He eventually came across a glass city known as Maski, built by a river, where he settled down in a house made of granite rock and feldspar. He was exhausted, underfed and very thirsty. He knelt by the river and drank himself into a deep sleep. When he woke, still exhausted, a man with a long beard was patting his face with a linen cloth. Days gave way to months until he finally felt strong enough to get to his feet. He got to know the man with the beard, a banished sorcerer who had fallen out of favour with the court. Stripped of his title as chief magician, he was forced to live in exile. It took him decades to build his home made of glass and hide his magic potions in the walls of his home. It was a ploy to hide his elevated secrets and, at the same time, to protect himself against the wrath of his former liege. When the old warrior recovered his strength, he took kindly to the old man. Because the two men were from different places, they could not understand one another at first, so they used sign language. The warrior was curious to know a sorcerer with such knowledge of magic, and he came to witness for himself that he was a skilled magician and healer. Over time, the warrior witnessed him heal many a stray traveller and natives of this town. The magician dedicated his life to helping those who managed to find him. His house was made of rock and glass – a most unusual combination – sometimes visible and at other times not. The warrior, while recovering, had seen him tend the wounds of a pregnant, terrified girl who arrived with her father – an old, broken man – who had been attacked by savages. The girl and her father became loyal servants to the magician, and when the child was born – a boy – the magician developed a fondness for the youngster. Slowly, the magician amassed a small band of followers who kept their master safe.

As time passed, the warrior learned the language well and explained to the magician how he made the journey from north to south. The magician smiled. He had heard of the wily empress. They had crossed paths when he trained her in the arts. The magician, he explained, had been taken in by her beauty and charm and never suspected that she would turn his potions into darker paths. The magician, who once had the ears of the emperor, was slowly eased out by her. The city was prosperous, and trade with neighbours kept everyone happy. Word spread that Maski turned glass into gold, which was untrue. The magician had managed in his free time to experiment with glass and rocks to give them a shine that reflected like gold, and people embellished this, creating the myth. Builders learnt from the magician the secret of making the plaster that covered the buildings shine, giving it a gold-like appearance to their buildings. Travellers who visited did not understand and were easily fooled, allowing the lie to spread. Maski's reputation grew as the wealthiest province among its neighbours. The truth is that all that shines was not really gold, and Maski was not an affluent city at all. However, it was beautiful.

When word spread further, invaders came from the north and east and stormed the palace. The small number of soldiers guarding the city were ill-prepared for a full-scale invasion, and many died. It was only when the invading mercenaries started to dismantle the houses that they realised that the decorative style was mere glass, which, once broken on the ground, became a shell of the splendour that was. They left corpses behind and returned from whence they came. The emperor summoned the magician and ordered him to leave the palace under penalty of death if he ever came back.

The warrior had listened to the tale. He had spent time learning some of the secrets of the magician whose life in exile made him yearn for the company of peers. He showed the warrior enough tricks to defend himself against predators and taught him how to camouflage himself against tigers and hyenas on his journey. After spending many months with the magician, he decided to move on and travelled further west as far as possible from familiar lands.

He passed through many terrains until he came across a peaceful place where he decided to stay. It overlooked a stream that gushed out of the earth, enabling him to plant crops nearby and hunt the abundant game. He continued to live a secluded life there until, one day, he spotted her.

If only he were the warrior that he once was, he thought, but old age was snapping at his heels. He had many wives and lovers in his bygone days, but his youth was long gone. The warrior's heart missed a beat when he first laid eyes on Osira. She raised her spear as he approached, but realising that he was old and no threat to her, she lowered it again. The warrior understood her look. He relaxed and invited her to join him in a meal of lamb he was preparing. They talked as they ate, exchanging stories in a common language. East and West had traded for centuries and used an official language to communicate. It was Akkadian, used by people living in Mesopotamia, where Osira found her temporary new home.

They slept fitfully till dawn, listening to the night sounds. Osira had told him of her quest, and he had promised to help. He had been on the move for nearly half a century and realised that those who sought him were probably long dead by now.

He knew a shortcut across the Tigris River. From there, they could set sail to an underwater pass directly below the palace.

The Spy – Nitocris had survived by a whisker. She, even now, continued to rebuild her lost Ka, that part of her soul which barely lived on, just as her plans to take over the kingdom were toppled when she burned in the temple grounds. Some of her remaining demons had been summoned to check on all who could come back to help rebuild another line to the throne of Egypt.

Priests in the kingdom of Egypt were conniving, some more than others, and Anhurmose was the most devious.

Nitocris still remembered the priest with the hungry eyes, Anhurmose, who she helped occupy a higher echelon among the king's inner circle. Anhurmose recruited help to carve tunnels as a retreat for the devilish queen across the temples in Abydos. She had already persuaded the chief architect of King Pepi, Ikhernofret, to work closely with Anhurmose. Once the architect was made aware of the subterranean passages below the temple, it was faster and simpler for the architect to furnish and secure a lavish hideout for the Queen. She was still too weak to reach those rooms below the temple of Abydos, those designed by Ikhernofret. She still, however, possessed the scent made of the breath of deities, which was secured by the loyal Assim, now dead, to guide her through the tunnels. She had bribed the priest with gold and silver to further win his loyalty, but she was now hardly recognisable to the demons below. Unable to reach her amulets and spells to help her regrow, she barely resembled her former self. However, even as she was dying, she had the foresight to cast her soul into Riva. She still needed her physical strength, her demonic spirit, but at least her soul was safe within the actress while she hid and plotted her return.

End of Vol.1

About the Author

- Started a career in media, at the age of nineteen, that lasted forty years, during which she was promoted to the most prestigious ranks.

- Joined the European Radio service, based in Egypt, in 1979.

- Audiences recognized her as a news reader, a short stories narrator, and a main host of live programs on the morning show.

- Worked as a television investigative journalist, a master of ceremonies and a simultaneous interpreter.

- Received a PhD in English and Comparative Literature from Cairo University.

- Era of Nitocris is her debut novel on the intriguing sorcery of ancient Egypt.

9 781739 297084

9 781835 667170